A Good Daughter's GHOST

A Good Daughter's GHOST

SAM WILKET

annick press
toronto • berkeley

Cover art by Marcela Bolívar, designed by Simin Dewji
Interior designed by Simin Dewji
Edited by Kaela Cadieux and Claire Caldwell

Expert read by Jae M. T
Copyedited by Linda Pruessen
Proofread by Mary Ann Blair

ONTARIO ARTS COUNCIL
CONSEIL DES ARTS DE L'ONTARIO
an Ontario government agency
un organisme du gouvernement de l'Ontario

Ontario

ONTARIO CREATES | ONTARIO CRÉATIF

Canada Council for the Arts | Conseil des arts du Canada

Canada

CERTIFIED CANADIAN PUBLISHER

This book is funded in part by the Government of Canada. *Ce livre est financé en partie par le gouvernement du Canada.* We acknowledge the support of the Canada Council for the Arts. *Nous remercions le Conseil des arts du Canada de son soutien.* We would like to acknowledge the funding support of the Ontario Arts Council (OAC) and the Government of Ontario for their support. We also acknowledge the support of the Government of Ontario through the Ontario Book Publishing Tax Credit, and through Ontario Creates.

Library and Archives Canada Cataloguing in Publication

Title: A good daughter's ghost / Sam Wilket.
Names: Wilket, Sam. author.
Identifiers: Canadiana (print) 20260142085 | Canadiana (ebook) 2026014844X | ISBN 9781834021157
(softcover) | ISBN 9781834021164 (EPUB) | ISBN 9781834021171 (PDF)
Subjects: LCGFT: Paranormal fiction. | LCGFT: Horror fiction. | LCGFT: Novels.
Classification: LCC PS8645.I4356 G66 2026 | DDC jC813/.6—dc23

Published in the U.S.A. by Annick Press (U.S.) Ltd.
Distributed in Canada by Jaguar Book Group.
Distributed in the U.S.A. by Publishers Group West.

Printed in Canada

annickpress.com | samwilket.com

MIX
Paper | Supporting responsible forestry
FSC www.fsc.org FSC® C103567

For Mike

CHAPTER ONE

TESTS SUCK AS A rule, but it's the silence that comes with them that settles on my chest like a pissed-off rhino. I guess, technically, there isn't a total lack of sound in Mr. Savoca's class. There's the rasp of twenty pencils scratching equations onto paper, the swish of someone turning a page, the *tick-tick-tick* of the clock limping toward noon.

But it's still too quiet, and without a track playing in my ear, my brain goes on a cruise, imagining how I'd score this scene if it were a movie: *The witch bitch of Brimley Collegiate sits in a generic high school classroom, staring blankly at the math test in front of her. It's obvious she's a loser from the all-black outfit, the long hair obscuring her face, the way her shoulders hunch like she's trying to melt into her desk. The students around her write furiously, but her pencil sits untouched, her hands clenched between her knees.*

To ramp up the anxiety, I'd play "The End" by the Doors. That slow tambourine at the beginning always rips a pit of dread open in my stomach.

Or, if it's a redemption arc, if she's about to pick up her pencil and fly through the exam, it would have to be the Sex Pistols. Any of their headbangers would do the trick.

But if something wild is about to turn this whole scene on its head—like an alien spaceship blowing the school's roof off—I'd pick "How Soon Is Now?" by the Smiths. That track is otherworldly.

I'd die to hear any of those songs right now. Honestly, I'd even take the cringy lounge music they play in my dentist's office. Anything would be better than silence.

Silence means something bad's about to happen. Not movie-worthy bad, just regular, everyday bad. It's my apartment after Wàipó dies, months of my mom staring at her bedroom ceiling. It's the moment my whole grade-five class notices the wet patch on the front of my pants. It's conversations stopping as I walk down the hall to find someone's scrawled *witch bitch* on my locker again. It's my mom's disappointment when I tell her I failed another test.

I shouldn't even be here. I knew pre-calculus would drown me. But how can I explain that to my mom, a woman who spends her free time taking online accounting classes?

The bell buzzes, and the classroom erupts in chatter and scraping chairs. The knot behind my ribs loosens as the noise washes over me. I pick up my half-finished test, drop it on Mr. Savoca's desk, and pop my earbuds in. One of Johnny Marr's iconic guitar riffs thrums through my skull, and it feels good to match my steps to the beat as I weave through the hall with my head down, my eyes on my combat boots.

It's a relief to spot the one person in this circus I actually like: Yas is leaning against my locker, a half-empty box of fries in her hand. Back when our age was a single digit and she went by her full name, Yanmin, I used to wish I looked more Chinese, because maybe then she and I could pass for sisters. We both had long, dark hair and people sometimes mixed us up from behind. But now she's almost a foot shorter than me, with blue hair that makes her look like a hot mermaid and an ever-changing, eternally on-trend manicure. This week her nails are chrome and coffin-shaped, sparkling as she pops a fry into her mouth. No one's mistaking us for sisters these days; most people can hardly believe we're friends. Sometimes *I* can hardly believe it.

"How was the test?" Yas asks.

I make a face and steal a fry in response.

"Same," she says. But we both know she's only saying that to make me feel better. On test days, Mr. Savoca lets you leave as soon as you finish, and Yas walked out at least twenty minutes ago.

"Is that what you're wearing to your interview?" Yas looks at my sweater and scrunches up her face.

"Uh . . . yeah?"

I'm in my best hoodie; it's plain black and freshly laundered. My jeans have rips in the knees, but they're not massive. There's a white film of road salt on my boots, but that's unavoidable when it's January in Toronto.

"Rachel!" Yas says my name like I suggested cheating on a test. "Don't you need this job to pay for Osheaga?"

Osheaga is the biggest music festival in Canada. It happens every August in Montreal, and this year LMK—a K-pop boy band Yas and I were *obsessed* with in elementary school—is playing. Though if anyone other than Yas asks, I've never heard of them. Yas's parents got her a car for her sweet sixteen, so this summer we're going to road trip to Quebec and ring in her seventeenth birthday with our preteen crushes and a sweaty, screaming crowd. I just need to, one, save up enough cash, and, two, pass driver's ed. Getting this job is critical for part one, and part two starts with our first class tomorrow.

Yas knows this, which is why she doesn't wait for me to answer before unzipping her backpack and pulling out one of the most "Yas" sweaters ever created: oversized, cream wool covered in rows of fuzzy cartoon peaches. It's disgustingly adorable. She holds it out to me, pointedly ignoring the face I'm making.

"You want me to go to an interview for a babysitting job covered in peach emojis?"

"Don't be gross," Yas says. "It's giving a super-cute kawaii vibe. Which is way more interview-appropriate than whatever eighties grunge music video you stepped out of."

She tugs at the hem of my hoodie until I take it off. I pull her sweater over my head, and when I pop out of the thick-knit cave of cuteness, Yas starts wiping at my wilting eyeliner with a makeup remover pad. A gaggle of grade nines walks by, and one of them whispers "That's her!" before they all break out in giggles. I squeeze my eyes shut and will my body not to blush. I don't know if Yas is truly immune or just oblivious, but she never seems affected by what other people think. I wish I could bottle her confidence. When the cool press of the cotton pad disappears, I open my eyes to find Yas squinting at me. She nudges me to turn so my back is to her and starts gathering my hair into a ponytail.

"Are you going to report him this time?" Yas speaks softly, but her words—and the pity underneath them—hit me like a steamroller. I guess she noticed those grade nines after all.

By "him" she means Cameron Edwards, the asshole who christened me *witch bitch* when we were in grade five. He's been finding new ways to make my life hell since he was a soft-bellied ten-year-old with a crooked bowl cut. Since we came back from winter break, he's been spamming the comments of my social accounts with walls of witch emojis. Compared to some of the other shit he's pulled, this is a vacation.

But Yas still insists I should report him. It's like she's erased the memory of the last time I followed her advice, back when it first started. Our principal said he couldn't do much about a "he said, she said" situation, so all he did was make Cameron apologize to me in front of my mom and his parents. That changed exactly nothing, except that my mom started randomly showing up at school to "check in" on me, which gave Cameron even more material to work with. Mom finally backed off when I started high school, and there's no way I'm risking her freaking out and starting that again.

Yas is convinced it will be different now. I'm convinced she's overestimating the Brimley Collegiate administration and underestimating my mom. So every time Cameron makes another asshole move, Yas and I have the same conversation.

"He's using throwaway accounts," I say. "There's no way to prove it's him. It could be Tanner, or Brad, or one of the Jakes." Cameron's friends read like a list from a douchebag name generator. "It's probably all of them. I've stopped posting anyway. They'll get tired of it soon."

"You can't just ignore your problems and hope they'll go away."

"I can and I will. And so will you."

"But I really think—"

"Just leave it, Yas. Okay?"

Yas huffs and pulls my ponytail tight with a sharp yank that makes my scalp sting. I shrug her off and examine myself in my locker mirror. With my hair slicked back, makeup gone, and cartoon peaches dotting my front, I look about twelve years old.

"I hate you," I say.

"Love you too." Yas pokes my shoulder. "Now, go get this job."

CHAPTER TWO

WHEN MY MOM SAYS *someday we'll have a nice place of our own*, I think this is the kind of house she has in mind. It's two stories of pretty red brick with white shutters, on a quiet street that dead-ends at a park. It has a covered front porch perfect for people-watching and garden beds that look neat even though all the plants are snow-covered and hibernating. Most importantly, it's separated from the sidewalk by a low wood fence that draws a clear line between *mine* and *yours*. As much as my mom adores gossiping with the neighbors in our apartment building, I know she dreams of a living room without someone else's TV blasting on the other side of the wall and a washing machine she doesn't have to wait in line for.

I turn my back to the icy wind and take out my phone to double-check the address. Yes, this is the place. Home of Sylvia and Hector Morin, and their eight-year-old daughter Blythe, who's destined to be my new best friend. The gate to their yard is unlocked, but it still feels like I'm trespassing when I unlatch it and step inside. Their front door has a wreath in the middle that smells like Christmas and a fancy keypad instead of a regular lock. I ring the bell, and a moment later the door swings open, revealing a blond wisp of a woman.

"You must be Rachel," she says, beaming at me. "I'm Sylvia."

Sylvia's handshake is warm and solid, as deliberate as everything else about her, from her pale pink lipstick, to the way her bob curves under her jaw, to how the sleeves of her oversized sweater are pushed up to her elbows. I half expect text to appear above her head promising *seven ways to live a happier life*, like in a lifestyle influencer video.

Yas was right to clean me up.

When I cross the threshold I'm enveloped in white. There's so little color and clutter, it feels like I've stepped into an art gallery. The main floor is open concept, the entryway morphing into a living room dominated by a fireplace and built-in bookshelves, which flows into the kitchen beyond. A massive abstract painting above the fireplace underscores the feeling of being in a gallery. The white canvas is covered in thick black lines, which ripple down in a way that makes it seem like they're moving. It gives me the creeps, though Yas would probably say I should *consider the artist's intentions*. How does a kid live here? When I worked for the Kings, the only art in their house was made by someone under ten, and there was always an overflowing laundry basket at the bottom of the stairs. Here, the stairs are clear and covered with marshmallow-colored carpet that wears the stripes of a fresh vacuum.

"Hector and Blythe will be home soon," Sylvia says. "But we have a little time to get to know each other first."

She takes my coat and I toe off my soggy boots, then follow her into the kitchen. I slide onto a barstool at the snow-colored island.

"What can I get you to drink?" Sylvia asks. "We have water, orange juice, and lots of tea. But nothing caffeinated! We're high on life." She chuckles at her joke, and I do too, though I can't imagine the monsters Mom and I would be without coffee.

"Water would be great," I say.

"Still or sparkling?"

Sylvia must see the confusion on my face because she smiles and clarifies.

"Bubbles or no bubbles?"

There's nothing teasing in her expression, but I blush anyway. She must think I'm an uncultured idiot. I force out a laugh.

"Bubbles would be nice," I say. "Please."

As Sylvia takes a bottle out of the fridge, I catch my reflection in the chrome double doors. They're completely bare: no magnets, no kids' drawings, not even the garbage pickup schedule. Just my face, distorted in the curved metal, my eyes too wide, too hungry. I sit up straighter and force my features into a more neutral expression.

"So." Sylvia slides a fizzing glass across to me and folds her hands on the counter. "Tell me why you're the right babysitter for Blythe."

Right down to the interview, then. My throat is tacky—I really want a sip of that water—but she's looking at me so expectantly. I ignore the glass and stretch my face into a smile, which I hope looks more sincere than nervous.

"As you saw on my résumé, I have a lot of experience," I say. "I've been babysitting since I was fourteen and I volunteered at a daycare before that. I worked exclusively for the Kings for the last year."

"I heard Celia and Clive were begging for you to move with them."

"They're great kids." My smile doesn't feel so forced this time.

Sylvia continues through a textbook list of questions, and I answer each one with growing confidence until we're interrupted by the sound of keys jangling in the front door.

"We're home!" Two voices—one a low rumble, the other high and reedy—call out their arrival together.

Blythe bounds into the kitchen and throws herself into her mom's arms, a ball of energy in a purple sweatsuit. Hector follows, a lanky man with wire-rimmed glasses. It seems like he's trying to make up for the receding hairline framing his pale forehead with the thick, dark beard that covers his chin. He grasps my hand firmly but looks over my shoulder instead of meeting my eyes.

"Did you know King John of England died from eating too many peaches?" Blythe is frowning at my sweater, her heart-shaped face framed by curtains of long, brown hair. I'm suddenly extremely aware that I'm wearing a cartoon fruit basket.

"Really?" I crouch down so we're at eye level. "I didn't know that. Did you know that in Chinese mythology, peach wood protects you from evil spirits?"

Blythe shakes her head, her eyes wide. I think she's a little impressed. Score one, me. Hector busies himself transferring things from the fridge into a blender, while Sylvia runs me through Blythe's after-school routine. Blythe has her arms around Sylvia's waist the whole time, pressing her head into her mom's stomach in a way that makes her seem a lot younger than eight. She doesn't move until Hector hands her a tall plastic cup, a reusable straw poking out of the thick, pink smoothie. She climbs up on a barstool and takes a long sip.

"When you finish your snack," Hector says to Blythe, as she slurps down her drink at a speed that must be giving her a brain freeze, "I'll help you with your homewo—"

Blythe explodes in a scream.

Pink droplets shoot out of her mouth, spraying her dad's dress shirt, as she sweeps her cup off the counter. Her smoothie splatters a strawberry arc on the floor. She leaps off her stool and throws it to the ground, the metal footrest slamming down with a teeth-rattling crash. The sound shakes me into action, and I jump up, backing away like she's a wild animal.

Blythe keeps screaming. The noise is all-consuming, crowding out every thought in my brain. As she bolts out of the kitchen, her scream morphs into high-pitched bursts. A door slams upstairs.

Then silence.

I can hear my own pulse thrumming wildly.

Sylvia and Hector are looking at each other like they're locked in some kind of grim staring contest. No one moves for one breath, two. Then Sylvia spins away and rushes after Blythe, leaving Hector and me alone in the kitchen.

Hector doesn't move. He keeps staring at the spot where Sylvia was, like she's still standing there. I focus on unclenching my fists, studying the half-moon indents my fingernails left in my palms. What the hell just happened? Why didn't they do anything? Was *I* supposed to do something?

"Did Sylvia tell you?" Hector's voice cuts through the tangled fog of my thoughts. His gaze drifts to the pink puddle on the floor.

"Uh . . ."

No, your wife didn't mention your kid was a screaming banshee.

"I'll take that as a no." Hector finally looks at me, a wan smile flickering across his face. I think he's trying to be reassuring, but it looks more like he's about to be sick.

"Blythe's older sister, Maddie, died last summer."

His words vaporize the muddle in my head, and the shock that remains is a vast, echoing emptiness.

Hector keeps speaking. He says that Blythe's never been an easy kid, but since Maddie died, she's been acting out: throwing tantrums, making up stories, clinging to him and Sylvia. He says this is normal for a grieving child; he's a psychologist, so he knows. He says Blythe's not a bad kid, she's just hurting. The best thing to do when she explodes is ignore her. He says what she needs—what they all need—is consistency and routine. He delivers this information in such a steady, matter-of-fact tone that he might be reading a shopping list, instead of describing how his youngest daughter is handling the death of her sister.

"I want to be completely honest with you," Hector says. "You're not the first sitter we've tried."

That's a bad sign. A stick of dynamite on top of a colossal mountain of bad signs. I should be freaking out, but I just feel numb. What am I supposed to say?

I'm saved by Sylvia striding back into the kitchen, looking surprisingly unruffled.

"Crisis averted!" She smiles an apology at me. "We try to limit Blythe's screen time, but sometimes it's the best medicine. We haven't had much luck getting her to do homework, but you don't need to worry about that. You leave that to us."

Hector looks like he wants to say something, but he swallows instead.

"I can't imagine what she's going through. What you're all going through." The words are wooden in my mouth, but at least I'm saying something half-coherent. "I'm sure you want the best for her, and I totally understand if I'm not what you're looking for."

Sylvia's eyes meet mine. Is that panic on her face? How many babysitters has this kid gone through?

"You're perfect, Rachel," she says. "The job is yours, if you want it."

• • •

If you want it.

Sylvia's words replay in my head the whole bus ride home; even the Clash's wild drums can't drown it out. Do I want it? On paper, the job is perfect. They'll pay me more money than the Kings, to watch one kid instead of two. It's a guaranteed once-in-a-lifetime trip to Osheaga. But I'm not sure spending every afternoon with a ticking time bomb is worth any amount of money. I should've known it was too good to be true.

I step off the bus in front of my apartment building, which looks even uglier than usual after the clean white lines of the Morin house. It's a twenty-story concrete block, created with the sole purpose of lasting for at least a hundred years. Even the balcony railings are cement slabs.

The tiles in the lobby are cracked, and one of the two elevators has sported an OUT OF ORDER sign for over a year. Still, the space smells crisply of vinegar, and the trash usually finds its way to the garbage bin by the door. There's even a leather loveseat with a fake palm tree next to it. But tonight, the harsh lights draw my eyes to the thousand tiny tears on the sagging couch and the thick layer of dust coating the tree's plastic leaves.

I ride the working elevator up to the fifteenth floor, where the hallway is lined with identical faux-wood doors, all blank except for ours, which is covered in a life-sized drawing of a heavyset Chinese man in a red tunic. He stares out with bulging eyes as he balances on one foot and holds a sword above his head. Mom says Zhong Kui is a famous exorcist who repels bad spirits and ill fortune. I say he's a freaky-looking dude who should work on repelling his neck-beard. Looking at his ridiculous cartoon face, I think longingly of the Morins' elegant wreath.

My mom has already left for her night shift at the warehouse, so our apartment is empty. The only signs she was here are the crumpled McDonald's wrappers on the table and the heady scent of incense. A thin tendril of smoke wafts up from the ancestral altar tucked in the corner of our living room. I'm sure the joss sticks my mom lit are just stubs now, but I still wish she wouldn't leave the house when things are actively burning.

The smoke curls around the framed photos of my dad and Wàipó, my grandmother, that sit in the middle of the altar. The peach-wood sword lying in front of the incense burner reminds me of my conversation with Blythe before she went supernova. *Peach wood protects you from evil spirits*. Did I really say that? I'm as bad as my mom.

Sword is a generous word for the slim, hand-carved piece of wood no longer than my palm. When I was little, I called it Wàipó's wand. When Wàipó died, my mom stayed in bed for months. She only got up to shamble to her shifts or dig a crumpled bill out of her purse so I could get groceries. But at least I knew Wàipó, and Mom will talk about her. The only thing my mom will say about my dad is that he died before he knew I existed but would have loved me very much.

I examine my dad's photograph, studying the familiar pink stripe of sunburn on his pale nose and the slight snaggletooth on the right side of his smile, which I also see when I look in the mirror. I can count the things Mom's told me about him on one hand. His name was Frank Jones. They met at the University of Toronto when she was in her first year of biochemistry. She was still living with her strict parents and had a 10 p.m. curfew, and he was a charming exchange student from England. They were together for only a couple months when he went to a conference and a drunk driver stopped him from ever coming back. A few weeks later, Mom found out she was pregnant with me and the rest of her life unraveled.

I used to ask about him, but the questions made Mom quiet and quiet Mom was weird. So I stopped asking. Everything else I know about him, I learned from the mixtape he gave my mom at the start of their brief, whirlwind romance. *Songs that changed my life*, he wrote on the CD in blue permanent marker. I wish I could tell him they changed my life too.

I've tried looking for info about him online, but he died before everyone started posting their lives on social media, and Mom doesn't know where his family was from, making it impossible to find him among the hundreds of white English guys named *Frank Jones*.

Maddie, though—

I pull out my phone and type *maddie morin* into the search bar. The first link opens to what looks like Maddie's yearbook photo. She's a stock image of a cool girl: pale skin, big brown eyes, dirty blond hair cascading over her shoulders in smooth waves, and the kind of delicate nose I've envied my whole life. She smiles with her lips closed, like she's holding in a secret. I bet she practiced that smile in the mirror, took a million selfies until she got the head tilt just right. I scroll down and guilt pinches me when I realize it's a news article about her death.

TEEN DIES IN FALL FROM SCARBOROUGH BLUFFS

CBC News, Toronto

The eastern end of the beach at Bluffer's Park was covered in candles, flowers, and police tape on Monday, in the wake of a tragic accident over the weekend.

In the early hours of Sunday morning, 17-year-old Madeline Morin fell off the 300-foot Scarborough Bluffs overlooking Lake Ontario. The police marine unit found the victim in the water at the base of the cliffs at 1:50 a.m. She was pronounced dead at the scene.

Police have ruled the fall an accident, calling it "death by misadventure." They are urging the public to respect the warning signs and fences intended to keep people away from the unstable cliff edge.

Every summer, the fire department rescues dozens of selfie-taking tourists who get trapped on the Bluffs when they get too close to the edge and the earth crumbles under their feet. But I've never heard of anyone dying.

Thinking of my mom, what happened to her after Wàipó died and the way she is about my dad . . . grief can make even grown adults do bizarre things. So an eight-year-old throwing a tantrum? It makes sense, given what Blythe's going through.

The question is, can I handle it?

CHAPTER THREE

AT 7:30 THE NEXT morning, I find my mom in the kitchen, scrolling through her phone with one hand and holding a spoon in the other, dripping cereal milk everywhere. She does an exaggerated double-take when she sees me, strands of dark hair falling out of her disheveled bun.

"What day is it?" she says. "It can't be Saturday; it's not even noon."

Ha ha. She's so predictable.

"Driver's ed starts today."

Our kitchen is a narrow corridor barely one adult wide, and my mom is between me and the coffee maker. She leans over the counter, spooning soggy no-name cinnamon squares into her mouth as I shimmy behind her. Her ID badge swings from the lanyard around her neck, and the bottom edge that reads *Jennifer Bei* is dangerously close to taking a swim in her breakfast. Or dinner? Whatever you call the meal after an overnight shift.

Mom straightens, though at her full height she still only reaches my shoulder. She's five foot three, and I've towered over her since grade seven. Her eyes drift up and to the right, the way they always do when she's about to say something she knows will annoy me. I pop the lid off the coffee tin and breathe in the bright, nutty scent, focusing on filling the machine with perfectly level scoops.

"I don't get why you're spending all your money on driver's ed," she says.

Here we go.

The coffee maker burbles as Mom runs through the list of talking points she's been repeating for the last month: We don't have a car and can't afford one; Yas is my friend, not a car rental company; public transit is way faster than sitting in Toronto traffic. This is exactly why I haven't mentioned Montreal yet. I need her to finish one lecture series before I give her a new topic to start on.

"Besides, you can learn to drive whenever. You know—"

"You learned when you were twenty-five. I remember."

"Exactly." Mom points her spoon at me and milk sprays my cheek. Ew. "You should be focusing on getting good grades and saving for university. You have a packed schedule with your credit recovery."

Heat floods up my neck and into my cheeks. No matter what topic we're talking about, my mom always finds a way to bring up the fact that I failed physics last term. It's like her superpower. She keeps talking at me as I pull a travel mug out of the cupboard. I look at the scratched stainless steel and imagine whipping it on the floor so hard it dents. Instead, I carefully place the mug on the counter and fill it to the brim with steaming coffee.

• • •

Donald's Driving Academy is above a Pizza Pizza, in a windowless room that smells like pepperoni and wet socks. It's crammed with old-school desks, the kind with wooden side tables attached to metal chairs. Surprisingly, most of them are already occupied. I guess Yas and I aren't the only ones who searched for *cheapest drivers ed in toronto.*

Yas waves at me from the back corner, pulling her bag off the desk next to her. Her hair is twisted into two perfect space buns. Even though I know she watched like twelve hours of tutorials to get this hairstyle just right, it's still annoying how effortlessly cool she looks. Especially since it's not even 9 a.m.

"How retro is this place?" Yas says in a stage whisper.

"It smells like sadness."

"And cheese. Blue cheese." She smirks. "How was the interview?"

"Oh god," I say with a groan. "They offered me the job. But the kid had a full meltdown while I was there. She *threw a chair*."

"Whoa!" Yas's eyes are wide. When she's locked in, she has this way of looking at you that makes you feel like you're the most interesting person on the planet.

"But *then*, her dad tells me her older sister died last summer. So obviously she's going through a lot." I rattle off the pro/con list I've been composing in my head: money versus hell child versus a lot of money. Yas nods as I speak, but her gaze wanders over my shoulder and suddenly she's beaming at the door with her hand up in the air.

The downside to Yas's ability to make you feel like the only person in the room is that she can also make you feel like you don't exist.

I twist around to see who she's waving at and my confidence fizzles out entirely.

"I didn't know Dell was coming." I try to sound unaffected.

"Didn't I tell you?" Yas plucks her mittens off another desk I didn't notice she was saving. "Now we can split the drive three ways!"

I have to fight to keep my face blank. Yas invited Dell on our trip? Wasn't this *our* plan? Shouldn't she have asked me first? Or am I being weird and possessive? I know "best friends" is a kindergarten thing—Yas is obviously allowed to hang out with other people. Plus, we're driving her car. But still . . .

"Hey Yas, hey Rachel." Dell unzips their hideous lime-green puffer jacket, which somehow looks straight off a runway when they wear it. Underneath is a sweatshirt printed with Van Gogh's famous self-portrait above the words *I can't hear the haters.*

We get it, Dell, you're an artist.

"Damn, this place is a time warp!"

"That's exactly what I said!" Yas laughs.

Dell grins and shakes their head, sending their curly mohawk bouncing. Mismatched earrings swing from their ears. One earring is a lightning bolt and the other is a hoop with a little star dangling from it. My stomach curdles as I glance back at Yas and find the identical, mismatched earrings hanging from her ears.

• • •

After five hours of demerit point math, road sign flashcards, and right of way quizzes, my brain is numb, and I'm dreading the physics assignment that's waiting for me at home.

"Are you coming to the park?" Yas asks, as we pack up our stuff.

"I can't."

"You *never* come." She pouts, her lower lip stuck out like a cartoon character. "Yujun's coming today."

"The guy who took you to the arcade?"

"No, that was David." Yas somehow manages to look sheepish and smug at the same time. "Yujun's from my photography class. The guy who looks like a K-pop star, remember? He's bringing a friend. Apparently Rishi's super into music—"

I give her an eye roll so exaggerated it makes me dizzy. There's no way I'm letting her set me up again. Yas means well, but every guy she meets falls for her within five minutes. She doesn't get what it's like for me.

"I can't," I say, cutting off her gushing.

"Why not?"

"I have to run some errands for my mom." Yas knows what my mom's schedule is like, so the excuse is basically a free pass. There's no way I'm telling Yas "Honor Roll" Wong that I failed a class.

I remember when I used to spend Saturdays at Yas's house, back when my mom worked at the grocery store. Mom always had Saturday shifts, so she could take Sundays off for Wàipó's weekly visits. Mom would drop me off at Yas's condo, and Yas and I would spend the day making up stupid dances to the latest LMK songs, binge-watching cartoons, and gorging ourselves on Mrs. Wong's homemade cookies.

But that ended when we turned thirteen, and Yas started spending her Saturdays in art classes and my mom decided I was old enough to stay home alone. Now, with the physics credit recovery looming over me, Saturday might as well be another school day.

When I get home, my mom's asleep on the couch, spooning her accounting textbook. She's halfway through the online certificate she started last year, and now whenever she's not working, she's studying. She calls the certificate her "ticket back to the land of the living." She dreams of a nine-to-five job the way some people dream of having a corner office or getting discovered on YouTube.

I slip my boots off and tiptoe into the living room, taking Mom's laptop from the coffee table. She sighs and I freeze, but her eyes stay closed. There's a small frown creasing her forehead and a smudge of what looks like chocolate on her chin. I pull the fuzzy blanket off the back of the couch and spread it over her, then head to my room as quietly as I can.

I'm waiting for the ancient laptop to start up when my phone buzzes. It's an email from Sylvia.

> Dear Rachel,
>
> It was such a pleasure to meet you yesterday. Blythe really took to you, and we think you'd be an excellent influence on her. If you decide to take the job, we'd like to offer you a signing bonus of $200 . . .

I stare at the words until they go blurry. Is she serious? That's nearly half my ticket to Osheaga, just for saying yes. I take a screenshot and send it to Yas. The Morins are obviously desperate; Blythe definitely didn't "take to me" at all. But can I blame them? They need help. And they actually seem very put together, given what they've been through. They're going to work, taking care of their kid, making fancy smoothies. Compared to how my mom was after Wàipó died, they're thriving. Blythe's still struggling, but she's only eight and she just lost her sister. Her tantrum yesterday was extreme, but I've dealt with tantrums before. I've been babysitting for years; I can handle it. I'd rather deal with one screaming kid than a line of screaming customers at some fast-food place, which is the only other job I'm likely to qualify for. I bet I can even win her over. And then a few months from now, I'll be staring up at the biggest stage I've ever seen, bass pulsing through my bones, surrounded by a surging crowd that doesn't care who I am—

My phone buzzes again. Yas's response is an incoherent mess of emojis, mostly money bags and exclamation marks. I can't stop the grin spreading across my face. She's right. I *need* to take this job. We're heading toward the summer of my dreams, and nothing is going to ruin it.

CHAPTER FOUR

WHEN THE LAST BELL rings on Monday, I burst out the front doors and take off at a speed walk. It's so cold that the hairs inside my nose freeze every time I breathe in. My cheeks and thighs are burning when the stony face of Cliffside Elementary School comes into view. The curb is lined with idling cars, and a swarm of adults in black jackets huddle around the school's entrance.

Which is still closed. I made it on time.

Sylvia waves, her hands covered by red mittens that match her hat. She starts toward me, weaving through the crowd.

"Hi, Rachel," she says. "Find it okay?"

I nod, trying to hide my panting.

The bell buzzes and the doors fling open, releasing a torrent of children in puffy snow suits and brightly colored hats. I don't see Blythe until she's right in front of us, almost unrecognizable with the fur-trimmed hood of her coat pulled up close around her face. The sound of her shrieking sears through my mind, but I shove it away and force myself to smile. I will not be intimidated by an eight-year-old.

"It's great to see you again, Blythe." I crouch down and unzip my backpack, pulling out the little treats I picked up at the dollar store:

a sheet of shiny unicorn stickers and a friendship bracelet kit. "These are for you."

Blythe stares at the gifts, unmoving, as the wind tries to rip the stickers out of my hand. Heat crawls up the back of my neck as the moment stretches into awkwardness. Sylvia nudges Blythe, who finally mumbles a thank-you. Sylvia beams at me as Blythe stuffs the presents into her backpack. Blythe might not be impressed, but Sylvia seems thrilled, and that's good enough for me.

• • •

The walk from Blythe's school to the Morins' home takes us through quiet streets lined by houses with two-car garages and hedges trimmed at perfect right angles. When we reach the park, the sidewalk becomes a path through it. To our right, the edge of the park is marked by an ancient wood-and-wire fence, a sagging line between the dead grass on this side and a thick tangle of bare shrubs on the other.

But beyond the bushes, the earth just . . . ends.

Hundreds of feet below, Lake Ontario churns all the way to the horizon. My eyes feel like they're stretching out of their sockets, like my brain doesn't know how to make sense of such a view after a day squinting at screens and notebooks.

In the middle of the park is a community center, where Blythe takes gymnastics on Tuesdays. Sylvia tells me it was just built a few years ago. The glass-walled building is beautiful, in a sleek, futuristic sort of way. But it looks out of place here, like someone plucked it from downtown and plopped it in the middle of this cute residential neighborhood.

When we reach the other end of the path, the Morins' house is right there. The fence around their backyard is *in* the park. I've never seen anything like it. Imagine having this view of the lake right outside your back door? It must be amazing in the summer, when you actually want to be outside. But today, it's a relief to step out of the biting wind and into the Morins' warm, pristine entryway.

Blythe is instantly glued to her tablet, planting herself at the dining table while Sylvia shows me how to make a smoothie. I try to nod at the right moments, but blending up a bunch of frozen fruit isn't that complicated. Sylvia presses a manicured finger to her lips and adds a handful of cauliflower. Yuck. She gives me a wink and flips the switch.

"Would you like some?" Sylvia asks, once the machine's grinding dies down.

"No thanks." I try not to sound disgusted.

"How about something else? Water?"

"I'm okay, thank you."

"Maybe something warmer? Tea?"

It doesn't seem like Sylvia is going to take no for an answer, so I nod. She turns on the kettle and opens a cupboard stuffed with glass mason jars of loose-leaf tea, a printed label fixed to each one like in a bougie café. She pulls a jar off the bottom shelf.

"This one's my favorite," Sylvia says. "Here, smell it."

She unscrews the lid and holds it out to me. I inhale the scent of sweet apples, roasted nuts, and cinnamon. I'm not usually into tea, but this smells like candy.

"That's amazing," I say, truthfully.

Sylvia smiles and spoons the tea into a metal steeper and pops it in a mug, while I make myself useful by pouring Blythe's cauliflower smoothie into a cup. Sylvia's filling the mug with hot water when her purse starts buzzing. She fishes her phone out, mouths an apology at me, and shuffles into the living room.

I pick up the smoothie and the mug of tea. I try to believe Blythe's as sweet and innocent as she looks, with her legs crossed on the chair and elbows splayed out on the dining table. She doesn't look up as I slide into the chair next to her. I stare out the wall of windows that lines the back of the house. A wide deck gives way to a patchy lawn. Fat, wet snowflakes float down, painting dark streaks on the fence that separates the Morins' backyard from the park beyond. I bet their lawn is perfectly green in the summer. They seem like the kind of people who have sprinklers on a timer.

Okay. Stop stalling.

I peek over Blythe's shoulder. Her face is so close to the screen that her breath fogs a circle on the glass.

"What're you playing?" I ask.

Blythe puts her tablet down. Without saying a word, she reaches for her backpack and pulls out the stickers and friendship bracelet kit I gave her. She looks me in the eye, walks over to the garbage can, and drops my gifts in.

"Stickers are for babies," Blythe says. "And you're not my friend."

My clenched jaw throbs in time with my pounding pulse.

Calm, I think. *Be calm.*

"I'm sorry," I say. "You're right . . . You're a bit old for stickers. And I know we're not friends yet, but I hope we can be."

The garbage lid bangs shut.

"No."

Blythe scoops up her tablet and resumes her game without so much as another glance in my direction. Like I don't even exist.

CHAPTER FIVE

IT'S ALMOST TIME TO pick Blythe up on my own for the first time, and I can't make my palms stop sweating. She's not the first kid who's been rude when their parents are out of sight. It sucks, but there's no reason I should be this anxious.

I stop at the cafeteria and buy myself a root beer for courage. The sweet fizz instantly makes me feel better. I haven't seen Yas all day, so I've been trying to explain what happened with Blythe over text, without seeming whiny or paranoid. I thumb open our messages.

the kid hates me

what did u do?

nothing!!!

did u say her music sucks 🤡

I would never

i gave her stickers but
she threw them out

did u get them at the dollar store?

i know u did

can't blame her for having standards

Yas is right. What was I thinking, giving a kid with her own tablet something from the dollar store? It was a stupid mistake, but I'm overthinking it. I start to type a message back, when something smacks me in the ribs and sends me stumbling sideways.

I crash into a jumble of bodies, the drink in my hand spilling all over my wrist and jacket. I apologize and back away, trying to shake the sticky liquid off.

"Don't curse me, it was an accident!"

Cameron Edwards cowers in mock fear, his hands raised in surrender. A bulky soccer bag hangs from his shoulder, definitely what nearly knocked me over. Tanner and Jake K. elbow each other, snickering "witch bitch" under their breath. Cameron's own personal laugh track.

The crowd morphs into a circle around us, all eyes on the four of us in the center. It teleports me right back to grade five: I'm ten years old, clutching a tiny wooden sword in front of me as a warm, damp patch spreads across the front of my pants. *What's that? A stick?* A shorter, pudgier Cameron smirks as our class giggles behind him. I've replayed the scene in my mind a million times. How different would my life be if I'd delivered a cutting comeback, made a joke, or stabbed him with Wàipó's stupid sword?

But there's no use imagining what might have happened.

Because what *did* happen is I yelled *it's a WAND!* and took off running.

It was literally the worst thing I could have done.

From that moment on, I was the freak who sees ghosts and pisses herself, the witch bitch who carries a wand in her backpack to curse people. I've cried, I've cussed them out, I've told an adult. But six years later, Cameron and his buddies are still blocking my way, sneering and making crosses with their fingers.

Do crosses even work against witches?

Morons.

I shove past Cameron, slamming my shoulder into his so hard it sends a sharp pain vibrating up my collarbone. A wave of *oooooooooooooo*s swells up as I push through the crowd, but I refuse to give them the satisfaction of looking back. Ignoring them is the only way to avoid making things worse. It's not quite the same as making things better, but I'll take what I can get. After next year, I'll be done with this high school hellscape, and I'll never have to see Cameron's face again. I'll go somewhere new, somewhere that no one's heard of Rachel the witch bitch. I'll start over.

I push the door open with all my strength, and it hits the wall with a satisfying smack. The sun is out today, but it's a trick. The wind is ice, and it fights me the whole way to Blythe's school, its sharp nails scraping my cheeks raw. I almost convince myself that's why my eyes are stinging. My hand is covered in a syrupy film, but I'm too late to stop to clean myself up.

By the time I arrive at Cliffside, the yard is already a zoo of kids reuniting with their parents. Blythe is sitting cross-legged on a bench, hunched over an open book—a real book, with paper pages the wind is trying to tear out of her hands. When she sees me coming, she snaps the book shut and shoots me a venomous look.

"You're late," she says.

Blythe leaps up and marches down the sidewalk, not waiting to see if I'm following. Halfway through the park, she veers off the path and up the steps to the community center. Right, it's Tuesday. She has gymnastics.

The atrium smells sharply of chlorine; there must be a pool somewhere. Blythe heads for the changeroom, but when I start to follow, she stops me with a glare that screams *stay the hell away from me.* The door swings shut behind her, and I'm alone in a corridor swarming with kids in brightly colored leotards.

I find a water fountain and rinse my hands, trading damp and sticky for plain old damp. I guess it's an improvement. The gymnasium is covered in blue mats, a wide-open space with balance beams and bars clustered off to the sides. I never took gymnastics; all the after-school stuff Mom put me in was utilitarian: daycare, Mandarin class, math tutoring. I take a seat on the bleachers and pop my headphones in. A lanky girl in bright red spandex takes a running start and launches herself into a series of impressive flips. I put on "Cherry Bomb" by the Runaways; that's definitely this kid's theme song. But she must be the keener of the group because all the other kids just lie on the ground, whispering and giggling. It's almost all girls, and most of them are sporting slicked-back ponytails fastened with matching silver scrunchies that twinkle under the fluorescent lights.

Blythe emerges from the changeroom and pauses at the edge of the mat, chewing on the limp end of her braid. No sparkly scrunchy for her. She seems so unsure, a completely different human from the one who looked like she might shank me earlier. As she slinks onto the mat, the kids closest to her shift away. It doesn't look coordinated. The way they lean in the other direction is almost unconscious, like there's a forcefield around Blythe repelling them.

Blythe pretends not to notice. She doesn't look at any of the kids, just sits down at the edge of the group and hugs her knees to her chest.

She might be a little monster, but no one deserves that.

• • •

Blythe watches me silently from the dining table as I bumble around the kitchen, measuring out frozen fruit and yogurt before dumping them into the blender, trying to get the proportions just right. So much for smoothies being easy. I compliment her on her splits—she really did go further than most of the kids—and she looks at me like I have six eyes. I guess it's a good thing that she's right back to her normal, prickly self.

I don't know how to sneak the cauliflower in with her staring at me, so I skip it. Hopefully Sylvia doesn't keep tabs on how much is in the bag. As the blender roars to life, I notice a mug on the counter with a yellow sticky note on it. It says *Rachel* in curly handwriting. There's a metal steeper sitting inside, and when I pick it up, I get a sweet whiff of Sylvia's candy tea. She put this out for me? Mrs. King let me eat some of whatever snack I put together for her kids, but this feels different. Special.

But the tea is going to have to wait.

I steel myself as I bring Blythe her smoothie. She's focused on her tablet, and the contents of her backpack are spread out on the table in front of her, a mountain of workbooks, colored pens, and pencil shavings. A thin black book pokes out of the pile, a cartoon skull grinning up from the cover. Red, dripping-blood letters spell *FRIGHTFUL: Terrifying, True Stories for Kids*.

That fits.

"This looks cool," I say, reaching for the book.

Blythe snatches it away and shoves it back in her bag.

"Is that where you learned about the king who died eating peaches?"

She ignores me.

"I like scary stories too," I continue, like we're having an actual conversation. "Maybe we can read some together later?"

Blythe grabs her tablet and backpack in one hand, her smoothie in the other, and stalks away. She stomps through the living room and up the stairs, her steps rumbling through the ceiling.

A door slams shut somewhere above me, then silence descends through the house.

BANG!

The knots in my shoulders tighten, and I look up.

The banging doesn't stop. It continues in a steady rhythm, and with every slam my annoyance sharpens further toward frustration. What is she doing? Her parents said to ignore her tantrums, but how long am I supposed to let this go on? What if she breaks something?

I close my eyes and start counting. If she stops by the time I get to ten, I'll let it go.

I'm at eight when another slam vibrates through the house with such force that the pictures on the dining room walls rattle.

My restraint snaps.

"Blythe!" I yell, racing out of the kitchen. "You absolutely *cannot* keep doing that!"

At the top of the stairs, I come face-to-face with a closed door with an engraved wooden sign that reads BLYTHE. Below it, a paper sign says KEEP OUT in thick, red marker. I'm reaching for the knob when movement flickers in the corner of my eye.

BANG!

I whip around just as a door at the other end of the hall slams shut, then swings wide open. I jog toward it and catch the door before it bangs closed again. It has a wooden sign on it that matches Blythe's, except this one says MADDIE.

I peer inside, but the room is empty. A gust of cold air sends goosebumps up my arms. There's a window across from me, and it's wide open, the curtains flapping wildly. I guess that solves the mystery of the banging door.

"Sorry, Blythe," I mutter.

The room is a mess. The bed is unmade, and the floor is barely visible between islands of clothes. It's like Sylvia and Hector are waiting for Maddie to walk back in any minute, so they can nag her to tidy up and finish her homework. The only clean surface is her desk, which sits under the open window.

I dart across the room, weaving around the clutter. The cold nips at my fingers as I yank the window down. My palms land in an icy puddle on the windowsill. Gross. I wipe my hands on my jeans, and silence descends like a weight.

I'm suddenly very aware that I'm in a dead girl's room.

When I turn back to the door, a pale face stares at me from the shadows. I jump and stumble into the wall.

Then I register the mirror.

My panic-stricken reflection melts into embarrassment.

"What are you doing?"

Blythe is in the doorway, her hands clenched in fists at her sides.

"The window was open," I say. "Didn't you hear the door banging?"

"You shouldn't be in here," Blythe says. "She wouldn't like it."

My mouth goes dry. For a second I think she means Maddie, but then my common sense kicks in. She means her mom, and she's probably right.

Blythe's eyes are unfocused, like she's looking through me. I glance over my shoulder, but there's nothing there. Only a dead girl's room, frozen in time, awaiting a return that will never come. It makes me think of my mom, and how she left the last container of leftovers

Wàipó made for us in the fridge for months. When I finally cleaned it out, the rice was covered in furry green polka dots.

Mom still yelled at me when she realized it was gone.

I turn back to Blythe, an apology halfway out of my mouth, but she's no longer there. Down the hall, a door clicks shut. I feel like I should go after her, but what would I say? I don't want to upset her more. I'll leave her alone for a little while, let her cool off.

• • •

I'm hunched over my homework when the front door opens and Sylvia swoops in, her face obscured by a big cardboard box that she barely has her arms around. I rush over and take the other side. Whatever is in here is heavy; I have to adjust my grip more than once as we shuffle through the living room and set it on the kitchen island.

"Thank you, Rachel!" Sylvia smiles at me through the wisps of blond hair that have escaped her stub of a ponytail. "Who knew jewelry could be this heavy?"

"This is all jewelry?"

Sylvia nods and reaches into the box, pulling out a plastic sandwich bag with a barcode on the side. Inside is a gold bangle, which Sylvia slips out and offers to me. I accept the bracelet with both hands, holding it like a raw egg. It's heavier than it looks and engraved with an ornate scrolling pattern that gleams when the light hits it. I bet it's real gold. It's probably the most expensive thing I've ever touched.

"Did you make this?" I ask.

"No, no. I do antiques appraisal and restoration. Basically, people bring me their old stuff and I tell them how much it's worth. That belonged to my client's mother. All this did." She gestures at the box.

"Are they going to sell it?"

Sylvia chuckles. "He thinks his mother's spirit is trying to communicate with him and that she's connected to a piece of her jewelry. He's had mediums and psychics and who-knows-what-else trying to figure out which one." She gives me a look that tells me just how ridiculous she thinks that is. "But all that 'investigating' is getting expensive, so he's planning to sell the pieces he's ruled out."

"Does a lot of the stuff you work with belong to people who, uh . . ." I think of Maddie's empty room and mentally kick myself.

"Died?"

Sylvia doesn't seem bothered at all. Maybe she's one of those people who's good at keeping a wall between her work and personal life.

"Yes, usually," she continues. "When I was younger, I was fascinated by different ideas about ghosts, hauntings, all that kind of stuff. It started when I was teaching English in Taiwan. They burn paper sculptures of things they think the dead will need on the other side. In some stores I saw paper cell phones, cars, even dentures! Isn't that wild?"

"Wow." I raise my eyebrows like I'm hearing about this for the first time, like I haven't sat around a fire with my mom and burned paper hell money to fund Wàipó's afterlife.

Sylvia's right anyway. It is wild.

"I started collecting unusual artifacts, getting a sense of how much they were worth. It's how I got into antiques. It earned me a bit of a reputation in the industry. And quite a lot of clients." She gives me a self-conscious smile.

"Do you think the stories are true?" I ask.

"I'm intrigued by the folktales, but that's all they are. As much as some people wish that were different."

We're interrupted by a thundering of feet, and Blythe races into the kitchen.

"Hi, honey," Sylvia says. "How was your day?"

Blythe doesn't say anything, just twines her arms around her mom's waist and squeezes. Sylvia laughs and turns her smile toward me.

"Did you two have a nice day?"

I push away the memory of Blythe standing at Maddie's bedroom door, eyes unfocused, hands clenched.

"It was great," I say. "Blythe was great."

CHAPTER SIX

THE REST OF THE week is a roller coaster. Cameron and his goons are still spamming all my social media posts with witches and other stupid comments. Since I stopped adding new photos, they've gone back through my entire feed instead. I turn off notifications and blast music to drown out the laughter that follows me through the school hallways. Yas does her best to distract me with Osheaga planning.

Then there's Blythe. On Wednesday, I catch her in the upstairs hallway with a lighter in her hand, talking to the flame. As soon as she sees me, she stuffs the lighter in her pocket and stomps into her room. I know that I should follow her, take the lighter, and give her a lecture on fire safety. But the thought of what she might do if I confront her makes me nauseous.

We do manage to have one actual conversation. On Thursday, I ask her to tell me the worst thing in the *FRIGHTFUL* book. She rolls her eyes but recites a gruesome story about a countess who kidnapped little girls and bathed in their blood because she thought it would keep her young. I must look shocked because Blythe grins like a demon. For the rest of the afternoon, she randomly pops up next to me with more creepy facts, watching my face closely to see if I'm rattled. It's weird, but at least she's not throwing chairs.

By Friday, I'm feeling more at home in the Morins' house. I key in the front door code by memory and make a strawberry-banana-cauliflower smoothie without measuring everything out. There's a mug of Sylvia's candy tea waiting for me by the kettle, in the same place it's been every day this week. Today the sticky note next to it asks me to fold the laundry in the living room.

Blythe disappears into her room with her smoothie and her tablet, and I flop on the couch and put an earbud in. The familiar opening chords of "This Perfect Day" by the Saints smooths the tension from my shoulders. Even though this song was released in 1977, it's just as ferocious today as it was then.

My phone pings with a message from Yas.

> i know u hate showing skin but how cute is this?

> we can get u a black one

The link takes me to a new post on our Osheaga mood board: a photo of a model-gorgeous girl in a red crochet crop top. Seriously, Yas? There's no way I can pull that off. Plus, it's $200. Yas isn't the kind of person to flaunt her family's wealth on purpose, but sometimes she does things without thinking that make it clear she exists in a completely different universe than I do. I send a skull emoji in response.

I get to work matching a mountain of miniature socks, and exhaustion settles over me like a weighted blanket. This week's been a lot, but I did get a B+ on my last physics assignment. To celebrate my best grade ever in the subject, Mom gave me money to get takeout tonight. Which means I'm looking forward to a BBQ chicken burrito and a movie marathon. Actually, I probably have enough to get two burritos. I send Yas a note to invite her over.

By the time Sylvia gets home, I'm surrounded by brightly colored balls of socks and a mountain of neatly folded T-shirts. Blythe bounds down the stairs and wraps herself around her mom's waist, clinging to her like a barnacle.

"Thank you for doing that." Sylvia smiles at me and tilts her head toward the piles of clothes on the couch. "Would you like to stay for dinner? It's taco night."

I glance at my phone. Nothing from Yas. She probably has way more exciting plans than hanging out on my couch with Netflix and a cheap burrito. Is that really how I want to spend *my* Friday night?

Sylvia is looking at me with a warm, almost hopeful expression, and homemade tacos sound pretty good. Maybe it will help if I spend more time with Blythe while her parents are around? If I can ignore the way she's glaring at me.

When I say yes, Sylvia beams.

The three of us head into the kitchen, and Sylvia assigns me to rinse the rice.

"A little trick I learned in Taiwan," she says. "It gets rid of the starch, makes the rice fluffier."

I don't mention that Wàipó always made me rinse the rice, though I never knew why. I'm pouring the rice into a pot when Hector walks into the kitchen. I haven't seen him all week; Sylvia always arrived home first. When he sees me standing at the sink, he does a double-take and my face goes hot. Is it weird that I'm here?

"Rachel's staying for dinner." Sylvia pecks him on the cheek like she doesn't feel the tension at all. "Can you and Blythe make the tortillas?"

Hector blinks and nods, turning away without acknowledging me. Blythe follows him to the dining table with a big bag of flour. I don't think I've ever had a tortilla that didn't come out of a bag. I'd be excited if this didn't feel so awkward. He definitely thinks it's weird that I'm here. But there's nothing I can do about it now except try to make myself useful.

Once the rice is on the stove, Sylvia points me toward a pile of tomatoes on the island. She opens a drawer and removes a large knife, slipping the protective sleeve off the blade and offering it to me handle-first.

"This was made by a Japanese company that started out making samurai swords," she says. "Nothing better for cutting tomatoes! Be careful, it's very sharp."

I take the knife gingerly, holding it like it might leap out of my hands and attack me. All our knives at home are so dull that they fold tomatoes more than slice them. But I barely press this blade against the skin and it opens like a zipper, revealing the pulpy flesh within.

"Learn anything interesting at school today?" Sylvia asks as she stirs a sizzling pan of vegetables. I wait for Blythe to answer, but she's busy chatting with her dad at the dining table. When I look at Sylvia, she's watching me expectantly. I hide my blush by focusing on the tomatoes.

"Not really." I shrug.

Sylvia chuckles, like it's an answer she's heard a thousand times before. She probably has. "You graduate next year, right? Do you know what you want to do after?"

"I'm trying to get into computer science at University of Toronto."

"What kind of job do you want?"

"I'm not sure. But my mom says it'll open a lot of doors."

I sound like one of the brochures my mom's always leaving in my room. From the long, thoughtful look Sylvia's giving me, it seems like she's thinking the same thing.

"What do *you* want to do?" Sylvia asks. "If you could do anything?"

"Anything?"

My mind goes blank. Has anyone ever asked me that before? For as long as I can remember, the plan has been for me to keep my grades up, get into a program my mom is satisfied with, and land a job that will—what? Pay the bills? I guess I know that's something I *should* want. I know how hard it is when you can't pay the bills. Still, it's not very exciting.

"It's okay if you don't know yet," Sylvia says. "You're still so young! But if you want my advice—and I know you didn't ask for it—but if you *did*, I'd say that if you don't know what you want, it's better to take some time to figure it out rather than jump into something you're not sure of. That's why I went to teach English in Taiwan."

Sylvia turns back to the stove and continues talking, explaining how she decided to take a break from school, how mad her parents were, but why it was one of the best decisions of her life. As the kitchen fills with chatter and spicy steam, I think of Wàipó. Have I cooked like this with anyone since she died?

My grandfather disowned my mom when she got pregnant, but my grandmother—Wàipó—refused to cut my mom out. But she wouldn't stand up to her husband either. Instead, she snuck over to our place every Sunday, while my grandfather was out playing cards. All afternoon, Wàipó would hold court on our couch, hosting a steady stream of guests who wanted advice from the spirit she said she could channel. In between, she took over the kitchen and I played her sous chef. By the time she left, our fridge was packed with leftovers and our apartment was cloudy with incense. Wàipó never made tacos, but the smell of steaming rice makes it possible to imagine that she's right behind me, chopping thick green stalks of gai lan or rolling out dough for dumplings.

A sharp sting shoots through my left hand, shocking me back to the present.

I drop the knife on the cutting board, where the tomato juice is quickly being overtaken by a pool of darker red liquid. My left palm is so smeared with blood that it takes me a moment to find the wound: a nasty-looking gash in the meat below my thumb.

As soon as I see it, it starts to burn.

"You're bleeding." Blythe's voice cuts through the fog.

Sylvia and Hector are next to me in an instant, their concerned voices mingling.

"I'm so sorry." I press my uninjured hand over the cut, but all that does is smear the blood around. "You said the knife was sharp—"

Hector hands me a wad of paper towels and Sylvia leads me to the bathroom, where she turns on the cold water and guides my bloody palm under the tap. Pain flares, then fades into numbness. Sylvia gives me strict instructions not to move and leaves me stooped over the sink. By the time she comes back with a first aid kit in hand, I've stopped bleeding. There's a long, gaping cut that runs from the base of my thumb almost to my wrist, but it doesn't look too deep.

"You're lucky." Sylvia shakes her head as she pats my skin dry. "I've seen knives like that cut down to the bone."

I feel so stupid. A little deeper, and I'd be on my way to the hospital right now. I try not to flinch as she pinches my skin together with a butterfly bandage and presses a bigger bandage on top.

"Good as new," Sylvia says.

But then she frowns, looking at my chest.

I'm wearing my X-Ray Spex band tee, and there's a streak of blood right through Poly Styrene's face. I'm caught off guard by the way my stomach twists and my eyes start to sting. What's wrong with me? It's just a T-shirt.

"I have a trick for getting blood out of clothes." The way Sylvia touches my elbow is a soothing balm. "Come on."

Upstairs, Sylvia flings Maddie's door open and strides in without a pause. I stand awkwardly at the threshold as Sylvia steps smoothly around the clothes on the floor and opens the closet.

"I'm sure you can find something in here." Sylvia's smile is stretched so wide across her jaw, it almost looks like it's hurting her. Maybe it is. "Bring your shirt down when you're done and I'll take care of it for you." Before I can think of anything to say, she slips out of the room, closing the door behind her.

She wouldn't like it, Blythe said the last time I was in here.

Well, she was wrong; her mom doesn't seem to mind at all.

But even with Sylvia's invitation, I feel like I'm trespassing. Still, what other options do I have? My shirt is starting to stiffen where the blood is drying.

I try to be respectful as I look through Maddie's overflowing closet, carefully sliding the hangers over one by one. I wouldn't pick up most of these tops in a store. I wouldn't even be *in* the kind of store where these clothes are sold. They sport brand names I recognize but definitely don't own. One of them is probably worth all my buy-one-get-one secondhand shirts combined.

I run my uninjured hand over a sherpa fleece sweater, my fingers sinking into the soft fuzz. It's teddy-bear brown with no logos I can see. Seems as good a choice as any. I start to pull it out when something sparkly catches my eye. Behind the sweater is a silver top made of a delicate material lined with rows of tiny rhinestones that wink in the light. It's gorgeous.

Yas's text runs through my head: *i know you hate showing skin*

Suddenly, it feels like a challenge.

I pull off my stained T-shirt and drop it on the floor. Carefully, I take the silver top off the hanger and slide it over my head. The fabric settles like cool liquid against my skin. I adjust the front so the loose folds drape over my chest and turn around to look in the mirror. The thin straps draw my gaze to the curve of my shoulder and the sharp outline of my collarbone. The slender strip of skin between the shirt's hem and the top of my jeans makes my waist look impossibly small.

I look different. I look . . . good.

Take that, Yas.

But this top is for dancing in hazy clubs with black walls, not for going downstairs and having a nice home-cooked meal with my employers. I toy with the hem, knowing I should take it off. But for a reason I can't name, I don't want to.

An idea swirls in my mind.

I pull the teddy-bear sweater on, zipping it all the way up to my chin. When I turn back to the mirror, I look like a cozy stuffed toy. There's no hint of the silver top below.

A thrilling shiver runs through me. For a moment, I can imagine what it must have felt like to be Maddie: the smell of dinner wafting up from the kitchen while she lounged on her bed and chatted with her friends until her parents called her down to eat. I bet she had a big group of friends, so she always had people to sit with at lunch, take notes for her if she was sick, and go out with on a Friday night. I bet Hector and Sylvia knew all her friends' names, drove her to and from sports practices or play rehearsals, asked her what she wanted to be when she grew up, and actually listened to the answer.

Am I envious of her? God, that's sick.

I turn away from my reflection in the mirror, but I don't take off either top.

When I walk into the kitchen, Hector is the first one to see me. He stumbles and sets down the stack of plates he's holding with a thud.

Sylvia's hand lifts, squeezing her shirt in a fist. Her eyes dart back and forth, like she's reading something in the air around me. Her lips form an O but no sound comes out.

Blythe doesn't even glance in my direction.

"It's yours." When Sylvia finally speaks, her voice is lace-thin. "It's meant to be yours."

I start to protest, but she silences me with a shake of her head.

"Please, keep it." She's almost pleading.

I look to Hector for confirmation, but he's setting the table now, his back to me. Sylvia lifts my stained T-shirt from my bandaged hand, and I mumble a thank-you. I wrap my arms around myself, my fingers sinking into the soft sweater. Underneath, the silver top is cool against my stomach.

"No," Sylvia whispers, squeezing my shoulder. "Thank *you*."

CHAPTER SEVEN

WHEN I SLIDE INTO bed and turn off the light, the whole week's worth of anxiety comes crashing down on me. My brain plays a highlight reel of the worst moments: standing covered in root beer in the middle of the cafeteria, the crowd snickering and whispering "witch bitch" as Cameron's sneer loomed in front of them all; Blythe's look of disgust as she threw my gifts into the trash; and Sylvia and Hector's horrified expressions as I bled all over their cutting board.

Yas finally replies to my message. She and Dell were at some art show where you had to lock up your phone to get in. She says I would've hated it. She's probably right, but it still stings that she didn't invite me. Yet one more thing for my racing mind to chew on.

The only cure I have for nights like this is listening to my dad's mixtape until I fall asleep. My mom gave me the CD for my thirteenth birthday. I'm not sure why Mom decided to do it then. I'd pretty much given up asking her about my dad by that point. Maybe she realized she couldn't dodge my questions forever. Maybe she knew I was having a hard time at school. Or maybe she just figured I was finally old enough to handle a band called the Sex Pistols.

Whatever her reason was, the morning of my birthday she gave me a box that held an ancient Discman and my dad's CD: *Songs that changed my life*. Mom said he was always trying to get her to listen to something other than Beyoncé.

"In *my* opinion, this noise has nothing on Queen Bey," she smirked. "But you might like it."

Listening to each song was like discovering a new piece of my dad.

Now I know the track list by heart, and even though I have the playlist on my phone, I never play it on shuffle. Listening to the songs in the order he put them in feels almost like reading a letter he wrote.

• • •

The trick works a little too well. I sleep through my alarm, and when I finally surface, my ears ache from wearing my earbuds all night. I have to sacrifice eyeliner and coffee, but I manage to slide into my seat at driver's ed with a minute to spare.

When class breaks for lunch, Yas whips around to face me. "What happened? Did the kid bite you?" She's staring at my left hand. The bandage Sylvia put on yesterday fell off overnight, and the no-name Band-Aids Mom buys wouldn't stick below my thumb. The only way I could cover the wound was to wrap gauze around the whole base of my hand. It makes it look worse than it is. So does the rust-colored stain that's appeared in the middle. I'm going to have to change that.

"What kid?" Dell asks. They've unwrapped a slice of cold pizza and are cutting it up with a knife and fork. Who eats pizza with cutlery?

"I just started babysitting for a new family," I say. "I cut myself cooking. Blythe's fine."

"Come *on.*" Yas elbows me. "She sounds like a monster."

"All kids are monsters," Dell says.

"Her older sister died last year," I snap. I'm surprised by the protectiveness suddenly pulsing through me.

"Shit." Yas sounds shocked, like this is new information. She really wasn't listening to me the other day, was she?

"That's awful," Dell agrees.

"Yeah." I dig through my backpack for my sandwich, effectively shutting down the conversation.

"Did you ask your mom about Osheaga?" Yas asks between bites of her salad.

"Not yet." My forehead starts to throb.

"Well, my mom wants to talk to her. Dell's parents too." Yas glances at Dell, who nods. How lucky that this isn't a big deal for either of them. "So when are you going to ask?"

"Soon." I press my fingers into my temple.

Yas looks like she wants to shake me.

"Oh!" Dell jumps in, grinning. "I wanted to tell you—I have a proposal for LMK."

Wait—did Yas tell them we're going to Osheaga to see LMK, like some basic K-pop groupies? The pounding in my head intensifies.

Dell sets their phone on their desk so we can all see. The mood board Yas and I started is glowing on the screen. Of course Yas shared it with them too. I'm not sure if I want to flip the desk or melt into the floor. Dell swipes to a screenshot from the "Electric Confetti" music video. The song isn't LMK's biggest hit, but one day, in grade three, it came on the radio in our after-school program, and I started singing along—and then another girl did too. That was how Yas and I became friends. Now Dell is zooming in on the dancers' outfits: baggy jeans and cropped denim vests covered in rows of matching pearls.

"I found a great deal on fake pearls," Dell continues. "We can buy a thousand for under ten dollars. Then all we have to do is sew them on!"

"Yes!" Yas gasps. "I love it."

I stare at her, my mind reeling. We decided months ago to do baggy black suits with leather accents, inspired by LMK's Thunder Rush tour. Didn't we? I already bought a suit secondhand.

But judging from the way Yas is zooming in on the photo, talking a mile a minute about a denim vest she has that would be *perfect* . . . I was wrong.

• • •

All kids are monsters. Dell's comment runs through my head for the rest of the afternoon. It's easier to hold on to the jolt of anger I felt when they talked about Blythe than it is to look too closely at whatever I'm feeling about this new wardrobe plan.

Blythe's sister is dead. Her behavior is frustrating, but it isn't about me. And it doesn't make her a monster. I know it's not the same, but I remember what it was like when Wàipó died. I just wanted someone to notice me, to ask if I was okay. Especially since my mom was too trapped in her own grief to think about me. Maybe I should make more of an effort with Blythe. Her parents are in a much better place, but that doesn't mean she doesn't still feel alone.

I remember the kids moving away from her in gymnastics class, and a plan starts to form in my mind. She hated the gifts I got her that first day, but Yas is right: I can't blame her for trashing cheap trinkets from the dollar store. What if—

A knock on our apartment door breaks my train of thought. I silently will the person on the other side to go away, but another series of knocks rings out, louder this time. I slouch over to the peephole and see a woman with a short, silver Afro staring back through tortoiseshell glasses. I open the door just enough to poke my head through.

"Hi, Mrs. Paul," I say.

"Hello, Rachel." A hesitant smile flits across her face. "Is your mom home?"

"Sorry, she's at work."

"Oh." Mrs. Paul purses her lips but doesn't move.

"I'll tell her you came by?"

Mrs. Paul nods but still doesn't leave. I want to close the door, but the tension in her posture and the way her eyes are darting around stops me.

"Are you okay?" I ask.

Her shoulders sag in relief, like that's the question she was waiting for.

"You know your mom's helping me with a . . . problem?"

Oh yes, I know.

Mrs. Paul's "problem" is that she thinks her late husband's ghost is haunting her.

My mom doesn't claim to be a spirit medium like Wàipó did, but after she died, her regular clients kept coming by. Mom couldn't turn them away, so she started inviting them in for coffee, and they started asking her questions. Before long, she was putting the things that Wàipó taught her to good use. Word got around, and more people started coming to my mom for help. People like Mrs. Paul, who first showed up at our door a month ago and has been a regular visitor since.

"Your mom gave me a coin," Mrs. Paul continues. "But when I went to get it this afternoon, it was gone. It gave me a bad feeling. I was hoping she might have another one, or something else—"

"Wait here," I say.

At our ancestral altar, I remove a small pouch from one of the drawers and fish out a coin-shaped charm. Mrs. Paul takes it from me with a grateful smile, running her fingertips over the Chinese characters inscribed around the square hole in the middle. "God of Thunder," they read, "use your thunderbolts to kill malicious ghosts."

With Wàipó gone, the main uses for my Mandarin skills are reading made-up spells and saying *No, that's actually my mom; yes, I know I don't look Chinese* when we go shopping together in Chinatown.

Mrs. Paul touches my forearm, her eyes glistening behind her glasses. I shut the door behind her and scribble a note to my mom.

I think Mrs. Paul is just lonely. She's new to our building, and my mom said her kids barely visit. She's looking for attention, and my mom's more than happy to oblige. How can she pass up the chance to hang out with someone else who believes in ghosts?

CHAPTER EIGHT

IT'S 8 A.M. ON Sunday, and my mom is knocking at my bedroom door. She plays a little tune: tap, tap, tap-tap. I lie still, squeezing my eyes shut, hoping she'll take the hint and go away.

The knocking starts again.

"What?!" I croak.

My mom takes that as an invitation and bursts into my room with a spotlight-bright smile. I throw my arm across my face. My mattress dips as she sits down, and the smooth, bitter smell of coffee fills my nostrils. My mouth starts to water.

"What do you want?"

"What makes you think I want something?"

I lift my arm just enough to shoot her a skeptical look.

After an overnight shift, Mom eats and goes straight to bed. She doesn't pop in to say hi. And she definitely doesn't bring me coffee.

"Okay, you caught me." She winces and holds the mug out like a peace offering. "I'm going over to Mrs. Paul's, and—"

"Mom!" I let my arm fall back over my eyes. I know exactly where she's going with this, and I don't want any part in it.

"I need you to come with me," she barrels on. "You know fújī won't work without my trusty assistant."

"I'm *sleeping*."

"You sound awake to me."

"This is my one day off. I'm exhausted." I know I've lost as soon as the words hit the air. Mom doesn't say anything, but she's looking at me with her eyebrows raised, unimpressed. *One of us is lying in bed*, her expression says, *and one of us just came off an overnight shift*.

I never win the "who's more tired" contest.

"It won't take long," she says.

I glare at her but sit up and take the steaming coffee from her hands.

• • •

Mom must really need my help because she doesn't say anything when I walk out in my pajama pants with the hood of my sweatshirt pulled up over my tangled hair. In the elevator, she pushes my hood off and motions for me to take my earbuds out, but doesn't make her usual comment about "the noise I call music" and tugs the hood back over my head after.

Mrs. Paul opens the door so fast she must have been waiting right on the other side. "Thank you for coming Jennifer, Rachel." She wrings her hands and tries to smile, but it doesn't stick.

Her apartment is a mirror of ours, and seeing the entryway to the kitchen on the right instead of the left is disorienting. Her living room is dominated by a big yellow couch and a wooden TV stand that takes up an entire wall, its shelves crowded with family photos.

"Okay, Rhonda," my mom says, once the three of us are settled on the couch. "Tell us what happened."

"Last night, when I was making dinner, the drawers in the kitchen kept coming open." Mrs. Paul's eyes are wide, magnified to a cartoonish size by her glasses. "My Anthony loved to cook, so it makes sense, him being with me in the kitchen. But . . ." Her hands clench and unclench in her lap. "All this is starting to scare me. What if it's not him? What if it's something else? Something evil?"

We used to have a drawer in our kitchen that wouldn't stay closed. The super kept saying he'd come look at it, but he never showed. In the end my mom fixed it with magnetic tape.

"I understand why you're scared, but I still think it's most likely your husband," Mom says. No magnetic tape today, I guess. "We can try to contact the spirit and ask if it's Anthony. If it is, we need to figure out what's keeping him here. When a spirit has been properly buried but doesn't move on to the next world, it's usually because they have unfinished business in this one."

"We can talk to him with that . . . Chinese Ouija board?" asks Mrs. Paul. At least she has enough sense to look skeptical.

"Fújī." Mom nods. "My mother was a medium, and she taught me how to use fújī to communicate with the spirit world."

I struggle not to roll my eyes as Mom explains how it's supposed to work. Mom's made me help with fújī dozens of times, but I haven't seen a single spirit say *boo*. Sure, someone writes stuff on the paper: my mom. Obviously. She's the *living human* holding the pen. But no matter how much I bug her, no matter what deity or prized possession I swear on that I'll take her secret to my grave, she still insists it isn't her. The closest thing she's given me to an admission is the time she said, *Sometimes fújī is more about what the living need to say to the dead.* I hate to admit it, but she might be on to something, given the way Mrs. Paul is nodding along like this is a completely normal conversation to have with your neighbors on a Sunday morning.

Mrs. Paul writes down two questions for the spirit, each on a separate sticky note, and hands them to me. The three of us cluster around the small table in the corner of her kitchen, as Mom pulls supplies out of her bag: a bundle of joss sticks and an incense burner, a package of tea lights and a lighter, a new red pen still encased in plastic wrap, and the dog-eared notebook with the red cover that holds everything Wàipó taught her about this kind of stuff.

Wàipó didn't speak much English, so Mom put me in Mandarin school and had me practice by playing translator. My brain is as full as that notebook with random stories about Chinese ghosts and demon-slaying heroes and magic spells. Very useful stuff.

Mom places a sheet of heavy, white paper on the table and sets the tea lights around it. Once the cluster of candles is glowing, she asks me to turn the kitchen lights off. The room plunges into darkness and the halo of light on the table seems to glow brighter. It feels impossible that it's not even noon.

"First, we bow to greet the spirit." Mom's voice is deeper than normal, like she's playing a part in an amateur horror movie. She bends low at the waist, and Mrs. Paul and I mimic her. Once we've bowed three times, Mom gestures for us to sit down.

"Next, I'll say a mantra to clear our minds and purify any negative emotions," Mom says. "Close your eyes, and focus on breathing steadily and listening to the sound of my voice."

The familiar notes of the mantra comfort me, but I know it's not magic. It's just meditation. When she's finished, she passes us a joss stick each. We light them in one of the candles' flames and place them in the incense burner. Curls of woody incense fill the air as the sticks start to smoke.

My mom removes the red pen from its plastic wrapper. I've tried to get her to reuse them—it feels so wasteful to use a new one every time—but she insists it's necessary. I guess the spirits don't believe in recycling.

Mom holds the pen above the center of the paper and looks at me sideways. I know my role well: I place the sticky notes with Mrs. Paul's questions in front of me, then lightly wrap the fingers of my good hand around the pen, above my mom's. Wàipó taught Mom that you need two people to conduct fújī, but she didn't say they both need to believe in it.

At my mom's signal, I read Mrs. Paul's first question: "Is this Anthony?"

The pen begins to tremble, and Mrs. Paul gasps. I can't see her eyes through the reflection of the candles on her glasses, but she seems transfixed. They always are.

This could be a decent side hustle, if Mom would charge people. I've read that some professional psychics make six figures. But I've never seen her take money in exchange for any of her little rituals. I think she'd be appalled if I suggested it. Sometimes she'll accept small things, like a container of homemade soup or a hand-knit scarf, but usually she gets absolutely nothing from this stuff. Except an ego boost.

"It's him." Mrs. Paul's voice is choked with tears. "It's really him."

The paper now reads YES in bold red letters. In my mom's handwriting, of course.

With her free hand, my mom slides a fresh sheet of paper under the pen. My arm is starting to go numb, but I will my muscles to stay locked in place. If I move the pen by accident, Mom will murder me.

At my mom's signal, I read Mrs. Paul's second question: "What are you trying to tell me?"

The pen trembles, but before my mom can write anything, a crash breaks the silence. We all jump, whipping our heads toward the sound.

The kitchen drawer closest to us hangs open, piles of silver cutlery within shining in the candlelight.

None of us move. The only sound in the room is our breathing.

I manage to bite back a joke about magnets, but a little laugh escapes me. I try unsuccessfully to cover it with a cough. Mom shoots me a glare and turns her gaze back to the paper.

"Thank you, Anthony," she says. "Farewell."

• • •

When we step back into the elevator, my mom nudges me with her shoulder.

"Thanks for coming," she says. "You go back to bed. I'll order us some pizza."

Wow, she must really be grateful. Mom rarely orders in. She usually says paying double to have something delivered is like flushing money down the toilet.

I think of Yas's exasperated stare. *Did you ask your mom about Osheaga?*

Mom's in a good mood. She owes me for this morning and she's not pestering me about school. There isn't going to be a better moment than this. But when I try to force the question out, the words stick in my throat. The closest I can get is, "Have you ever been to Montreal?"

Mom blinks at me, like I've never asked her a question before.

"No," she says. "But I've been to Quebec City. We went for a school trip in grade nine."

"That's cool." Is my voice as shaky as it sounds in my head? "You know, Montreal hosts the biggest music festival in Canada every year."

"Is that right?" The way she says it sounds like *no*.

I'm trying to figure out what to say next when she looks at the bandage wrapped around my left hand.

"What happened to you?" She takes my hand in hers, turning it over to inspect the thick gauze. Good thing I changed the bandage last night.

"Nothing," I say. I pull my hand away but resist the urge to hide it behind my back. "I was just cutting tomatoes. The Morins have this really sharp knife—"

"The family you're babysitting for? They're making you cook too?"

"It's fine." It comes out harsher than I intend, but why does she have to question everything I do? "They're paying me so much, I'd sort their garbage by color if they wanted."

"Rachel—"

"Oh my god. They're obviously not making me do that. They invited me to stay for dinner, so I was helping."

Mom's eyebrows shoot up. "Well, be careful not to overstay your welcome." The elevator doors open and she walks out, leaving me standing there, gaping.

So much for her being in a good mood.

CHAPTER NINE

A STAPLED STACK OF papers lands on my desk.

"See me after class," Mr. Savoca says. His frown is so deep that his bushy eyebrows merge into a single gray caterpillar in the middle of his forehead.

My throat closes up. It's my test from last week, with a big, red *32%* circled in the corner. I shove it under my textbook.

When the bell rings, Mr. Savoca calls my name, like he doesn't trust me not to sneak out.

"Hot date?" Cameron hisses as he walks by.

I ignore him and focus on packing up my things, keeping my eyes down to avoid the heads turning my way. Especially Yas's.

The classroom door clicks shut, muffling the chaos in the halls as I shuffle up to Mr. Savoca's desk. He's a notoriously serious teacher. His smiles are rare, and I don't think I've ever heard him laugh. People say he once threw a mug at a student who talked back to him, but my theory is he started that rumor himself to keep us in line.

"Rachel, I'm going to be direct with you." Mr. Savoca is stone-faced beneath the outrageous tangle of his eyebrows. "We both know you're struggling. You have a couple of options. You can switch into the applied course—"

I shake my head, panic clawing at my ribs, and he pauses.

"I have to take calculus next year." My voice is brittle; I barely recognize it.

For a moment, I think he might laugh in my face.

But instead, he nods and suggests I get a tutor. "The school board runs free programs online," he says, holding out a flyer. "But no amount of tutoring can make up for motivation. If you're serious about passing this class *and* calculus next year, you need to put in the work."

I nod and take the flyer from him, folding it in half to hide the way my hands are trembling. At the meeting my mom and I had with my physics teacher after I failed her class, the two of them talked about motivation and discipline and study strategies like I wasn't in the room. Mom was so disappointed she didn't look me in the eye for weeks. It was awful. I can't do that again.

"Rachel." Mr. Savoca's tone asks me to look at him. His gentle expression makes my stomach twist. He feels sorry for me.

God, this is humiliating.

"You can still pass this class," he says. "You need to work hard, but you don't need to do it alone. I'm here to help you. If there's something you're having trouble with, let me know. Don't wait until it shows up on a test."

"Okay." I'm already halfway to the door. "Thank you." I give him a stilted wave and rush out of the room without looking back.

• • •

Yas texts me, asking what Mr. Savoca wanted, but I leave it on read. The image of the red 32% keeps flashing in my mind as I plow through the rest of my classes and pick up Blythe on autopilot.

Blythe is silent on the walk home, which is just fine with me. She beelines for the kitchen—or, more precisely, her tablet, which sits in its charger on the counter. There's a note from Sylvia asking me to fold the laundry in the living room again, along with the mug and steeper filled with her candy tea. I make Blythe's smoothie and fill the mug with hot water, the sweet scent soothing my frayed nerves.

Blythe doesn't look up from her tablet when I set her smoothie down. She's guiding a big cartoon shark across the screen with her finger. I almost leave her to it, but then I remember I resolved to make more of an effort. So instead, I sit next to her and watch as she brings the shark underneath a swimmer.

The shark opens its jaws and bites the man in half. Over-the-top cartoon blood sprays across the screen. I can't stop myself from laughing, and Blythe looks up at me, surprise on her face.

"That's awesome," I say.

Blythe looks back at the screen but not before I catch her lips twisting into a smile.

"Did you know sharks can't chew?" Blythe makes her shark eat another swimmer, then an entire school of yellow fish. "They have to swallow their food whole."

"Whoa. They're pretty scary, huh?"

"Not really." Blythe shrugs. "You're more likely to get killed by a falling coconut than a shark."

I glance out the window at the backyard, where the grass has frozen into a skating rink and the fence is covered in mean-looking icicles.

"I think we're pretty safe from both of those, for now."

Blythe rolls her eyes, but the smile is still tugging at the corners of her mouth. Is this progress? I'm going to call it progress.

I have an idea I want to try tomorrow, so I better quit while I'm ahead.

I leave Blythe to her game and head for the basket of clean sheets that Sylvia asked me to fold. I pop an earbud in, and the rhythm of the music and the mundane task calms me. I'm nearly done when I pull out a sheet that's twisted itself into a rope. I shake it free, and something hits the ground with a thud.

I don't see anything on the floor, so I drop to my knees and peer under the couch. There isn't a single dust bunny, but there is a small plastic bag with its zip-top gaping open. A gold locket on a thin chain is curled next to it.

I reach under the couch, and when my fingers wrap around the necklace, my pores tingle and an itchy heat ripples up my arm. When I stand up, the world tilts sideways, darkness flickering at the edges of my vision. I close my eyes to steady myself. The feeling passes as quickly as it started. I must have gotten up too fast.

When the locket comes back into focus, I see it's an oval that fills almost half my palm. It's pretty, even though the gold is tarnished, almost black in places. I slide the necklace back into its plastic bag, which has a barcode on the side like the one Sylvia showed me the other day. I wonder if this also belonged to that guy's mom.

When I finish with the laundry, I look up the tutoring class Mr. Savoca mentioned. It's online, but my stomach sinks when I see it's after school on Wednesdays. Would Sylvia and Hector mind if I joined while I'm watching Blythe? I hate to admit it, but Mr. Savoca's right. I need help to pass his class. Yas is too wrapped up in photography and debate club and dating, and whatever else is keeping her so busy these days, to help me more than she already is. My mom would freak out if she knew how close I am to failing another class. This feels like my only option; I have to ask.

My thumb stings, the nail ragged. I didn't even know I was biting it.

When Sylvia comes home, I follow her into the kitchen, waiting for the right moment to ask about the tutoring. I linger as she catches up with Blythe, waiting for an opening. I pick up Blythe's empty smoothie cup and put it in the dishwasher, just for something to do.

When Blythe takes off to get something upstairs, I seize the chance.

"Sylvia? Can I talk to you for a minute?"

Sylvia stiffens and grips the back of the couch, looking slightly panicked. "Is something wrong?"

"No, everything's fine." I rush to reassure her. "It's . . . my math teacher wants me to do this tutoring thing. It's online but only on Wednesdays. While I'm with Blythe."

Sylvia looks confused, which frays my nerves further.

Words keep tumbling out of my mouth. "It would just be an hour, once a week. I can call in from the same room as Blythe, so I can still watch her. But I totally understand if you're not comfortable with it . . ."

"Oh." Sylvia blinks, and I can see the gears turning in her head. Then she smiles. "Of course," she says. "That's fine."

"Thank you so much." My limbs feel suddenly light with relief.

"No problem at all." As Sylvia waves off my thanks, her eyes land on the coffee table. I follow her gaze to the locket in the plastic bag.

"I found that in the laundry basket." It comes out in a rush that makes me sound guilty. I hope she doesn't think I took it from somewhere.

But Sylvia doesn't seem to notice. "I remember this piece." She holds the bag up to inspect it in the light. "The client who brought it in never came to pick it up."

"People do that?"

"More often than you'd think." Sylvia shrugs. "I always try to contact them, but there's a reason I put a time limit in my contracts."

The necklace shines through the clear plastic. How could someone just abandon it? It's old and worn, but it's still beautiful.

"Do you like it?" Sylvia asks, like she's reading my mind.

"It's cool." I struggle not to squirm under the intensity of her gaze.

"Would you like it?"

I stare at her. She can't be serious.

Sylvia chuckles but not unkindly. "It's yours, if you want it."

"That's so nice of you, but I can't—"

"Of course you can. It may not be worth much, but it deserves a good home."

A loud, resounding *yes* bubbles up in my throat.

But instead I say, "Are you sure?"

Sylvia smiles in response and opens the bag, tilting it so that the necklace spills into her palm. She undoes the chain and motions for me to turn around. I gather my hair up in my hands and lift it out of the way.

"Thank you." My voice cracks, and there's a quiet click as Sylvia fastens the clasp. The necklace settles against my chest, and my skin suddenly flares hot, like the locket is a burning coal.

I gasp and jerk away.

"Are you okay?" Sylvia asks. "Did I catch your hair?"

The burning feeling is already gone, replaced by a twinge of embarrassment. "Yeah, I think so. It's okay." I wrap my hand around the locket, tracing the smooth face with my thumb. "Thank you so much."

CHAPTER TEN

THE WARM FEELING LASTS until the elevator doors screech open on our floor, and then I remember the failed test in my bag and the pity on Mr. Savoca's face. I can't let Mom find out about this. She already can't stop talking about how I messed up with physics and how important the credit recovery is; I can't give her another failure to obsess over.

Zhong Kui glares at me from our apartment door like he knows my secret. His bulging cartoon eyes erase any lingering warmth from the candy tea and Sylvia's gift.

Why can't we have a nice wreath? Or nothing, like normal people?

Why does my mom insist on being weird so *loudly*?

A ball of anger flares hot behind my ribs, squeezing up into my throat. I grab the top edge of the poster and yank. It tears with a satisfying sound and Zhong Kui's hideous face rips in half. I glare at his one remaining eye, panting like I just ran a race.

The anger slips away as my breathing slows, and guilt swells up in its place.

Shit. I guess I'm not handling all this stress so well.

I peel the rest of the poster off the door, crumpling the ruined paper into a ball. By the time I'm tossing it in the recycling bin, I have a note to my mom composed in my head. I'll tell her I found it this way when I got home. It's not the first time something like this has happened in our building. When I place the sticky note on top of my mom's accounting textbook, I almost believe that's what actually happened.

I follow Sylvia's instructions for cleaning the necklace, filling a small bowl with warm water and adding a couple drops of dish soap. I leave the locket to soak while I take a shower. As the water heats up, I unwrap the bandage around my hand. It doesn't hurt too much. The skin around the cut is still red, but it's starting to scab.

When I come back to the necklace, the water is murky with soap scum and something darker. I lift it out, and the locket sparkles as it breaks the surface, like I've caught the reflection of a star. I unwrap a new toothbrush and gently scrub each part of it, even the dents that warp the locket's latch and hinges shut. I try to pry it open, but all I manage to do is chip a fingernail.

I polish every bit of the necklace with our softest towel, and when I'm done, it's unrecognizable. The locket is shining, buttery gold, not a trace of tarnish in sight. It looks like it belongs on a red carpet. I've never held a piece of jewelry like this, never mind being able to call it mine. My mom got me real gold hoops for my last birthday, but this is an entirely different level. I fiddle with the clasp for a minute, and then the necklace is once again secure around my neck. The weight below my collarbone already feels familiar. As I study myself in the bathroom mirror, an idea bursts into my mind. I dart back into my bedroom and dig around in my closet for Maddie's top.

I can't remember the last time I smiled at my reflection, but I'm beaming now. My collarbones curve beneath the gold chain, and the delicate, sparkling top makes my pale skin shimmer. My tangled hair falls over my shoulders in a way that seems intentionally tousled, and my cheeks are dewy and flushed. I barely recognize myself.

I raise my hand to touch the locket, and the fact that the girl in the mirror does the same is the only reason I believe it's truly me.

• • •

I snap awake, every muscle in my body tense. The orange orbs of the streetlamps outside my window come into focus first, then the familiar shape of my bedroom solidifies around me. There's a flicker of movement by my bedroom door, and I turn my head to get a better look.

Or I try to.

But I can't move.

My muscles refuse to obey me.

I'm locked in place, a statue on my bed. The only things I can move are my eyes. The sensation of being watched grows in me, along with a galloping panic. There's a hum in the air that reminds me of the sound my mom's laptop makes when it overheats. My heart strains against my ribs like it's trying to escape my body as desperately as I'm trying to move just one finger or just one toe.

But nothing happens.

I'm certain something is standing over me, something menacing and dangerous. But I can't see it, I can't run, I can't even shout for help.

It's just a dream, I tell myself.

I close my eyes and force myself to focus on breathing, zeroing in on the sensation of cool air brushing my skin as it flows into my nose and out again.

Breathe in. Breathe out.

Breathe in. Breathe out.

I repeat the words over and over in my mind until the darkness of sleep finally rescues me.

• • •

The soft whir of my vibrating phone tugs me awake, and I grope around for it with my eyes half closed. I finally manage to turn the alarm off, ignoring the unread messages blinking at me. My mouth is dry and sour, and my sweaty hair is pasted to my throbbing temples. My limbs are concrete slabs sinking into my rumpled sheets. I rub a damp hand over my face and snippets of the nightmare surface: glowing streetlamps peering through my blinds, not being able to move my body, a deep, overwhelming dread.

Every time I have sleep paralysis it feels like the first time. For as long as I can remember, my mind's been waking up before my body, leaving me unable to move and drowning in panic. Knowing what it is doesn't make it any less frightening.

Wàipó taught me to breathe through the nightmares, to quiet my mind so my body would go back to sleep. *Your breath is the key to a calm mind*, she said. *And a calm mind is magic.* Sometimes I go for months without a nightmare; sometimes I get them every day for weeks. I hope this isn't the start of another marathon.

There's no time to think about that now. If I'm not walking out the front door in ten minutes, I'm going to be late for school. I imagine myself swearing, throwing my phone at the wall, slamming my door open and stomping out of my room.

But the apartment is silent, which means Mom's already sleeping. Waking her up after an overnight shift is a sure way to make this morning twice the disaster it already is. So I suppress the urge to regress into a Blythe-like tantrum and move quietly into the start of my day.

• • •

"Did you get my message?" Yas skips up as I open my locker.

"Oh . . ." I reach for my phone. "Sorry, I was running super late this morning—"

"It was an important update!" Yas clucks her tongue and leans in close, speaking in a stage whisper. "Yesterday we were doing critiques in photography class, and Eric said my composition was *masterful.*"

"Is Eric . . . the teacher?"

"No!" Yas flicks my arm. "He's that hot guy I told you about, remember?"

"The K-pop star?"

"No, that's Yujun. Keep up!"

"I thought you liked K-pop Guy?"

"I do? Maybe? But Eric, he's so unique. Like, he does his own nail art."

"So you want him for the free manicures."

Yas laughs. Then her gaze lands on my neck.

"What's *that*?"

I follow her eyes down to the locket clanking against the zipper of my hoodie. I had it tucked under my shirt, but it must've escaped.

"Sylvia gave it to me." I shrug.

Yas's wide eyes snap up to mine.

"Sylvia? As in the mom you're babysitting for?"

"Yeah, she's super nice. But it's not a big deal." I roll my eyes and sling my bag over my shoulder. "She's an antiques dealer or something. She said the owner didn't want it and it's not worth much. But I liked it, so she gave it to me."

Yas reaches for the necklace and I jerk back. Her eyebrows knit together as I slide the necklace back inside my shirt. I brace for the cold metal against my skin, but the locket is surprisingly warm, almost comforting.

"Is it real gold?"

"No way!" I scoff. "Come on, who'd give a real gold necklace to their babysitter?"

Yas's eyes narrow.

"It's not a big deal," I repeat.

Yas sighs heavily, but the buzzing of her phone interrupts whatever she was about to say.

"Dell wants to get subs for lunch. Wanna come?"

Doesn't she remember I have to save every dollar for Osheaga? I can't just buy lunch whenever I want to. Besides, the thought of listening to the two of them drone on about Eric's nails or whatever sounds torturous.

But I don't say any of that.

I just say, "No."

• • •

I'm so tired that I forget about the next phase of my "make an effort with Blythe" plan until I'm in the community center's atrium, breathing in a lungful of chlorinated air and watching Blythe march away from me.

"Wait!"

She spins around, scowling.

"I have something for you."

I pull two brand-new scrunchies out of my bag, the tags still on. One is the same as those the girls in her class had last week, covered in shiny silver sequins. It took my whole Sunday afternoon scouring the mall to find the right one, but if this works it'll be worth it. The other scrunchie is black and printed with small, grinning white skulls. It reminded me of the *FRIGHTFUL* book, and the store had a buy-one-get-one deal, so I thought *why not*. I need to save as much money as I can, but I won't *have* any money to save if Blythe drives me out of this job. I'm thinking of it as an investment in workplace health.

Assuming it works.

I hold them out to her, trying to ignore the nervous flutter in my gut. Blythe stares at the silver scrunchie with distaste, but she smiles when she sees the skulls. She mumbles a thank-you and dashes into the changeroom.

Blythe steps onto the mat with skulls grinning from the root of her high ponytail and strides right over to the silver scrunchie girls. The other kids look a bit surprised, but they shuffle to make room. Then Blythe says something, and suddenly the whole group is giggling and Blythe's all smiles. Kids can be mean, but they can be pretty great too.

When we leave the community center, it's started snowing fat, wet flakes that float down lazily and melt as soon as they touch the ground. I hunch under my hood, but Blythe bounces ahead of me, chattering nonstop, seemingly oblivious to how soaked her hair is getting, skull scrunchie and all. She's practically a different kid.

"Cynthia said she'll help me with my cartwheel next week," she says. "She's the only one who can do a handstand without the wall."

"That's awesome."

"Maddie can do a cartwheel with one hand. She says—" Blythe stiffens and tugs on her damp ponytail. "Sorry."

"Why are you sorry?" I try to keep my voice gentle. *Please don't freak out. This is going so well.*

"I'm not supposed to talk about her."

"Who told you that?"

"No one. It's just—" Her voice is so soft that I have to lean down to hear her, sending cold water sliding off my hood and down my neck. "Mom gets weird if I mention her. And Dad gets really sad."

"Well, I don't mind if you talk about Maddie."

"You didn't know her."

"I know. But she's important to you. I'd like to know more about her."

Blythe considers this for a moment.

"We used to do our homework together," she says. "After she picked me up from school. She set a timer and, if we worked until it went off, we could have a treat after. She had a secret stash of junk food in her room. Stuff mom would never buy."

"I bet doing homework makes you miss her, huh?"

Blythe nods.

As we climb the front steps to her house, the air is suddenly sickly sweet. It smells like flowers when they're left in a vase too long and mold starts to grow in the water. I cover my nose with one hand and glance at Blythe. It doesn't look like she smells anything off; it looks like she's wondering why we're still standing outside. I punch the code into the door and rush into the house, where the air is warm and fresh.

Blythe perches on the couch and pulls some worksheets out of her bag. I make her smoothie, and she's still there when I bring it over. Okay. This is definitely progress. I settle down beside her with my history textbook open in my lap and one earbud in, but it's hard to focus with Blythe quietly working next to me. It's so strange to see her without her tablet.

We're still there an hour later, when the front door opens and, to my surprise, Hector walks in. Blythe bounds over to show off her new scrunchie. His face softens as he looks at her, and when he smiles at me, it feels like the first time he's really seeing me.

"She's in a good mood," Hector says, as Blythe rushes off to get her tablet to show him something. He points to my hoodie. "You like Siouxsie Sioux?"

A button with Siouxsie Sioux's trademark black-lined eyes is fixed to my hoodie between an oversized safety pin and another sporting the Ramones logo.

"Um, yeah. She's cool."

Siouxsie Sioux is only the goddess of British post-punk. "Spellbound" is track four on my dad's mixtape. Yas thinks my button collection is "eighties overkill," but putting them on this morning felt like the armor I needed after that nightmare.

I'm not a complete idiot though. I left my Sex Pistols and Damned buttons at home.

Hector motions for me to follow him to the long wooden sideboard by the dining table. He opens the top to reveal an old-fashioned record player, then slides the cupboard door open. It's crammed with the most vinyl I've ever seen outside a record store. He runs a finger along the spines and carefully slides a record out. The cover is a mass of black-and-white scribbles that looks like ripped-up sheet music. I can't hold back a grin when I read the title: *Siouxsie and the Banshees: Juju*.

"Awesome." This is the album "Spellbound" is on. "It's between this one and *Tinderbox*, for me."

Hector's grin sends a warm spark through my chest. He slides the record out and places it on the turntable, and a slow, deep bass line rumbles through the room.

"You're welcome to listen to anything you want when you're here. Just be careful with the records and don't turn the volume up too loud."

"Thank you." I'm stammering, staring at the treasure trove of music in front of me. I've read that everything sounds better on vinyl, but I've never had a chance to listen for myself. I scan the records. There are lots of bands I haven't heard of, but also—

"You like Billie Eilish?" I can't keep the surprise out of my voice.

Hector smirks. "I know I'm old, but I *have* heard some music made after 2000."

"She's playing at Osheaga this summer. It's this music festival in Montreal; I'm going with my friend Yas."

"Osheaga is a great time. I haven't been in—" He shakes his head. "I don't want to do the math. We thought about taking the girls . . ."

"DAD!"

Blythe's shriek saves me from having to respond.

We both spin toward her as she races in with her tablet held high. She grabs Hector by the hand and drags him over to the couch, talking a mile a minute, leaving me to listen to the echo of their voices and Siouxsie's haunting wail.

CHAPTER ELEVEN

THE ADRENALINE FROM TURNING a corner with Blythe and nerding out about music with Hector wanes when I sit down on the bus. Exhaustion from my terrible sleep hits me like a wall. By the time I get home, my head is pounding and my eyes are itchy from the effort of keeping them open. I stumble straight into my bedroom and under the covers.

What feels like a breath later, I wake to darkness so complete I think my eyes are still closed. Then the world slides sideways and down, and I'm looking at a pair of bare feet with toes painted deep purple, half-illuminated by a thin line of light streaming in through the bottom of a door.

My toes.

My carpet.

My bedroom door.

My right hand drifts up, but I'm not moving it. As my eyes adjust to the dim light, I watch my fingers close around the doorknob, but I don't feel the cool metal or the dent on the left side of the handle. It's like one of those first-person video games, where you watch through the character's eyes as they glide through the world, their disembodied hands fluttering up to loot a chest or cast a spell.

I watch my hand grip the knob so hard my knuckles go white. With one violent motion, my hand twists and yanks the door toward me.

Pain explodes in my left foot and rockets up my calf.

I crumple to the floor, clutching my toes until the sharp spear subsides to a dull throb. My foot is a blotchy shadow in the dim glow of the nightlight in the hall. The tip of my big toenail is ripped almost completely off; it's pointing straight up and the purple nail polish makes it look like a claw. A dark bead of blood wells up underneath. I touch the ragged nail gingerly, sucking in a breath at the sting. I look up at the door, then back down at my hands. The strange video game feeling is gone, rapidly evaporating like my dreams always do when I wake up.

I limp into the bathroom, soak up the blood with a tissue, and clip off the ripped nail and wrap my toe in a bandaid. I haven't gone sleepwalking since I was about ten. The first time, I walked into a wall and gave myself a nosebleed. That was the start of—

No. That's not what's happening here.

I got over all that, thanks to therapy and the tools it gave me. Maybe those tools will help me now.

Back in bed, I pull the covers up to my chin. I close my eyes and start to count backward from a thousand. I've never made it past eight hundred before falling asleep.

When I reach four hundred, a tendril of anxiety coils in my stomach.

When I hit two hundred, a cold bead of sweat rolls down my neck.

When I hit one, I open my eyes.

Dread gnaws a hole in my gut, a dark abyss that grows deeper and deeper, threatening to suck me in. I watch the shadows dance across my ceiling until the sunrise sweeps them away.

• • •

I'm exhausted the entire day, but I manage not to fall asleep during any of my classes. Later, at the Morins' dining room table, I join the virtual tutoring group while Blythe slurps her smoothie and does worksheets beside me. I squint at the tutor in the tiny square on my phone screen and scribble the example problems into my notebook. By the end of the hour, the equations are blurry but don't seem like an entirely foreign language. Maybe I won't fail math after all.

When the class ends, I pop my earbuds out and turn to Blythe.

"I think we deserve a break," I say. "Want to watch a movie?"

"Can I pick?" Blythe asks.

"Sure." When her grin turns wicked, I rush to add, "But it has to be something that's okay for kids."

She rolls her eyes, like she wasn't just scheming. "Can we have popcorn?"

"Definitely. You set the TV up and I'll get snacks."

The microwave hums as the bag spins, inflates, and begins to pop. Something moves in the corner of my eye, and my gaze catches on the abstract painting above the fireplace.

The thick black lines running down the canvas make my skin crawl. I try to avoid looking at it. But now, I realize what it reminds me of: the music video for "Peek-a-Boo," a track by Siouxsie and the Banshees. The song is stellar, but the video gives me the creeps. It cuts between close-ups of disembodied eyes and lips and silhouettes of shadowed faces jerking with inhuman movements. The thickest of the painting's ominous dark lines looks like one of those creepy shadow faces in profile. Yes, that's exactly what it reminds me of. No wonder I hate it.

The shadow face in the painting turns toward me.

I flinch away, smacking my left hand against the counter.

Pain ripples up my arm and I gasp, my vision blurring.

When the worst of it subsides, I look down and see a thin line of blood seeping from my palm. I must have ripped off the scab. I grab a paper towel and press it on the wound. A wave of nausea runs through me as the splotch of red expands across the white towel. I stare at the floor until it stops swimming.

Somehow I find the courage to glance back at the painting.

The abstract lines might be tentacles or wings, but there's nothing there that suggests a face. My tired brain is just playing tricks on me.

The microwave beeps.

I pour the popcorn in a bowl and head down to the cozy home theater the Morins have set up in their basement. The TV takes up one entire wall, and the couch is bigger than my bed at home. I've been dying to watch a movie down here since Sylvia showed it to me on the tour last week.

But when I reach the bottom of the stairs, the TV is off and Blythe is standing in the middle of the room with her back to me. The bright orange reflection of a flame flickers in the dark screen.

"Blythe?" I step up beside her, but she doesn't move, doesn't seem to see me at all. She's holding a lighter in front of her face and whispering something, her voice too low to make out the words. My stomach does a somersault.

"Blythe?" I say again, louder this time.

Blythe recoils with a gasp and shoves the lighter in her pocket.

"Are you okay?"

"She doesn't want you here." Blythe won't meet my eyes. Her cheeks are wet. Was she crying?

"Who?"

Instead of answering, Blythe dashes up the stairs.

I stand there a long time, staring at the blank TV screen as the popcorn cools in the bowl. What did she mean, *She doesn't want you here*? Is she talking about herself? Or her mom? Or . . . Maddie? Maybe this is what Hector meant when he said Blythe's been making up stories. I really thought we were moving forward, but I guess we're in a new phase. Just when I was starting to think that things were going to work out, that the next few months wouldn't be so terrible after all . . . Why is she doing this to me?

My pulse is rioting in my neck, and my hands are balled in sweaty fists. No—not sweat. My cut's still bleeding. I suck in a shaky breath. Getting angry at Blythe isn't going to help. She's grieving. I need to calm down, be the adult.

I head back to the kitchen and clean myself up. My hand stops bleeding pretty quickly, but I find the big bandages Sylvia used and stick one over it anyway. There's no sign of Blythe on the main floor. I consider looking for her upstairs, but the thought of another confrontation drains what little energy I have left.

Outside, the sky is dark and hurling sheets of hail. As ice pellets pound against the roof, I remember what Hector said about his record collection. It's the perfect distraction. I spend a long time looking at the records, crunching handfuls of popcorn. There are only a few albums I recognize. Running my fingers along the spines, I wonder how many of these albums my dad would have known. Eventually, I choose one with a bright pink jacket. When I slide the record out, the vinyl is the same donut-icing color. Yellow text on the front tells me it's called *Pottymouth*, by a band called Bratmobile.

Ridiculous.

I love it already.

A fast-paced guitar riff takes off, and a woman's voice snarls over top. I perch on the couch and scroll through social media, carefully avoiding reading the comments, just tapping the heart button over and over, barely taking in the photos. I somehow end up looking back through Yas's pictures, and I find an old collection from that summer when her parents got two-for-one passes to Canada's Wonderland and we went every weekend.

There we are eating a massive funnel cake, strawberry sauce dripping down our chins; waiting in line for the Bat roller coaster, making over-the-top terrified faces; and watching fireworks explode over the fake mountain in the middle of the park. It makes me miss her.

Which is silly; I see her almost every day.

• • •

Sylvia offers to drive me home. I protest a little, but a warm car sounds way nicer than getting battered by hail while I wait for the bus. As she types my address into her phone, I wonder if I should say something about Blythe. Today started off so well and then . . . ended so strangely.

But Sylvia's humming to herself, tapping her fingers on the steering wheel in time to the pop song on the radio. She seems so content. Is what happened today worth bringing up, spoiling her good mood? Blythe's going through a lot, but Sylvia already knows that. And *she's* going through a lot too. I'm supposed to be making her life a little easier. What happened with Blythe was odd, but it wasn't dangerous. I'm not concerned for Blythe's safety. I can handle it.

"I hear you're going to Osheaga this summer?" Sylvia's question silences my inner monologue. "Hector and I went once. You're going to love it."

"I can't wait." I wish that's what Mom would say when I finally ask her.

"How are you getting there? Taking the train?"

"Road trip. My best friend and I are taking driver's ed now, so we can get our licenses in time."

"That's so fun! If you ever want to practice, I'd be happy to take you out."

"You would?"

"Of course! I'd offer you the wheel today, if it wasn't so gross out. Next time."

Sylvia pulls up to the curb, and embarrassment twinges in my gut as she glances up at the ugly concrete building I live in.

"Thanks for the ride," I say. "Goodnight."

"Goodnight, Maddie."

I freeze. But when I look back at Sylvia, she's smiling softly at me, her fingers still drumming on the steering wheel. My heart sinks. I don't think she knows what she just said. What am I supposed to say?

What can I possibly say, except thank-you and see you tomorrow?

CHAPTER TWELVE

I START TO NOTICE little things about Sylvia, small signs that maybe were always there but that I didn't see before she called me Maddie by mistake. The way she sometimes loses her train of thought and drifts off mid-sentence; the way she always makes a point of asking me how my day was but sometimes asks the same question twice in a row; the way I sometimes find part of the stairs vacuumed or a half-empty dishwasher sitting open. She's struggling, but she's trying. She might be the strongest person I've ever met.

I do my best to help. I empty the dishwasher and finish vacuuming the stairs without being asked, I thank her for the tea she leaves me every day, and I try to connect with Blythe. Unfortunately, the kid is a fortress. After the incident in the basement, Blythe's back to being glued to her tablet the whole time we're together. I didn't think it was possible, but it's even worse than it was before. She doesn't speak to me at all; she only grunts or points when she absolutely needs to communicate something to me. The one positive is that she hasn't had a tantrum in a while. But I'm still on high alert around her, expecting the calm to snap at any moment.

Not being able to sleep isn't helping either. I get an hour at most before I jolt awake, sweating from a nightmare I barely remember and a feeling of deep dread I can't shake. I'm way more familiar with the migration of shadows across my ceiling between 2 and 7 a.m. than I ever wanted to be. I find myself clutching the locket, and sometimes the press of the chain against my neck and the smooth metal in my palm feel like the only things keeping me sane.

When Friday comes around, I'm jittery and dazed. After driver's ed tomorrow, I'm not leaving my bed. Hopefully, sleeping for two days straight will be the hard reset I need to feel normal again.

But first I need to get through today.

Yas is waiting for me by my locker. Her face is grave, and I'm not sure if she's about to ream me out or hug me. I apologize pre-emptively, explaining that I haven't messaged her back because I've been busy and haven't been sleeping super well. Yas says it's okay, and I think I might tell her about the nightmares if she asks. But she doesn't. Instead, she asks if I've talked to my mom about Montreal.

"Not yet," I say. "I've barely seen her all week."

Mostly because I'm avoiding her, since I have no idea how to bring up Osheaga. I've recorded and deleted a dozen practice voice notes, but no matter how I start, I can't see how it ends in anything but a "no" wrapped up in a lengthy lecture.

"My parents are talking to Dell's parents this weekend," Yas says. "Hopefully that'll be enough for now. But they *know you*, Rachel. You've got to ask soon."

"I know!" It comes out louder than I expect, and heads turn toward us.

They don't look away once my voice fades. Most of the people in the hall are staring at us—no, at me—and whispering. Laughing behind their hands.

"Yas . . ." A tingling sensation runs up the back of my neck. "What's going on?"

"What do you mean?"

"Why is everyone looking at me?"

"I don't know?" Yas licks her lips. She's stalling.

I pull her into the bathroom, which is mercifully empty, and look at her expectantly. As I watch the slow, reluctant way Yas takes out her phone, the back of my throat starts to ache. She clicks around for a few seconds, then turns the screen toward me. It's open to a social media account, a picture filling the screen.

A picture of me.

But it's not me, not exactly. It's my face, on the poster for *The Shining*—my head where Jack Nicholson's should be, peering menacingly through the door while his wife cowers in the corner. I swipe to the next photo.

It's me, projectile vomiting in *The Exorcist*.

Me, bald and snarling with vampire teeth protruding from my mouth.

Me, glaring out from behind a black curtain of hair, the ghost girl in *The Ring*.

"What is this?"

Yas winces. "Someone made the account last night."

"You weren't going to tell me?" My skin flushes hot, like my pores are on fire. How could she let me walk around totally unaware that the whole school is laughing at me, again?

"I was!" Yas glares at me, defensive. "*And* I was going to say we should go to the principal."

"Absolutely not." I give her the phone back.

"Come on," Yas groans. "He's been harassing you for *years*—"

"And telling people about it made it worse."

"It was different back then. We're at a new school, and this kind of stuff is taken more seriously now."

"What if my mom freaks out again? What if she thinks this means it's not safe for me to go to Osheaga?"

"That won't happen—"

"You can't know that. Leave it alone, okay?"

For a moment, Yas looks like she's going to argue. The muscles in my shoulders bunch into knots, and I clutch her arm, mirroring the tightness in my throat.

"Please."

Finally, slowly, Yas bites her lip and nods.

• • •

I keep my head down the rest of the day, and my earbuds almost block out the whispers that follow me through the halls. I somehow manage to avoid Cameron, though I expect to see him smirking at me every time I turn a corner. Over lunch, I lock myself in a bathroom stall and scroll through the pictures obsessively, poring over every like, every comment, until my eyes are scratchy.

Enough.

I delete the app.

I shamble from my school to Blythe's and then to the Morins' like a zombie. I'm woozy with exhaustion by the time Blythe finishes her smoothie and slinks up to her bedroom with her tablet in hand. I'm grateful she's ignoring me today.

I find the Doors' self-titled album in Hector's record collection and let the familiar notes soothe me as I look out into the backyard. Or try to. The sun is already setting, and the approaching darkness has turned the windows into a wall of mirrors.

The girl reflected in the glass looks like she belongs here, standing next to the spinning turntable in sock feet and a messy bun. She looks like someone who posts "get ready with me" videos online and gets a thousand likes, not someone whose face gets pasted onto monsters. She looks like she could leave her open textbooks and eraser shavings on the table until morning and head upstairs to bed, mumbling an apology when her parents poke their heads in to say goodnight.

I wish I was that girl. But I know I'm not.

My head feels so heavy. I make a pillow of my arms on the dining table, the wood cool against my cheek, and sink into the soft place between sleeping and waking, the music fading behind the sound of my breath.

I dream of a shadow peeling itself off the wall and floating toward me, stretching across the table, flooding the surface like spilt ink.

I start awake to the sound of the front door opening. I fumble a book out of my bag, just in time to look busy as Hector walks into the kitchen. He pauses and tilts his head, as Jim Morrison croons from the speakers.

"You picked a classic today," he says. "Did you know that the band licensed 'Light My Fire' for a Buick ad without telling Jim? When he found out, he threatened to smash a Buick with a sledgehammer at every show."

"No way." I grin. "How do you know so much about music?"

"I'm mostly a fan." He shrugs. "But I also minored in it."

"What do you play?"

"Nothing," he laughs. I think it's the first time I've heard him make that sound. It's strange but also nice. "My minor was in media studies, with a focus on pop music and culture. I know, it sounds made up." He makes a face, and I chuckle.

But then his expression turns serious.

"Can I ask you . . ." He hesitates, glancing over his shoulder.

Blythe is nowhere to be seen. Still, Hector lowers his voice and I have to lean forward to hear him. "How's she doing? Really?"

"Blythe? She's . . ." I wrack my brain for an answer. Being with her is such an unpredictable ride, but Hector knows that. I promised myself the other day that I wouldn't make the Morins worry for no reason. But he is asking.

Maybe I can tell him a little more without setting off an alarm.

"She told me a story about Maddie the other day. She said she wished she could talk about her more."

"That's good." Hector is looking over my shoulder again, tugging absently at his shirt cuffs. "That's good she can talk to you. I wish—" He's cut off by the front door opening and Blythe thundering down the stairs. I never get to hear his wish.

CHAPTER THIRTEEN

SYLVIA INVITES ME TO stay for dinner again, and the *yes* is out of my mouth before I know I'm going to say it. After today, going home to my empty apartment and eating instant ramen with only my thoughts for company is the opposite of appealing.

I don't usually mind having the place to myself. Without Mom asleep in her room, I can listen to whatever I want without headphones and watch shows on the actual TV instead of my phone. But right now, I want to stay in this warm, bright bubble, answering Sylvia's questions or swapping music trivia with Hector, and avoid the anxious monologue in my mind for as long as possible.

Tonight's menu is homemade burgers. Hector pulls his parka on, announcing that he's going to get the barbecue started. Sylvia follows him to the back door. She pokes her head out, but her sock feet stay inside. I've heard of people who barbecue in the middle of winter, but this is the first time I've met any.

The record stops, and as I go to flip it, a frosty breeze floats in through the door, along with Hector and Sylvia's voices.

"—been six months." Hector's voice is a pleading whisper. "I thought we could all go to the beach—"

"She's not there anymore," Sylvia snaps.

"I know that. But I think it might—"

I place the needle on the record and dart back into the kitchen, forcing myself to focus on putting together a salad. Sylvia gave me a different knife than last time and there are no tomatoes in sight. Blythe is on the opposite side of the island, squeezing ground beef into balls and mashing them flat with the palm of her hand.

"She doesn't want you here," Blythe says quietly. She stares at me, unsmiling. I put down the knife and will myself to be calm.

"What are you talking about?"

"She wants you gone."

I look over at Sylvia, whose back is to us as she sets the dining table.

"I don't think that's true." I try to keep my tone gentle, but there's an edge to my words that I can't fully soften.

"Not her." Blythe balls her hands into fists. Raw, pink flesh oozes between her fingers like some kind of grotesque playdough.

"Then who? You?"

"No!" She presses her lips together. "My sister."

Her gaze darts over my shoulder, and I instinctively turn my head to look behind me. Something slimy smacks me in the face. It slides down my cheek, leaving a cold trail, and some of it sticks to my lips. I swipe the raw beef off before it can get in my mouth. It hits the floor with a disgusting, wet thud.

I imagine myself reaching across the counter, grabbing Blythe by her hair, and smashing her face into the mound of raw meat in front of her. It takes everything in me to ignore the impulse and walk over to the sink instead.

I scrub at my face, then cup my hands and rinse my mouth out once, twice. I'm frightened by the violence of what I just imagined, but blood is still pounding in my ears. My injured hand is clamped around the locket. The dull ache under the scab feels good, and the metal is warm, almost hot, like it's absorbing my anger. I focus on the sensation, and it anchors me, the feeling fading from the first sharp snap into a simmer.

I swing back toward Blythe.

"I didn't—" Blythe's eyes flick to her parents, who are talking by the open back door, oblivious.

I grip the edge of the counter and lean in close.

"You can tell *your sister* that I'm not going anywhere."

I've never heard my voice like this, low and blade-sharp. It feels good to see Blythe's mouth fall open.

"You're stuck with me, Blythe. It's fine if you don't like me, but you need to be respectful. I like you, though. I still hope we can be friends."

I pick up my knife and resume slicing a cucumber into slim, even circles, pretending Blythe is invisible. Let's see how she likes it.

• • •

When I get home, laughter greets me from the other side of our apartment door, my mom's high-pitched giggle joined by a low, musical chuckle. Oh, good. The perfect way to end a messed-up day. What's she doing home?

I peek into the living room, where my mom and Mrs. Paul are chatting on the couch. I sneak into the kitchen and find an open bottle of red wine on the counter, next to a pile of dirty dishes and a big plastic container half filled with chicken and rice that smells deliciously spicy. A big blob of red sauce is splattered next to it.

Looking at the hurricane on our counter, I think of the Morins' kitchen: its pristine marble island and gleaming chrome appliances. I resist the urge to start cleaning, forcing myself to grab a glass of water and turn my back on the chaos. I nearly run into my mom as she swoops into the kitchen with two empty wine glasses.

"There you are!" She's glowing, her cheeks flushed from the wine. "How was your day?"

I shrug. "Fine."

Mom sticks her tongue out at me. What is she, five?

"What are you doing home?"

"Shift got cancelled." She sloshes red wine into the glasses. "Mrs. Paul brought dinner."

"I already ate." Shouldn't she be more worried? If she doesn't work, she doesn't get paid. But here she is, smiling like it's a surprise vacation.

"Come say hi anyway."

"I was going to—"

"Just come for a minute." She means, *Don't argue with me while we have company.*

I trail my mom into the living room and say hello to Mrs. Paul, who's wearing a maroon sweater dress and big gold hoops. She looks way too nice to be hanging out on our sagging couch, with *MasterChef* playing on mute and dirty dishes littering the coffee table.

"Rachel!" Mrs. Paul smiles and accepts the glass of wine my mom offers her. "Jennifer was just saying you're going into computer science."

I give her a tight smile and take a slow step toward the hallway.

"We're pretty set on U of T," Mom says. "But she'll still apply to all the top schools in Toronto and Vancouver."

"My Tyrone went to U of T. He's an optometrist." Mrs. Paul taps the tortoiseshell frames perched on her nose. "He has his own clinic in Ajax. Nicole is out in Calgary. She's a paramedic now."

"You must be very proud," my mom says.

"I am." Mrs. Paul's lips press together in a way that makes me wonder if she's telling the truth. Mom did say Mrs. Paul's kids don't visit much.

"I was going to be a dentist," Mom says.

"Ew. Why?" The words slip out before I can catch them.

"It's one of the highest-paying jobs in Canada, that's why," she snaps. "Plus no one times your pee breaks."

My face heats up and I look away, taking a sip of my water.

"Not that you'll have to worry about that." Mom's smile is thin, her voice straining for lightness. "You'll get a degree, get a good job. You'll have health insurance—"

"All the exciting things in life," I say dryly.

Mom frowns. "All the important things in life."

The muscles in my jaw twitch as I swallow the protests building in my throat. Doesn't she know that a university degree doesn't guarantee any of that anymore?

Mrs. Paul hums in agreement. "Anthony's insurance was a godsend when he got sick. We were lucky." She swallows thickly. Then her eyes light up, like someone flicked a switch. "That reminds me!"

She reaches for her purse and takes out a box of matches with a red bird on the front. But instead of matchsticks, the box is filled with bubble wrap. She unfolds the plastic, and nestled in the middle is a gleaming, silver watch.

"This was in the back of the cutlery drawer." Mrs. Paul picks the watch up gingerly and flips it over. "Errol was Anthony's grandfather. I had no idea he had this." She hands the watch to my mom.

"It must be what he wanted you to find." Mom sounds a bit breathless as she runs her fingers over the back of the watch.

Mrs. Paul nods. "I'm going to take it in somewhere, find out how much it's worth."

"Do you think you'll sell it?" Mom passes the watch to me. It's cool in my hand, and the engraving on the back reads *Errol Paul for 25 years of distinguished service.*

"I don't know," Mrs. Paul says. The look on her face tells me she won't.

For a moment, I consider telling Mrs. Paul to take it to Sylvia . . . but no. I like that there's a line between this world and that one. Work/life balance is healthy, right?

"It was nice to see you, Mrs. Paul, but I'm exhausted." I stand up and force a smile as I hand the watch back to her. "I'm glad you found what you were looking for."

• • •

Searing white light. It pulses in time with the low hum that fills my throbbing skull. I try to close my eyes, but they ignore me. They remain open and the piercing glare persists. Slowly, shapes come into focus, solidifying into glass shelves, a jar of peanut butter, a carton of orange juice: the inside of a fridge.

My fridge.

In front of me, glowing in the stark light, two pale hands move in jerky motions.

My hands.

But I'm not moving them. Even when I try, my body disobeys me.

My hands tear into something in my lap, scooping handfuls toward my mouth. I can't see what it is, but I hear chewing. The thick, wet sound turns my stomach. Or it would, if I could feel it. But I can't feel my jaw working, can't taste whatever is sliding down my throat, can't smell the crisp air wafting from the open fridge in front of me.

When my right hand rises into the fluorescent light, it's covered in sticky red from fingertips to wrist. My body moves of its own volition, bringing my hand to my mouth to lick the glistening red off each finger, one by one. *Wake up, wake up*, I plead in my mind, watching my tongue smear across the flat of my stained palm.

I struggle to close my eyes or turn my head, anything to cut off the sickening scene playing out in front of me, but it continues. I try to focus on breathing like Wàipó taught me, but I can't feel my breath. I can't feel anything.

A feral sound fills the air, a cross between a moan and a growl, and I know it's coming from me. If I could move, I would be running. I would be screaming. *It's just a dream.* I repeat the words in my mind, willing myself to believe them. *Just a dream, just a dream—*

• • •

I gasp awake, drenched in cold sweat. The darkness in my room is almost complete. I take a shuddering breath, and feeling my lungs expand with air makes my eyes sting in relief. The nightmare is already leaving me, but I try to grasp the threads that linger—harsh white light, my hands stained red. I can't hold on to them. The memories slip away, and soon all that's left is the sour slosh of dread, disgust, and panic churning in my stomach.

I reach for the glass on my bedside table. The water slows my fluttering pulse. But there's something spongy stuck between my back teeth. I run my tongue along my molars. Whatever it is, it's wedged in too firmly. I reach into my mouth with my fingers, which makes me gag. When the feeling passes, I try again and manage to grab the wet, stringy thing between my thumb and index finger. With one firm yank, it comes free.

I turn on my bedside lamp and hold my open hand under the warm light. A dark pink glob sits in my palm, about the size of a quarter. When I poke the shapeless, lopsided mass, it's rubbery and wet. Bile rises in the back of my mouth as I realize what it is.

Meat.

It's raw meat.

I dash to the bathroom and fling the chewed-up glob into the toilet.

I collapse on the floor, dry-heaving and clutching the bath mat with all my strength. When my stomach settles, I wipe my mouth with my hand and flush the toilet without looking in the bowl again. I haul myself up and turn the sink on full blast. What is happening to me? How did that thing get in my mouth?

A pinching feeling in the back of my mind says it has something to do with the nightmare, but when I try to remember it, the flimsy memories disintegrate further. I stare at the rush of water flowing down the drain, gripping the locket and listening to the torrent like it might whisper the answer.

I stand there until dawn, but it never does.

CHAPTER FOURTEEN

I DRAG MYSELF TO driver's ed, my head pounding like something's trying to hammer its way out. I fold my arms into a pillow on my desk as Yas and Dell chatter around me, their voices blending into a fuzzy murmur that lulls me deeper into the darkness behind my eyelids.

Yas pokes my shoulder. "What are you doing next Saturday?"

I shrug without lifting my head.

"Eric's having a party," she says. "You should come."

"No thanks," I mumble into my sweater.

"Everyone will be from Maplewood or Watson. No one from Brimley but us."

I shrug again. I feel the weight of Yas's stare on the back of my head. I know she wants to ask me if I've talked to my mom about Montreal.

But what she says is "Are you okay?"

When I don't answer, she continues in a whisper.

"I'm worried about you. You didn't text me back last night."

"Sorry, I was at dinner."

"Where?"

"The Morins'."

"Really?" The surprise in her voice grates me. "You've been spending a lot of time with them." What's that supposed to mean? Is it that shocking that someone other than her might want my company?

Donald claps his hands to get our attention, and I shove myself back up to sitting, grateful for the interruption. After today, just one more of these classes left. Then it's on to the in-car lessons. My hands tingle when I imagine gripping a steering wheel, but I push the thought from my mind and try to focus on the slides. One thing at a time.

• • •

I head directly to bed after class. I have another assignment for my physics credit recovery course due soon and I haven't looked at the website in days, but I can't keep my eyes open another second.

Yet when I crawl under the covers, sleep eludes me. I drift into a fuzzy half-consciousness, but every time I'm close to dozing off, I snap awake with my heart thundering behind my ribs. My head throbs. The streetlamps outside blink on and then off. Eventually, the front door opens. Mom's home.

I pick up my phone to check the time: 6:54 a.m.

Have I really been awake all night?

The muffled sounds of pots clanging and the familiar honey notes of a Destiny's Child song travel through my door. I press my face into my pillow and lay there for a while, somewhere between sleeping and waking.

Then I smell burning.

Am I dreaming? I roll over onto my back and my neck cracks like a gunshot. No, I'm awake. Which means that smoke is real.

I leap out of bed and race to the kitchen.

Mom's standing over the sink, scraping burnt goop out of a pan, swaying her hips, and humming off-key.

"Mom?"

She doesn't hear me.

"Mom!"

She gasps and the pan crashes into the sink.

"Rachel!" She presses a hand against her chest, laughing. "You scared me."

"What's burning?" I scoop her phone off the counter and turn the volume down. I try to peer into the pan, but she turns the tap on and steam puffs into the air with a sizzle.

"I'm making pancakes! That one was my tester."

"Why are you making pancakes?" Have I woken up in an alternate universe?

"Why do I need a reason?" Mom laughs as she pulls out a new pan and sets it on the stove. "Can't I make my favorite daughter her favorite breakfast on a Sunday morning? It feels like a year since we've eaten together!" She wraps her hands around my biceps, beaming up at me. "Are you taller? Are your boobs bigger?"

"Oh my god."

I shake her off and stalk to the end of the kitchen, where by some miracle there's a hot pot of coffee waiting for me. As my first sips start to clear the cobwebs away, I realize that Mom's also drinking from a steaming mug as she watches the blobs of batter solidify in the pan.

"Why are you drinking coffee?" I give her a look and she grins.

"Okay, fine. I have a surprise. I'll tell you while we eat."

This can't be good. I want to nag her for more details, but the new pan is already starting to smoke. I nudge her away from the stove, flipping the pancakes just in time to save them from turning completely black. Mom doesn't even pretend to protest; she just pinches my arm and starts scraping charred gunk out of the first pan.

Thanks for breakfast, Mom.

Still, dropping the batter into almost perfect circles and watching bubbles start to form is almost meditative. While I'm scraping the last of the batter out of the bowl, Mom grabs a pancake off the top of the stack, pops it on a small plate, tops it with a swirl of whipped cream from a can, and walks it over to the altar.

"Do ghosts like pancakes?"

"Everyone likes pancakes!" Her voice is muffled because she's on her knees in front of the altar, her forehead touching the floor. She sits up, then bows twice more. As I flip the pancakes, I hear the scratch of a match being struck. Then the thick scent of incense fills the air.

We sit down at the table and I douse my pancakes in maple syrup while my mom digs through her purse. She pulls out a handful of crumpled napkins, chewed-up pens, gum wrappers, hair ties, and . . . Wàipó's peach-wood sword? She's carrying it around with her now? Good lord.

Finally, she retrieves a somewhat battered envelope with a University of Toronto sticker on the front. She slides it across to me with an encouraging nod. It's already been opened.

The first thing I pull out is a glossy brochure, featuring an ancient-looking stone building with a green domed roof.

"That's Convocation Hall." Mom's voice is almost reverent. "They hold graduation ceremonies there. It's like a cathedral inside."

She doesn't say that she never wore a cap and gown in that building, that she never walked across the stage to accept the degree she earned as her parents beamed with pride in the audience. She doesn't say that she would have, if they hadn't kicked her out because of the screaming baby she was saddled with, leaving her searching for the best job she could get with a high-school diploma and trying to find a place to live that would leave some cash for groceries after rent.

Mom's told me that she wouldn't change a thing, but it's hard to believe when she's staring at this photo like the building's a holy temple.

The second thing in the envelope is a piece of paper branded with U of T letterhead. *Dear Rachel Bei,* the typed text reads. *Congratulations on your acceptance to the University of Toronto Summer Coding Academy.*

Um . . . what?

"This is the program Grace's daughter did." Mom has that laser-beam intensity she always gets after working overnight, when she's wired and less than ten minutes from keeling over. "She's in the computer science program now, doing a co-op placement at Google! They have catered lunch every day. *Poke bowls* once a week."

"You applied for me?" I fold the paper in half, running my thumbnail across the crease.

She dismisses me with a wave of her hand. "It was just a little form."

"Isn't it expensive?" I fold the paper in half again.

"Don't worry about that. Isn't it exciting?!"

There are a lot of feelings coursing through me, but none of them are excitement.

"Will it be a lot of math?" It's getting harder to bend the paper, but I force the edges together one more time and pinch the fold so they stay that way.

"A bit." Mom shrugs. "But you're good at math, like me. You just need to apply yourself more."

I picture the giant red 32% at the top of my last test, and a hot flush of anger flows through me. I just need to *apply myself*? No, I need a different brain. I'm nothing like her.

"Excuse me?" Mom's staring at me like I've grown a second head.

Did I say that out loud?

The mix of disbelief and hurt in her face suggests that I did.

"Rachel." I hate how gentle her tone is. "What do you mean?"

My stomach drops and tears well up in my eyes. She wouldn't sound this way if I answered her question honestly. I mean, I hate math. I mean, I don't want to study computer science—maybe I don't want to go to university at all. I mean, you'd know all this if you ever actually *listened* to me, instead of trying to make my life a do-over for the one you screwed up.

But I can't say any of that, can I?

If I did, she would yell or cry or both, and I'd feel ungrateful and guilty. I'd end up apologizing, swearing I didn't mean it, and she'd accept it because that's what she wants to be true. Then we'd be right back where we are now. So what's the point?

A hot fist clutches my sternum, and I press my fingers to the spot, finding the locket resting under my shirt.

"Are you okay?" Mom looks concerned now, like she's worried I might throw up.

"Sorry," I mumble. "I'm not feeling great."

"Oh." Her smile deflates. "Why don't you go lie down? We can talk about this later."

I manage a nod and leave her at the table with the folded-up letter and a stack of cold pancakes.

• • •

I flop back on my bed and stare at the ceiling. I imagine my anger like a ball of flame, raging within my ribs. I picture it getting smaller and smaller, until it can fit inside the locket.

Why doesn't she ever listen to me? She's drawn this map of my entire future without asking where I want to go. I've only known Sylvia for, like, two weeks, but I swear she already knows me better than my own mom. Because Sylvia asks me questions and actually listens to the answers. How revolutionary.

Would things have been different if Dad were here?

Exhaustion washes over me and my eyes droop closed. But instead of darkness behind my eyelids, a burst of cold, white light shoots panic up my spine and spreads the taste of iron in my mouth.

I sit up with a jolt. My tongue throbs, and when I touch it, my fingers come away with a watery drop of red. I've hardly slept at all these last few days, and I know that can mess with your head. I'm not the first person in history who's been sleep-deprived. I'm sure there's something I can do about it. I curl into a ball on my side and search *sleep deprivation* on my phone. The common causes read like a pretty accurate description of my life right now: high stress levels; disruptive sleep disorders like night terrors, sleep paralysis, or sleepwalking.

Of course I'm stressed. I spend every afternoon with a kid who's convinced her dead sister hates me, I'm teetering on the edge of failing another class, I'm trying to learn to drive, and I have no idea how to ask my mom about Osheaga, when all she wants to talk about is how she plans to turn me into some kind of computer whiz. It makes sense that I'm having trouble sleeping.

I scroll down to the list of sleep deprivation symptoms: daytime sleepiness, irritability, trouble focusing, headaches. Check, check, check, check. It says that the longer sleep deprivation persists, the worse it gets: *The most severe symptoms may look like the effects of alcohol intoxication, including tremors, visual and tactile hallucinations, and impulsive behavior.*

I'm so tired, I'm drunk. Perfect. Now, what to do about it? I skip ahead to the section on treatment. A consistent bedtime routine, no electronics before bed, staying physically active . . . It's all frustratingly common sense. The recommended treatments for sleepwalking are no better. The top two are meditation and therapy. Neither of which solve my immediate problem. I need to sleep *now.*

I find a message board dedicated to sleep issues, where people exchange stories and advice about insomnia, sleep paralysis, night terrors, and everything in between. In a post titled *what is the strongest over-the-counter sleeping pill?* the drug with the most mentions is a common allergy medication. I can pick it up at any pharmacy.

Thank you, internet.

I keep scrolling through the posts, where people behind anonymous usernames bare their deepest struggles to strangers.

I've been awake for almost 3 days straight—

I turned the stove on in my sleep—

Typing this at 4:15 a.m.—

I think I'm going insane—

I feel a little bad that I'm comforted by how much worse these stories are than mine. My eyelids get heavy as I scroll, and the screen in front of me blurs. But as soon as my eyes close, that searing white light flashes, jarring me awake.

It's dark outside. How is it 6 p.m.?

At least I don't have to face my mom, I think, as I pull myself out of bed and head for the nearest pharmacy.

CHAPTER FIFTEEN

THE INSISTENT BUZZING OF my alarm pulls me out of sleep slowly. I took two of those allergy pills, and they put me down hard. I'm groggier than when I got into bed, but there's only darkness between my memories of closing my eyes and opening them again. I'm calling that a win.

My left hand feels oddly stiff, and I lift it to find my palm caked in dried blood. The cut below my thumb gapes, the skin around it swollen and tender. It must have opened up again overnight. As I clean and rebandage the wound, an unsettling shard of memory scrapes at the back of my mind. Did I have another dream where I was moving? Watching myself move? I can't quite touch it, but it lingers there, troubling me.

I move through the day in a haze. Stares and stifled giggles follow me through the school corridors. What monster have they made me into this time? I never thought I'd say it, but I preferred it when Cameron was being an asshole to my face. Back in grade nine, he and his friends made a game out of trying to trip me. I collected bruises for a week, until I figured out that if I stayed as close to the wall as possible and kept them in sight when we were in the same room, I could usually avoid their traps.

But this stuff online . . . there's no beating it. If I try to keep up with what they're posting, I'll doomscroll myself into oblivion. But not knowing is making me twitchy. I debate texting Yas to ask what she's seen, or reinstalling the app so I can look myself, but I don't end up doing either.

When Blythe and I get to her house, she darts up to her room and I head into the kitchen to make her smoothie. I move around the Morins' kitchen on autopilot, zoning out as the blender swirls in a purple blur. Blythe hasn't reappeared by the time it's ready, so I pour her drink into a glass and start upstairs.

"I don't understand!"

I freeze at the sound of Blythe's voice, low but distinct.

"Why?" Her voice trembles, but I can't tell if it's fear or frustration.

I take the rest of the stairs two by two and find Blythe standing in front of Maddie's open bedroom door. She stares intently into Maddie's room, both of her hands clasped around the lighter that she's holding in front of her face.

"Maddie, please . . ."

My stomach sinks.

"Blythe?"

Blythe jumps and drops the lighter, the flame winking out. She swivels around, eyes wide and mouth open. Her face is streaked with tears.

"Blythe," I say, crouching down so I'm at her eye level, "what happened?"

"You won't believe me," she whispers.

"Try me."

Blythe tenses and looks away. I think she's going to run, but instead she says, "Sometimes . . . I see her."

"Who?" I think I know, but I need to hear her say it.

"Maddie."

My chest aches as Blythe whispers her sister's name at the floor.

"She comes closer if I have a candle. Or this." Blythe nudges the lighter with her toe.

"Okay," I say.

Blythe looks at me, her chin quivering. "You think I'm making it up."

"I didn't say that."

"But you're *thinking* it. Mom said that's what would happen." Blythe pushes her shoulders back, her face twisting into a determined grimace. "But it's the *truth*. I'll show you." She picks up the lighter, flicking it on as she stares into Maddie's dark room, calling her sister's name.

I hold my breath, not because I expect a ghost to appear but because of the desperate hope on her face. After a minute, I put my hand on her shoulder. She shakes me off, brushing past me and down the stairs. I follow her to the living room, where she crouches in front of one of the cupboards next to the fireplace. I settle on the floor next to her, as she flings the cupboard doors open.

Inside sits a framed photograph of Maddie. It's a familiar picture: her graduation photo, the same one that I saw in the news article about her death but blown up almost to life-size. Maddie stares right at the camera and smiles with her lips pressed together, her ivory skin and perfectly waved hair even more magazine-worthy than I remember. It's hard to believe that someone my age, someone who looks so alive, is dead.

The photograph is surrounded by a sea of trinkets. There's a stuffed whale, a pair of pearl-covered hairclips, a card that says *happy mother's day* in a child's handwriting, and a dozen other keepsakes. It's a shrine, or maybe an altar. It's not so different from the one we have at home.

Except it's locked away, hidden. It must be too painful for Sylvia and Hector to look at every day. No wonder Blythe feels like she can't talk about her sister.

Blythe reaches into the cupboard and pulls out a tall, red candle that was tucked into the corner. Behind it are three small jars sealed with wax. One jar has a lock of dark hair floating in a yellow-brown liquid. Next to it is a fancy pink perfume bottle, half full of rusty nails and sticks.

The third jar is brown and opaque. A worn, yellow piece of paper curves around the neck covered in smudged Chinese characters. The only one I can make out is "bind." What does that mean? I wonder what significance these objects hold, to be placed here alongside all these memories of Maddie.

"Don't!"

Blythe grabs my arm, which I'm surprised to find is reaching for the brown jar.

"It's a spirit jar. If you touch it, the ghost inside can possess you."

From the way Blythe is trembling, I think she believes what she's saying. I draw my hands into my lap and sit back on my heels, as Blythe flicks the lighter on and lights the candle's wick. When Wàipó died, I wasn't much older than she is now. Would things be different for me if I'd known someone who understood what I was going through?

"I used to think I could see ghosts," I say.

I keep my eyes on the candle, the flame flickering, softening the wax around the edges. Out of the corner of my eye, I see Blythe turn toward me.

"I was about your age. It started after my wàipó—that's what I called my grandma—died. My mom got really, really sad. I wished, harder than I'd ever wished for anything, that Wàipó would come back. I thought that maybe then my mom would get better. Then, one night . . . I had this feeling. Kind of a . . . tingling all over my skin? Like something was watching me."

• • •

The first time I saw Wàipó's ghost, I was half asleep.

I was moving through the dark void between the night-light outside my room and the one setting the bathroom aglow, running my hand along the wall so I wouldn't have to turn the big light on and risk waking Mom.

There was a flicker of movement at the end of the hall, a shadow where there shouldn't have been a shadow. Then Wàipó was there, with her cloud of gray hair and pink slippers, beckoning me to join her in the kitchen like it was an ordinary Sunday afternoon. It only lasted a moment, and then she was gone.

My mom cried when I told her. But she also got out of bed and went straight to the altar. We started lighting incense for Wàipó every day, and Mom started to get better.

But I kept feeling like I was being watched by something I couldn't see and seeing shadows where there shouldn't be any. I only saw Wàipó one more time, in the same place as that first night. But the feeling didn't go away. It started to scare me.

One night, the shadows tried to grab me. I freaked out, woke up my mom, and she scoured her notebook and the internet for advice. She put the Zhong Kui poster on the front door, began to leave a fresh cup of water on our altar every morning, and gave me a coin charm and then Wàipó's peach-wood sword to carry around for protection.

One day I was in class, coloring. I remember I had a yellow crayon. One second everything was fine, then the next there was something dark and furious behind me. I could *feel it*, like ice water down the back of my neck. I tried to convince myself it wasn't real, but somehow my body *knew* it was coming closer, and it was going to grab me—I leapt up, holding the peach-wood sword in front of me, striking at . . . nothing.

There was no monster, no shadow.

Just my classmates' stunned faces and silence.

Then Cameron started to laugh.

What's that? A stick?

It's a WAND!

After that, my fate as the *witch bitch* and Cameron's punching bag was set.

To this day, I think my mom believes Wàipó came back to save her, to get her out of bed and back into the world. I don't think it's occurred to her that the one who actually did that was me.

• • •

Blythe is looking at me with an intensity that, up until now, I've only seen directed at her tablet.

"What really made things better is when I started talking to a bunch of other kids who were struggling too." The school referred me to a therapy group, and for three months Mom took me once a week. That, plus learning about Cameron's bullying shortly after, ignited the overprotective streak in her that I've been fighting ever since.

"We had different problems, but we were all kind of the same. I learned that our minds and bodies . . . sometimes they take the hard things you're feeling, like stress or sadness or fear, and make them into something else. For me, it felt like being haunted. And I guess I was, in a way. Just not by ghosts."

"You don't think ghosts are real?" Blythe wraps her arms around herself. "Even after everything that happened to you?"

I know what she wants from me, and it's so tempting to give it to her. It seems like such a harmless white lie, like Santa Claus or the Tooth Fairy. Except I know it's not harmless. It might make her feel better in the moment, but it'll only hurt her in the long run. My mom and the peach-wood sword taught me that the hard way.

I shake my head.

"But I *see her*, Rachel. She's trying to tell me something."

"What do you think she's trying to tell you?"

"I can't hear her voice. She's like . . . a shadow. I try to read her lips. But since you came . . . I think she's angry? She points at you. Like she's mad. Like she doesn't want you here. I don't know why. If I could just talk to her . . ." Blythe grabs my arm, hope flaring in her eyes. "I was thinking, maybe with a Ouija board—"

"Blythe." I put my hand over hers. "I know it seems real. I know you might even want it to be. But it isn't." I grip her hand and look her in the eyes, trying to convey how I truly want to help her, even if I don't know what to do from here. "Maybe if you talk to your parents—"

Blythe shakes me off with a huff and jumps to her feet, stomping upstairs. Her door slams, and the vibration rumbles heavily through me, weighing me down like my bones are made of cement. I just proved her right, didn't I? She said I wouldn't believe her, and I didn't. I don't.

I know that feeding into her fantasy won't help her. But I'm not sure what I said instead did either.

"This would be easier if you *were* here," I mutter to Maddie's picture.

I freeze.

Maddie's face is twisted in a snarl and pressed so close to the camera that it fills the whole frame. Her look is pure violence, like she's about to leap out and strangle me. I scramble back, the sharp edge of the coffee table striking between my shoulder blades. I squeeze my eyes shut, counting my gasping breaths.

It's not until I hit fifty that my heart no longer feels like it's going to fall out of my mouth. I open my eyes and slowly look back at the photograph.

Which is now perfectly normal. I blink rapidly, my eyes glued to the picture.

Maddie keeps smiling her secretive smile.

• • •

Sylvia offers me a ride home, and I immediately say yes. After what happened today . . . I think I need to tell her about Blythe. I'm still reluctant to worry her, but the conversation with Blythe this afternoon was a whole other level.

Yet when I'm buckled in the passenger seat and houses are whipping by outside the window, I can't find the words. How do I describe what happened today? I'm so lost in thought, it takes me a moment to realize that we've stopped. We're in the middle of an empty school parking lot.

"Want to try?" Sylvia smiles broadly at me.

It takes a beat for me to figure out what she means. By the time it sinks in, Sylvia's already opening my door with a joking half-bow.

It's weird being on the driver's side, with the wheel jutting toward my lap. I've only driven once before, when Yas first got her car and convinced her mom to let me try driving down their street. Even though I went super slow and didn't come close to hitting anything,

Mrs. Wong gripped the emergency brake so hard I thought it might come off in her hand.

But Sylvia is relaxed and patient as she walks me through the pedals at my feet, and the buttons and levers around the steering wheel. It feels more natural than I expected it to, and my confidence grows as I follow Sylvia's instructions and guide the car in slow loops around the lot, signaling to invisible traffic before I turn left or right. Soon, I can't believe I was ever worried about mixing up the gas and brake pedals. After a while, she has me reverse into a parking spot, which is easy with the backup camera. I put the car in park and look over at Sylvia.

"Great job." The proud gleam in Sylvia's eye sends sends a flush of warmth up my neck. "Keep this up and soon you'll be driving me around."

I'm unable to control the grin spreading across my face. We switch seats again, and I'm so giddy that the rest of the trip home flies by, Sylvia regaling me with stories from the summer she spent driving from Toronto to Vancouver.

It's not until we're stopped in front of my apartment building that everything that happened with Blythe today comes rushing back. Sylvia is smiling warmly, almost expectantly, at me. I don't want to ruin this moment. But I have to say something.

I can't think of a way to bring it up casually, so I just blurt it out.

"Blythe thinks she sees Maddie."

Sylvia stiffens and her mouth twists. "Thank you for telling me," she says. "I'll talk to her." She tries to smile again, but it looks more like a cringe.

The back of my throat aches. She's going through so much, trying to keep her life together, trying to keep her grief locked away like the altar in her living room. I wish I hadn't had to give her more bad news. But it was the right thing to do. Wasn't it?

CHAPTER SIXTEEN

THE NEXT AFTERNOON, BLYTHE is back to ignoring me completely. She trudges right from the front door to the dining table, eyes immediately glued to her tablet. The peace offering I brought weighs heavy in my pocket. I want her to know that I didn't mean to shut her down and that she's not alone. There are other people who believe in ghosts, even if I'm not one of them. Maybe it's stupid to think this can communicate all that, but I have to try.

I sit down next to her and place the coin charm on the table between us.

"My mom says this can protect you from spirits who mean harm." I trace my fingers over the square hole in the middle of the coin. "I thought you might like it."

Blythe doesn't show any sign that she hears me or that she knows I'm here at all.

I might as well be a ghost.

After a few moments, I leave her to her game. I want to kick myself for the way I handled things yesterday. I had an opportunity to help her, and I blew it. As my candy tea steeps, I rack my brain for other ways to bridge the growing gulf between us.

When I glance back at Blythe, the coin charm is gone.

Maybe I didn't mess up as badly as I thought.

But instead of that making me feel better, I find myself on edge for the rest of the afternoon. I feel like there are eyes in the walls, following me everywhere. Despite what I said to Blythe, despite what I *believe*, it's like the idea of Maddie's ghost has infected me.

What if Maddie is *haunting her house?* my mind whispers.

What if she does *want me gone?*

I put a record on to drown out my inner monologue. The Ramones' hyper energy helps ease my nerves a little.

But it gets worse as the week goes on. A tingling sensation crawls up my spine when I approach the Morins' front door. I think I smell molding flowers when I sit on the couch, but the scent disappears as soon as I try to find its source. I can't shake the sensation I'm being watched, the weight of invisible eyes drilling into the back of my neck. I feel silly, but I start to avoid the living room, speed-walking through when necessary and keeping as far away from the hidden altar as possible. I find myself staying in the dining room with music playing at all times, jumping at the slightest creak, until Sylvia or Hector walks in and the din of their evening routine eases the anxiety in my veins.

Logically, I know it's just exhaustion. But my imagination won't listen to reason. I'm doing everything I can to get more sleep. I've gotten into the habit of popping two allergy pills before bed, and they submerge me in sweet darkness until my alarm drags me out on the other side. But I don't wake up any more rested.

When I peel my eyes open, my head pounds like my brain's trying to punch its way out of my skull. My hands shake so badly that I give up on eyeliner entirely. It feels like my head is full of static, and even my favorite songs can't drown out the white noise. I have bruises I can't explain and sometimes I wake up in weird places, like face down on the carpet in front of our altar or standing in the bathroom in the dark. The one comfort is that I almost always wake up holding the locket. Its familiar weight confirms that I'm real, and whatever happens in my dreams is not.

But in the early hours of Saturday morning, I wake up outside our apartment, barefoot on the grungy hall carpet with the door lolling open behind me and a thin streak of blood trailing down my left wrist. The cut on my hand is open again. There's a red smear on the doorjamb where I must have torn the scab off.

The thought that I might leave the house in my sleep scares me enough that I look up Dr. Lorimer, who ran the therapy group I went to as a kid. My heart sinks when I find out she closed her practice two years ago. I take a breath, but the air gets stuck halfway. I keep trying, focusing on the sensation of the cool air on my skin as it flows in and out of my nose. *Breath is the key to a calm mind.*

I set my left hand on my lap and force my eyes to focus on it. I cleaned it, but the skin around the reopened cut is puffy, and there's a red line where the scab was. I take a deep breath and start another breathing exercise I learned in therapy, tracing the outside of my left hand with the index finger of my right, breathing in when I trace up a finger and out when I trace down. When I'm finally taking full, steady breaths, what I need to do is clear.

I need to tell my mom.

• • •

I get my chance a few hours later, when I walk out of my room and find Mom on the couch, tearing open a package of LED tea lights. There's a red origami flower as big as my hand on the coffee table. Mom and I used to make those for the Hungry Ghost Festival. We'd fold a bunch, then choose the best ones to take down to the lake, where we'd put a candle in the middle of the paper flower and release it onto the water. Mom says the flame helps guide lost ghosts to the afterlife. But the Hungry Ghost Festival is in the summer, not January.

"What's that for?" I ask.

"Mrs. Paul." Mom flicks the switch on the bottom of a candle, and its fake flame glows yellow. "Now that she's received Anthony's message, it's time to guide him home." She places the lit candle in the center of the paper flower, making the red petals glow.

"Do you seriously think he came back from the dead to give her a watch?" It comes out more cutting than I intended. But it's also satisfying to say what I'm really thinking for once.

My mom looks up at me, her face dangerously calm.

"When were you going to tell me about your little Montreal trip?"

Shit.

"Yas's mom called me," she continues. "Apparently she and another parent met to discuss it last weekend. She wanted to know if I could join them next time. Since the three of you are driving down together."

"I was going to ask you." Words tumble out of my mouth in a panicked jumble. "It's just for a long weekend, four days, and I can pay for the whole trip; I have a bunch saved already and I'll have more than enough by the time we go. We're staying with Yas's cousin, Alice. Remember her? She's going to McGill and she said she'll give us a tour of campus."

"Sounds like you have it all planned out," Mom says mildly.

My word vomiting has dried up, and now I can't say anything. It feels like my lungs are wrapped in rubber bands.

Mom looks at me with her head tilted to the side, her face unreadable as the silence drags on.

"Well . . ."

My heart shrivels.

"I guess, if you pass physics—"

I scream and dive onto the couch, crushing her in a hug. The two of us tumble back into the cushions, and the tension dissolves into laughter.

"This isn't a *yes*," Mom says once we catch our breath, only half succeeding in rearranging her expression to look stern. "It's a maybe, *with conditions*. You need to pass physics. You need to do well in *all* your classes this semester. You need to stay out of trouble."

She counts the requirements out on her fingers and I nod along.

"And you need to go to the Coding Academy this summer."

"Okay! Yes." My cheeks ache from grinning so hard. "Whatever you want!"

"Really?" Mom's eyebrows shoot up. "If I'd known all I had to do was take you to a LMK concert—"

"Oh my god," I groan. "We're not just going to see them."

"Remember you and Yas used to make up dances to their songs? You made tickets for your shows, and you made Mrs. Wong and me give them to you before you'd let us sit down."

Giggling on the couch while Mom teases me, I feel hopeful for the first time in a long time. I'm going to Osheaga.

It isn't until I'm halfway to driver's ed that I remember I was going to tell Mom about the sleepwalking. But there's no way I can do that now. She'll freak out, and she might change her mind about Montreal. She hasn't even said yes yet, not for real. But this is way closer than I ever thought I'd get.

Plus, this is one of the things that's been majorly stressing me out. Since talking to her about the trip went so well, maybe the nightmares will stop on their own.

• • •

I'm so excited, it's like all my senses have sharpened to superhuman levels. A flock of brown sparrows shiver on a power line, and I see their tiny talons curled around the wire. The Velvet Underground pine for "Pale Blue Eyes," and I peel back each layer of the melody, separating the melancholic strum of the guitar from the jangle of the tambourine from Lou Reed's rough voice. Every scratch on the stairs up to driver's ed looks like an abstract work of art.

As soon as I spot Yas and Dell, the news comes bursting out of me. "My mom said yes! I'm going to Osheaga!"

The two of them grin. Dell pumps their fist in the air and Yas squeezes my hand. But it's not the squealing, jumping-up-and-down reaction I expected. Their energy feels more agitated than excited. Something is off.

"We have news too." Yas glances sideways at Dell, and the adrenaline coursing through me sours. "You will *not* believe what Dell heard."

"About what?"

"The kid you're babysitting—her sister died last summer, right? Fell off the bluffs?"

"Yeah?"

"Is her name Madeline?"

"They called her Maddie, but—"

"But this is her, right?"

Yas turns her phone, and there's Maddie in her graduation gown. When I nod, Yas barrels on. Apparently Maddie went to school with Dell's cousin, who filled them in on the gossip last night.

"After Maddie died, her mom was down at the spot where she drowned for, like, a whole week straight," Dell says. "The cops eventually threatened to ticket her so she would leave."

“So?” I frown. “Her daughter just died.”

Yas shakes her head and swipes to a string of posts on a message board.

r/Toronto

TEEN DIES IN FALL FROM SCARBOROUGH BLUFFS: CBC NEWS

ski444
Such a tragedy. RIP Madeline.

treatortrick
Heartbreaking.

[deleted]
This is exactly why you don’t fucking climb the bluffs.

lateryogurt
I walk my dog on this beach 2x a day and the girl’s mother hasn’t moved since it happened. She just sits and stares at the lake.

ski444
So sad. I hope she has support.

nightyknight
That’s creepy shit.

1mag1n3
She just lost her kid asshole.

lateryogurt
Two weeks later and the mother’s still there. I was on the beach at 10pm and she had hundreds of candles lit around her, like some kind of cult ritual.

1mag1n3
Ok that is creepy.

skii444
“The only cure for grief is to grieve.”—Earl Grollman

This post has been locked by community moderators.

I try to swallow, but it gets stuck halfway. How devastated Sylvia must have been to be unable to leave the spot where her daughter died.

"Isn't it weird?" Yas says. "It's like she was trying to be some kind of witch—"

Every muscle in my body goes rigid.

Witch bitch.

How often has that word been flung at me? *That's* what Yas is taking away from this?

"What are you saying?" I grip the locket, the curved edges branding my palm. "You think I should quit?"

Yas presses her lips together but doesn't say anything.

She knows there's no way I can afford Montreal without this job. Does she even want me to come to Osheaga anymore? I thought she would be thrilled that my mom said yes, but as I watch her and Dell exchange a look, I'm not so sure. Do they have some kind of telepathic link now? I bet they'd both be glad if I didn't come. Then the two of them could talk about photography and fashion and whatever, without Yas's loser friend tagging along.

"We just thought you should know." Dell's eyes shift from me to Yas and back again. "That's all."

"Well, now I know."

It looks like Yas might say more, but I don't want to hear it. The anger simmering beneath my skin feels like a snake coiled inside me, rearing back to strike. What would happen if I let it go?

Instead, I channel the energy into violently searching my backpack for my notebook.

When Donald claps his hands to get our attention, Yas leans toward me.

"You're coming to the party tonight, right?" She means *I'm sorry.*

The pressure in my gut eases a little, and I nod.

• • •

My phone buzzes in my hand, startling me awake. I peel my face off the couch cushion, leaving a puddle of drool behind. It's just after 7 p.m. Did I manage to take a nap? I don't remember the last time I slept for more than five minutes without a pill. Maybe talking to my mom about Osheaga really was the cure.

I wipe my mouth with the back of my hand and thumb open a string of messages from Yas.

pregame at the park at 9

you're coming right?

you promised

don't make me come over there

i'll make u wear a skirt

hello

rachel

hi

hi

hellooooooooo

I huff out a laugh, but warmth spreads in my stomach like sunlight. Yas is trying to apologize. She doesn't know the Morins like I do, so that story Dell heard made her worry. I probably overreacted too. But she's still my friend, and she still wants me at Osheaga—and at the party tonight.

calm down stalker I was sleeping, I write back. *I'll be there*.

I pull up my music app and start my dad's playlist. The opening riff of "Pretty Vacant" blasts out of the speaker and Johnny Rotten's snarl sends a bolt of energy through me. In this video, Johnny's wearing sunglasses and this weird shirt with super-long sleeves that cover his hands, twitching more than dancing as he yells into the mic. It's like he knew he was going to be a legend but didn't give two shits if anyone else agreed. God, they were so badass. I bet that's why my dad liked them.

I bang my head to the beat all the way to my closet. I stare at the sea of rumpled band T-shirts, secondhand sweaters, and scratchy discount tank tops. Should I ask Yas what she's wearing? But how would that help me? Our wardrobes are total opposites. Will her photography friends dress up for a house party? They're artsy; maybe a band T-shirt is fine. Why do I even care? I won't know anyone. But the problem is that I do care, and my enthusiasm splinters into defeat as I riffle through my sad wardrobe.

Then a sparkle catches my eye.

Maddie's silver tank top. I still don't know why I took it. I thought about returning it, but how would I get it into her room without anyone seeing me? So I shoved it in the back of my closet, like maybe it would magically teleport itself home if I forgot about it.

But now, with the delicate silver material sparkling in my hands, that same sharp craving that overtook me the first time I saw it grabs hold of me again.

I already have it. It's not like Maddie's missing it.

She can't be—because ghosts aren't real.

The shimmering shirt transforms me into a version of myself I don't recognize. The locket rests against my chest, drawing attention to the way the neckline folds and dips, revealing far more skin than

I'm used to. But instead of igniting my anxiety, it gives me a surge of confidence. I try on a smile, pressing my lips together and tilting the corners of my mouth up just slightly.

Like I'm holding in a secret.

CHAPTER SEVENTEEN

THE LINING OF MY winter coat brushes against my bare arms and the wind whips my hair into my face, but somehow I'm not cold as I head into the park. It might have something to do with the shot I had while I was getting ready. I don't drink that often, since I don't go out much. The one time I got drunk alone, I ended up ugly crying to Taylor Swift's *Red* album. But I like the way that alcohol silences the twitchy monologue in my head, and I really needed that tonight. Deciding to willingly walk into a house full of strangers got my brain running worst-case scenarios at three-times speed.

The jungle gym in the middle of the playground is shaped like a pirate ship, but at this time of night it hunches like a hungry beast. The swing set is occupied by two figures whose laughter bounces wildly through the empty playground. Yas lets out a whoop when she spots me, leaping off the swing and wrapping her arms around my middle.

"You came!" Her breath smells of cinnamon and alcohol. When she pulls back, her face is flushed red and her grin is lopsided. "Your hair is *amazing*!"

It took me over an hour watching YouTube videos and fighting with the curling iron to get the waves just right. But the effort was worth it. I perch on the wobbly edge of the merry-go-round and pull a water bottle out of my pocket.

"What've you got?" Dell asks.

"Orange juice and gin." I shrug. "It's all my mom had."

Yas and Dell's faces crumple in twin cringes. Dell jumps up and offers me a bottle with a sunset-orange label. Their fingers are long and elegant, and I wonder if they play the piano. I don't know much about them at all, do I? They shake the bottle and the golden liquid inside swirls.

"What is it?" I ask.

"Fireball whisky."

I take a slow sip and the hot-sweet flavor of cinnamon hearts bursts across my tongue. But as I swallow, the hot takes over and all traces of candy are consumed by a searing fire that burns my throat. I choke out a cough as Dell cackles and Yas grins, kicking her feet in the air. I take another long swig before passing the bottle back.

The orange juice and gin tastes like sour plastic after that sweet rush of heat, but I force it down. When my water bottle's empty, Yas grabs the whisky and tops me up with a wink.

By the time we arrive at a bungalow with a pretty blue door, the world is pleasantly fuzzy around the edges. I can feel the bass rumbling through my feet as we walk up the front steps. Yas rings the doorbell and we shuffle nervously as we wait. When no one answers after the second ring, Yas pulls her phone out and rapidly types a text. The tip of my nose is numb when the door finally swings open.

A wave of heat and warm light tumbles out from behind the guy grinning down at us. He looks like a dictionary definition of a jock: tall, broad-shouldered, even wearing a navy-blue letterman jacket. Blond hair falls into his eyes, and when he shoves it back I notice his nails. Each one is intricately painted like a different kind of sports ball.

There's the black and white hexagons of a soccer ball, the neon green and white of a tennis ball, a white baseball with red seams . . .

This must be Eric.

My gaze sweeps over his outfit again. The jacket is worn around the collar, probably vintage. He must know how this whole getup makes him look. Is he being ironic? I brush away a strange impulse to ask him.

"Hey! You made it." Eric steps back so we can crowd into the warmth. He gives each of us a high five as we pass. I hope my cheeks are red enough from the cold to cover up my blush. As I take my coat off, Yas slides up next to me.

"This top is *hot*! I never thought you'd wear anything that shows your *shoulders*!" She's trying to whisper but not really succeeding. "I wasn't even sure you *had* shoulders."

I shrug like it's no big deal, but the glow already thrumming through my body flares brighter.

Every inch of the house is packed, but Eric is so tall it's easy to follow him as he weaves through the crush. He leads us to a counter piled with stacks of red Solo cups, giant bottles of pop, and dozens of half-empty liquor bottles. Against the back wall, cases of beer are piled into a tower almost as tall as I am. I've never seen this much booze in one place.

"Shots?" Eric leans against the beer tower with a mischievous smile.

A minute later, the four of us are raising our plastic cups and yelling *cheers!* with one voice. The tequila stings on the way down, but the tart slice of lime I bite into after provides more relief than I expected. Dell catches my eye and we grin at each other, the limes covering our teeth and transforming our mouths into green monstrosities. We laugh until we're gasping.

Yas, Dell, and I mix drinks in red plastic cups and head to the basement, which has been transformed into a club. Once we close the door to upstairs, the only lights are the neon glowsticks shining from dancers' bodies and the Christmas lights framing the makeshift DJ booth. The humid air pulses, heavy with the rhythmic thud of bass and the scent of sweat and beer. Dell grabs Yas, who grabs me, and we elbow our way into the middle of the grooving mass.

I brace myself for the fluttery, hollow feeling that usually rises in my stomach when I'm surrounded by a crowd, but it doesn't come. Instead, my entire body fizzes with tiny, giddy bubbles that make my skin tingle whenever someone brushes against me. I tilt my head back and gulp the rest of my drink, closing my eyes and moving my limbs to the pulsing sound. I imagine I'm at Osheaga and LMK is tearing up the stage, the music vibrating through the crowd, every individual deliciously anonymous and free.

When I open my eyes, the others are gone. Strangers dance around me, a sea of unfamiliar shadows. I try to act casual, but a knot of panic twists behind my ribs. I shove my way to the stairs, and the room tilts slightly. Halfway up, I pause and lean against the cool wall, focusing on taking deep breaths.

"Hey." A deep voice rumbles in my ear. "You okay?"

I look up and meet Eric's blue eyes. I'm a couple steps above him, so we're the same height. He looks worried.

"I'm good," I say. He shakes his head and leans toward me. Maybe he can't hear me over the music? I speak a little louder. "Just needed some air."

"Yeah, it's packed down here." He tilts his chin at the empty cup in my hand. "Want a refill?"

A bead of sweat slides across his temple, down the side of his throat, and disappears under the damp collar of his T-shirt. Sweaty guys are usually gross, but he's glowing. There's a small mole on the side of his neck. I wonder if his skin is salty. He's looking at me intently. Because he asked me something. Oh. Right. What was the question?

"Yes," I say.

He plucks the cup from my hand and intertwines my now-empty fingers with his. Our slick palms slide over one another and I start to pull away, but he tightens his hold.

"I'm Eric," he says.

I know who you are, I think. *Everyone does.*

"Hi, Eric." I smile with my lips closed. Do I look stupid? He's going to laugh at me any second. Someone's going to turn the lights on and everyone will be staring, pointing at me.

But Eric grins and leans closer. "Hi . . . ?"

A question hangs on the end of the word, and an answer slips out of my mouth before my brain catches up.

"Maddie."

The thrill of the lie courses through me like electricity, every nerve ending sparking like a live wire. The feeling only intensifies when his thumb strokes the back of my hand.

"Hi, Maddie." His warm breath tickles my cheek. "I think I have something you'll like. Come on."

We weave between the people clustered throughout his house. I spot Yas on the couch between Dell and a guy with a jaw so sharp he might be made of marble. Yas leans into the guy, biting her lip as he whispers into her ear. She reaches up and runs her fingers through his sleek, black hair. *K-pop Guy?* my fuzzy brain supplies before Eric pulls me away.

Eric pauses in the kitchen to open a cooler and grab a couple of tall cans, then guides us into the hall. We end up at the back of the house, both of us searching the buzzing crowd for somewhere to sit.

Every cushion, every chair, even most of the floor is occupied. I'm about to suggest we try to squish in by the couch, when Eric tugs me over to the wall between two closed doors and slides down to sit on the floor with a grin. He squeezes my hand and I follow, settling onto the hardwood floor next to him.

Our knees knock together and he looks at me sideways, the corner of his mouth turning up. It's quieter down here, like we're below the current of the music and chatter. My mouth is suddenly dry, and I wonder what Yas would think if she walked around the corner. Then I remember I just saw her, snuggled on the couch with her hands in that hot guy's hair. She's busy. And she'd probably tell me to go for it anyway; she barely said hi to Eric tonight.

Eric offers one of the cans to me.

"Tastes like peach iced tea."

He opens the other and gives me a smile as we cheers. I take a tentative sip, and my teeth tingle as the cold, tart tea floods my mouth. It's sweet and I can't taste the alcohol at all. I'm suddenly fiercely thirsty, and I tilt my head back to take a long drink.

Eric's free hand rests on the hardwood between us. His nail polish is even more detailed than I realized. The baseball is decorated with dozens of symmetrical red stitches, and the black lines on the soccer ball are impossibly straight. I take my index finger and trace his cuticles, one by one. How am I just touching him? My skin hums in all the places where it meets his. When I look up, he's staring at me with his lips parted, his eyes intensely focused on mine.

"Did you do these yourself?" I ask. "They're so good."

"They're just decals." Is he blushing?

"Really?"

I look down again and slide my fingers underneath his hand so I can lift it up toward my face. As I examine the designs on his nails more closely, my vision blurs and the room lists sideways. I grasp his fingers to steady myself and his hand tightens around mine, drawing me toward him. When the world rights itself, our clasped hands are trapped between our chests. His eyes flick down to my lips.

An alarm blares in the back of my brain. Is this a bad idea?

Then he's kissing me, and my thoughts dissolve into sensation: the tang of peaches and tequila, the warm slide of his tongue against mine, the low sigh that vibrates through his lips. It's not my first kiss, but the few I've had always made me more nervous than anything, my mind racing with worry about which way to tilt my head and if there's too much spit in my mouth or not enough. But as Eric slides his hand up my bare shoulder and cups the back of my neck, my mind is still.

I'm consumed by all the places where his skin touches mine, by the steadily increasing hum pulsing through every pore in my body. It's like I'm floating outside myself, watching the confident, carefree girl I've been playing tonight kiss a boy who can't take his eyes off of her.

I watch her swing her leg over his and crawl onto his lap, kissing him deeply as she presses him back against the wall. One of his hands tangles in her hair and the other slides up her back, disappearing beneath her shimmering shirt.

Then he jerks back with a yelp and shoves her off of him, scrambling away. His eyes are wide. His fingers touch his mouth.

They come back red.

The girl with my face watches him from the floor, leaning back on her elbows with a feral grin. The locket around her neck shines like a beacon. Her tongue darts out to lick the blood off her front teeth, then a sharp, vacant smile spreads across her glistening lips. She rises slowly, settling into a crouch more animal than human, like she's preparing to pounce. Her foot slides back on the wood floor and she flinches—

The world shifts.

A shooting pain courses up the sole of my right foot, and my fingernails warp as they dig into the wood floor.

I blink rapidly, trying to bring the blur into focus. Then Eric's wild eyes are above me, his face slack with disbelief. A thick red bead wells on his ruined bottom lip and slides down his chin.

My heart is rioting, like it's trying to break my ribcage open.

I taste iron, and an acidic horror expands in my stomach. The sounds of the party fade, until all I can hear is my own panting breath. My eyes are fixed on the red streaks marring Eric's chin.

Rage flares in my belly, filling me with a sudden urge to lash out, to *hurt*. Every muscle in my body is a coiled spring, vibrating with an urge to give in to the instinct. Then a tear slips out of the corner of Eric's eye, and the feeling burns out as fast as it appeared. All that remains in me is a black hole, a bottomless pit of shock and shame.

I do the only thing I can do.

I turn, and I run.

CHAPTER EIGHTEEN

I WAKE UP WITH a mouth like sour sandpaper. I pry my sticky eyes open, but all I see is a gray blur. I blink and the world slides into focus: the coarse carpet under my cheek, the leg of my nightstand in front of me.

My bedroom.

Thank god.

I push myself up to sitting, but the movement makes my stomach lurch and I collapse against the edge of my bed. I close my eyes and gulp in air until the nausea subsides.

Okay.

I need to assess the damage.

I'm wearing the same clothes from last night. That's fine.

There's a suspicious burgundy stain on the front of the silver top. I rip the shirt off and toss it toward my laundry basket, stumbling up to do the same with my jeans. I briefly debate a shower, but I don't think I can stand for that long. I pull my pajamas on instead. My right foot aches, and I pick a nasty splinter out from the bottom of it. But otherwise I seem uninjured.

When I check my phone, there are no new messages. For some

reason, that makes my stomach churn with dread, like my body knows something my mind doesn't. My pulse pounds in my ears as I stare at my phone, thinking back to last night, trying to remember.

What happened at the party? How did I get home?

I feel numb as I prod the blank space where my memories of the evening should be. Only a few images surface: running my fingertips across Eric's hand, Eric's half-smile as he leans in to kiss me, his tenderness morphing into shock as he touches his torn lip, the warm salt of blood in my mouth—

My phone hits the floor with a dull thud. My fingers dig into my forehead like I can pull the awful pictures out of my skull.

Was that real? There's no way that could be real—

Mom bursts into my room, my keys in one hand and the bottle of gin in the other.

"You left these in the door." She flings the keys on my bed. "And I see you helped yourself to enough of *this* to redecorate the bathroom." She shakes the gin in my direction, and the sound of the liquid makes my stomach turn.

"Do you have anything to say?"

"Sorry," I mumble at the ground.

"What?"

"I'm sorry!" I can feel the heat of her glare, but I can't look at her face. She's wearing mismatched socks, one white and one neon yellow.

"The front door was open! Do you have any idea how that made me feel?" She's muttering, talking more to herself than to me. "And you wanted to go to Montreal *by yourself* this summer . . ."

My stomach drops. "What?"

"I told you, it was a maybe. *With conditions*. Conditions that you've now puked all over."

"But Mom—"

"But nothing." Her lips press into a thin line. "Montreal is off the table. The first thing you're going to do today is clean the bathroom until it sparkles. You're grounded for two weeks. You'll come straight home from work every day, no hanging out with Yas or whoever."

Mom holds out her hand and looks at my phone meaningfully. I hesitate for a beat before I pass it to her. She doesn't hide the screen as she sets it up to share my location with her and protects it with a password to keep me from turning the feature off.

She knows I can just put my phone on airplane mode, right?

What does she think I'm doing that she has to stalk me?

The image of Eric's bloody lip flits through my mind. But there's no way that happened. It has to be another nightmare. All I *actually* did was forget to lock the door and throw up in the bathroom.

"I made one mistake!" I've never done anything like this and I'm *sixteen.*

"One mistake is all it takes."

Her words are like a slap in the face. I don't know if it's what she meant, but my mind goes to the one mistake she made that blew up her entire life.

Me.

A bitter taste rises in the back of my throat, and I grab the garbage can just in time.

• • •

After I clean the bathroom, I lie in bed until the streetlamps are glowing outside my window. I still haven't heard from Yas. My curser blinks below the last message I sent, before I met her at the park last night. Maybe I should call her?

In a few minutes.

I flick back to YouTube and sink into the endless stream of videos. I watch concerts in train stations, behind a tiny desk, at the Super Bowl; actors eating hot wings, petting puppies, putting makeup on; tips on how to line your lips, straighten your hair, curl your eyelashes.

I forget each one the moment I scroll to the next.

When I look at the time, it's been Monday for twenty minutes. I feel a dread that surprises me with its force. I have to be at school in a few hours. There's no way my mom will let me stay home sick, and if I skip they might call her and I'll be in even more shit than I am already. I need to get some sleep.

I put my phone down and pop the last two allergy pills out of the pack, swallowing them dry. They stick in my throat as I think of Eric's hand, his painted nails gleaming in the dim light as he reaches for me, then again as he lifts his fingers to his lips and they come away red . . . no. That part was a dream. It has to be.

Right?

Yas is just hungover. She's probably been sleeping all day. I'll see her in the morning, and she'll confirm I imagined the whole Eric thing. We'll laugh about how drunk we were. Maybe together, we can figure out how to change my mom's mind about Osheaga. Everything will be fine.

CHAPTER NINETEEN

WHEN I WAKE UP, there's still no message from Yas. I make a double-strong pot of coffee, tuck the locket into my shirt, and pull the hood of my sweater up, telling myself *it will be fine* over and over until I almost believe it. I cling to that thin thread of hope until I walk through my school's front doors and every face snaps toward me.

The crowd grows denser the closer I get to my locker; people are staring openly at me and whispering to each other. My feet are heavy, like I'm walking through knee-deep mud.

I should turn around. I should get out of here now.

When Cameron and his buddies see me, they gasp and clutch each other, shrinking away in mock horror. Cameron raises a big wooden cross with a golden figure crucified on it—did he steal that from a church?—holding it out like a shield. Fury flares in my chest.

No. I won't let them see me run.

I shoulder past them and the crowd backs up like a many-legged monster, a glinting multitude of eyes and phones trained on me.

My locker is drenched in blood.

Up close, it's clear that it's not real. But it's still thick and red and dripping down the dented door, framing a printout of my face on a snarling vampire's body. I recognize the image. It was one of the pictures from that anonymous account. Cameron's account. There's a mountain of garlic piled on the floor, a heap of white bulbs and crushed cloves that fill the air with their foul stink. My eyes burn as I glance sideways at the crowd. They're watching, waiting, taut with anticipation.

I make my face carefully blank and fish a handful of tissues out of my backpack. I wipe the blood off of my lock, focusing on carefully scraping the red out of every number and notch on the dial. The streaks of red on the tissue make me think of Eric's shocked face, a fat bead of blood welling on his lip. But that can't be what this is about because that didn't happen.

Right?

It takes me three tries to spin my combination correctly, with the way my hands are shaking. When I risk a glance around, most of the crowd has drifted away. I guess they were expecting more of a show. I grab the books I need as fast as I can without getting fake blood all over my stuff.

I spot Yas's blue hair bobbing down the hall, and I'm not sure if it's relief or the garlic making my eyes water. I jog to catch up with her, saying her name as I touch her shoulder.

Yas yanks away and wheels around, her face contorted in a glare.

"Hi, *Maddie*." Yas's hiss pierces me like a needle. "Did you have fun at the party?"

"What?"

"So you hooked up with Eric. Then you bit him? Kinky."

No.

No, that was a dream. A nightmare.

Something that definitely didn't happen in the real world . . .

But the look on Yas's face tells a different story.

"Yas, I— I don't remember."

"You made out with the guy *I told you I liked*, and you don't even remember? Wow."

I notice heads turning toward us and I lower my voice. "I was drunk—"

"That's not an excuse."

She isn't listening to me. Why doesn't she ever listen to me?

"*He* hit on *me*."

"Oh! Why didn't you say so? That changes everything."

Why is she making this such a big deal? Didn't she see what they did to me? She should be on my side. She should be asking how *I* am.

"How was I supposed to know you *actually* liked him? You have a new crush, like, every three seconds."

"You could've asked?" Yas has never looked at me like this before; the hostility makes her face unrecognizable. "Why did you say your name was Maddie? That's fucked up, Rachel."

My throat feels thick, but I make myself swallow through it. I don't know why I said my name was Maddie. It was stupid, but so what? People get drunk and do stupid things all the time. I don't need another person thinking I'm some kind of freak, another person telling me how messed up I am. The palm of my hand throbs where it presses on the locket through my sweater.

Yas's eyes narrow. "Something is seriously wrong with you."

The world goes white.

I don't feel myself move, but I hear Yas's yelp and a clang.

Then she's cowering against the lockers, her hands raised defensively between us. My arms ache and I'm panting, my hands curled into claws. Fear pulses in Yas's eyes, an echo of Eric's stunned, bloody face. I take a step back, trembling.

Did I push her? What am I doing?

The volume cranks up on the jeers and laughter from the crowd as it closes in again, and I know Cameron is there somewhere, riding high off my disgrace.

In another ugly echo of one of the few memories I have of that night, I turn and I run.

• • •

The rest of the day is a blur of humiliation. Cloves of garlic appear on my desk in every class. I get called to the office, where the vice principal heaves a sigh as deep as the bags under his eyes and says he expects my locker to look brand new by the end of the day. He doesn't ask any questions, and I don't volunteer any information, because it doesn't sound like he's going to call my mom and I want to keep it that way. I just nod and spend my lunch hour staining a whole roll of paper towels red.

When the last bell rings, I'm the first one out the door. Frigid gray fog hangs low over the sidewalk, and my head pulses in time with my steps. I can't even summon the energy to put my earbuds in. When I get to Blythe's school, I pull up my coat's heavy hood and slouch against the chain-link fence, letting my eyes slip closed. The cold wind makes my cheeks sting, but it feels good after hours trapped by stale air and stares.

"Are you okay?"

Blythe is staring up at me.

I didn't hear the bell ring, but the yard is in full motion now, swarming with kids and parents.

Blythe frowns, three little lines appearing between her eyebrows. What does she see?

Me, leaning against this fence like it's the only thing holding me up. I haven't slept properly in weeks, I mauled a guy who kissed me, everyone at school thinks I'm a freak, my best friend hates me, my mom hates me, and worst of all . . . I think they might be right.

"I'm fine," I say. "I just have a stomachache."

Blythe doesn't look convinced. "Did you drink too much?"

My mind short-circuits. What am I supposed to say to that?

"Maddie used to drink too much," she clarifies.

Her sister's name makes me think of Yas's accusing glare.

"She would stay in bed all day because she had a stomachache." Blythe looks down at her boots. "It happened so much I thought maybe she had, like, cancer or something? But when I asked her, she said she just drank too much. I started being careful about how much I was drinking, 'cause I didn't want to get sick too. But then my dad told me Maddie meant she drank too much alcohol."

I don't know what to say to that.

Blythe's barely spoken to me since the day I told her about Wàipó's ghost, and this is the most she's ever said about her sister. Maybe more than she's ever said about anything.

I don't want to screw this up again.

"Maddie got grounded all the time, but she always found a way to sneak out. Last summer, dad put an alarm on the front door, so she started going out my window. I never told on her. Never."

"You're a good sister."

"No." Blythe shakes her head, her eyes filling with tears. "Mostly she went to parties, but sometimes she went down to our spot on the beach. I knew that's where she was going. She wanted me to come see the full moon, but I was too scared. When she didn't come home, I should have—"

Whoa. I crouch down so I can look her in the eye.

"Blythe, it's not your fault."

"I need to talk to her."

"Blythe—"

"I DO!" Blythe explodes with a shriek. "She wants to tell me something! I need to talk to her!"

"Blythe, stop." I glance around, hoping no one's watching us. "Calm down."

Blythe does not calm down. Instead, she opens her mouth and lets out a feral scream that shoots splinters into my eardrums. Hot flecks of spit fly from her mouth into my face.

Then my mouth is open and I'm roaring back like a wild beast, my fingers digging into the soft flesh of her arms, fury and frustration thundering out of my mouth in a hot rush of sound.

It stops only when I run out of breath.

Blythe's stricken face is inches away from mine, her face contorted with the same shock that's thrumming through my body. We stare at each other for one breath, two.

Then the dam breaks.

Blythe's face crumples and tears stream down her flushed cheeks.

"You—screamed—at—me!" Blythe howls between hiccups.

"I'm so sorry—"

She shrinks away and I let go of her arms. What's wrong with me?

There are only a couple of parents left in the schoolyard, but they're looking at us, frowning in a way that makes my mouth taste like bitter cotton. Are they going to come over? What if one of them tells the Morins?

But I don't have time to worry about that because now Blythe is sprinting down the sidewalk. I take off after her, calling her name. Blythe picks up speed and momentum takes over as the hill curves down, her limbs starting to flail. I know she's going to fall before she does, and I yell a warning but it's too late. Her backpack goes one way, and her body goes the other. She slams into the concrete, on her hands and knees. She's sobbing when I reach her, staring at the grimy bits of road salt and gravel embedded in her palms. When she looks up at me, I see another scream building in her lungs.

"I know how to talk to Maddie." The words tumble out in a rush.

Blythe blinks, stunned into silence. Her fury evaporates, and she's just a kid again, hesitant and hurting, and a little hopeful.

I ignore the guilt gnawing in my stomach, brush the dirt off her jacket, and lead her home.

CHAPTER TWENTY

BLYTHE LETS ME CLEAN her scraped hands with soap and water; luckily none of the cuts are deep. She goes to find a red pen as I rip a piece of paper out of my notebook and place two fat, vanilla-scented candles I found in the bathroom on either side. Blythe reappears and puts a red pen with a chewed-up lid on the table, along with the tall red candle from Maddie's altar.

I see Maddie's snarling face, pressed against the picture frame, and I shiver. I shove the image away and dim the lights to near darkness. Blythe lights the candles and, as the too-sweet vanilla fills the air, I feel a pang of longing for the smell of incense. My mom would definitely not approve of this haphazard setup—though she'd say it's the spirits who'd be offended—but it's going to have to do.

"This is called fújī. It's a Chinese game to try to talk to spirits. Kind of like a Ouija board." I explain what we have to do, conscious of my voice stumbling over my mom's words.

"Cool," Blythe says when I finish, and starts writing down her questions for Maddie on a scrap piece of paper.

"It might not work," I warn.

I don't say it *can't* work, since ghosts aren't real, because my mom's voice is playing in my mind. *Sometimes it's more about what the living need to say to the dead.*

But how does she believe that, if she's also writing messages and pretending they're from spirits? Still, it seemed to help Mrs. Paul. And Mom's clients keep coming back, week after week. Even if it helps Blythe a little bit, it will be worth it. If it stops her screaming at me too, well . . . that's a bonus.

But am I prepared to fake a message from Maddie to make that happen?

I don't know. I'm not sure I can take it that far.

"Blythe? Did you hear me?" I look at her until she meets my eyes. "Maddie might not say anything back. But that doesn't mean she's not listening. Okay?"

Blythe bites her lip, nodding slowly.

Blythe and I bow three times, then sit down at the table.

"Next, I'm going to chant a mantra to clear our minds." But rather than comforting me like the mantra usually does, the sound of my thin voice cracking awkwardly over the notes makes me uneasy. I'm glad that Blythe has her eyes closed.

Since I don't have any incense to light, when I finish I just pick up the pen. Blythe's hand grasps it above mine, and we hold the tip so it just touches the middle of the paper.

"Is this Maddie? What are you trying to tell me?"

Blythe reads both her questions at once, but I don't bother to correct her. It doesn't really matter. What matters is whether or not I'm going to fake a response. My heart is thudding in my ears. I have no idea what to do. The candles flicker, sending shadows swaying in the dim corners of the dining room.

Sudden sleepiness sweeps through me and my eyelids droop.

"Did you see that?" Blythe hisses. I force my eyes open. "It moved!"

My hand is clammy; the pen probably just slipped.

I try to tell her that, but I can't quite manage the words. My whole body is flushed, and it feels like there's a hot coal in the middle of my chest. The pen twitches, and the dot beneath the tip grows wider.

"Stop moving it." I force the words out, but they burn like my throat is full of broken glass.

"I'm not."

The pen loops in a circle, curving over and over in a spiral that grows larger with every stroke.

"Blythe—"

"I'm not doing it!"

Every atom of my being rejects what I see. The world outside the candles and the paper blurs.

It feels like I'm outside of my body, watching over my own shoulder as the flames dance shadows up the walls and the pen circles and circles and circles. Dizziness rushes over me, and the smell of molding flowers floods my nostrils, making my eyes water.

I close my eyes, but instead of darkness there's a hot white light.

"Maddie?" Blythe's voice is faint, like she's speaking from deep inside a cave.

When I open my eyes, I'm watching us from the other side of the table. Blythe and I are hunched over, the candlelight casting us in an eerie glow. The pen skitters across the paper, dragging our hands along with it. How can I be there but watching from here?

Am I dreaming?

This must be a dream.

"I'm so sorry, Maddie," Blythe chokes out. "I should have gone with you. I should have told them when you didn't come home—"

All the kitchen cupboards fling open and slam shut, like some kind of twisted Disney dance. Blythe glances around, eyes bulging, but keeps hold of the pen.

My body doesn't show any reaction at all.

"What are you trying to tell me?" Blythe asks.

Her eyes snap up to the seat across from her and she gasps. The chair is obscured by a black stain of shadow, so dark it almost seems solid, and Blythe stares at it, transfixed, her mouth making the shape of her sister's name.

The pen keeps moving across the page, switching from circles to waves to loops, the tip never leaving the paper.

I watch tears slide down Blythe's cheeks.

In front of me, my body is bent over the paper like a gargoyle, my eyes narrowed in fierce slits of focus. The table starts to tremble; the candles threaten to tip over. The shadow expands, stretching from the chair across the table, darkness obscuring the paper, our hands, shrouding the twisted face that isn't my face. The shaking in the table grows more furious, spreads through the whole house. The pen jerks from one side of the page to the other. I don't understand how Blythe and I are still holding it.

I don't understand a lot of things.

But as the room rattles like an eighteen-wheeler is driving through it, the one thing I do know is that nothing good is happening here.

Stop this, I plead. *Stop!*

But I can't hear my voice, and Blythe doesn't seem to either.

I can no longer see the paper through the unnatural darkness enveloping the entire room, but I can tell the pen is still spasming, pulling our hands along with it.

Suddenly, the pen draws a straight line across the whole page.

It traces and retraces the line, moving back and forth with such force that I hear the paper rip. The table rocks violently, its legs coming inches off the ground.

The pen flies out of our hands, whipping against the wall of windows like we threw it with all our strength.

My vision blurs and lurches.

Somewhere in the distance, the pen clatters to the floor.

I'm back at the table next to Blythe, the paper a jumble of scribbles in front of us.

The candles flicker. The only shadows in the room are the ones that belong there.

My hand is cold and wet. The paper is almost soaked through, the ink a blurry mess, like someone spilled a full glass of water on it.

A drop of red falls on the paper, landing in a puddle where it spreads into pink.

The scab under my thumb is gone, leaving beads of blood where the fresh, pink skin has ripped open again. I press it with my other hand, and the jolt of pain brings me back to the present.

Blythe is panting next to me. What just happened?

Did it *work*? Did Maddie's ghost try to talk to us?

There has to be another explanation. Was Blythe playing a trick?

"Thank you, Maddie," I croak. "Farewell."

"Farewell," Blythe repeats.

I wipe my wet palms on my jeans, careful to avoid the reopened wound. Did I sweat that much? How is that even possible? How is *any of this* possible?

"I saw her." Blythe is staring at the seat on the other side of the table. "She was right there. Then, she was behind you." Blythe looks up at me, her eyes wide and frightened. "She had her hands around your neck, like she was trying to—"

When I touch my neck, my skin is clammy and cold. Blythe saw her sister's ghost try to . . . what? Strangle me? That's impossible. Blythe takes a shuddering breath and looks down at the paper, pulling it closer with trembling fingers. "What does it mean?"

I start to make an excuse, but when my eyes land on the page, the words turn to ash in my mouth. Disbelief twists in my gut as my brain re-examines what I thought were random scribbles.

They're not random at all.

Even with the water-blurred ink, they form two unmistakable, vigorously underlined words:

"Do you think she's trapped somewhere?" Blythe's voice shakes. "What if she's hurt?"

I open my mouth, but nothing comes out. I don't know what to think. I didn't expect this to happen. I didn't expect *anything* to happen.

It was always my mom who wrote the messages.

It *had* to be, because ghosts aren't real.

Right?

"You saw her this time, right?" Blythe's voice is shrill, desperate. "The shadow—you saw it, didn't you, Rachel?"

I want to blame it on sleep deprivation, add it to my growing list of strange, exhausted experiences, and lock it away. But the words are right in front of me, and I know I didn't write them. Given the way Blythe's looking at me, I don't think she did either. Even if she *did*, she couldn't have made the house shake like that.

And I *did* see a shadow.

I focus on the hand I have pressed against my chest, tracing the familiar shape of the locket through my sweater, and I remind myself to breathe, to follow the rise and fall of my lungs filling and emptying.

I think back to all the strange things that have happened at the Morins' house since I started working there. The doors slamming, the shadows where there shouldn't be shadows, the strange rotting flower smell, Maddie's twisted face in her photo.

Blythe saying she sees Maddie, and that her dead sister's trying to tell her something.

She wants you gone. What if Maddie *is* trapped? What if she feels like I'm trying to take her place? That would make anyone angry . . .

My whole sense of reality slides sideways. The only thing that keeps me grounded is Blythe's pale face, looking at me for reassurance. I search for the right thing to say to her and find my mom's words.

"Sometimes, spirits get stuck between this world and the next. Usually because they weren't properly honored after their death, like if there was no funeral. But sometimes spirits choose to stay, if they have unfinished business. They might try to make contact with the living, to ask for help to fix whatever's wrong."

I leave out the part about the ones who are just angry, spirits who haunt and hurt the living for no reason other than they can, eventually transforming into demons of pure spite and violence. I don't think Maddie would do that. But I don't know her, do I?

Do I even believe any of this?

I don't know that, either. I don't know anything anymore.

"We didn't have a funeral," Blythe whispers. "I heard Mom tell Dad it was too much."

I turn this piece of information over in my mind. My mom would say that funeral rites help spirits find their way to the afterlife. Maddie's tragic death could have made her spirit linger, and without a funeral . . . Maddie could have gotten lost. If she couldn't find her way to the afterlife, she would be trapped in our world.

Then where would she go?

Home, of course. She would come here, to this house.

"Where was she buried?"

Instead of answering, Blythe stands up. She leads me to the living room, where she stops in front of the fireplace. I look at the abstract painting that's given me the creeps since my first day here. I thought I saw a face in it. Did that actually happen? Was that Maddie?

Peeeeek-a-boo, Siouxsie keens in my mind. *Peeeeek-a-boo.*

Blythe points to a long wooden box sitting on the mantel.

I've never noticed it before. It blends into the wooden candlesticks and dried flowers around it. Even now that it has my attention there isn't much to it. It's simple and unassuming, smooth wood stained a rich brown.

But slowly, understanding dawns on me.

"Is that . . . ?"

Blythe nods.

The two of us stare at the box, the urn that holds Maddie's ashes.

"What do we do, Rachel?" Blythe's voice is small. "We have to help her."

Blythe seems so fragile. Is this the same kid who was screaming in my face just over an hour ago? This morning, I would have laughed myself hoarse at the ideas now running through my mind. But now . . . everything is different.

"I don't know," I say. "But I know someone who might."

CHAPTER TWENTY-ONE

TALKING TO MY MOM seems like a great idea until I walk into our empty apartment and find the half-empty gin bottle beside the kitchen sink. Reality comes crashing back. My mom's already furious. What would she think of me and an eight-year-old trying to contact a ghost on our own?

Irresponsible. Stupid.

Dangerous.

I sink to my knees in front of our altar and pick up the photo of my grandmother. Wàipó stares back at me from the frame, her gaze calm, knowing. *You'd know what to do, wouldn't you? I wish you were here.*

I set her picture back down, next to the one of my dad. *What would you make of all this?*

I imagine the two of them would have very different takes.

I light a joss stick and bow, pressing my forehead to the scratchy carpet. My eyes sting and I squeeze them shut, breathing in the incense as it swirls around me. The stinging melts into hot tears. When I finally sit up, the rug has branded itself on my face and all that's left of the joss stick is a smoldering stub.

This afternoon feels like a dream.

What if it *was* Blythe moving the pen? What if she's trying to get rid of me, trying to scare me away?

But then I remember the look on her face when we read the words on the paper. She's not that good an actor. No one is.

As the last tendrils of incense waft up, I think of Mom's notebook. Maybe it can help me figure out what to do, and I won't have to tell her about this at all.

I don't remember the last time I was in my mom's room. It feels like entering a secret passageway, a part of our home I forgot existed. Her bedsheets are rumpled, the pillow still indented in the shape of her head. In all the years we've lived here, she hasn't done anything to make the room her own. The walls are bare, except for a lonely nail sticking out above her headboard, a relic of the last tenant's decorations.

I open the drawers in her bedside table, but they're all empty. Nothing under the bed either, except a single blue sock that I leave untouched. I slide her closet doors open, and a densely packed row of hanging clothes swings out. The fabric smells like my mom: oatmeal lotion and joss sticks.

There's a tower of shoe boxes piled against the back wall. Maybe her notebook is in one of those? The box on top is navy blue and so heavy that I almost drop it when I try to lift it with one hand. I slide the lid off and there's the scratched red cover of Mom's notebook, on top of a jumble of papers.

The notebook's pages are dog-eared and full of my mom's familiar slanted scrawl, haphazard arrows, and roughly drawn diagrams. As I flip through it, magazine clippings and loose printouts of webpages threaten to slip out. There are smaller bits of paper too, sticky notes and scraps of three-hole-punch paper, some yellowed with age and covered in Chinese characters.

I find the page describing fújī, bullet-point notes next to a printed illustration of an ornate temple where two mediums hold a stylus over a tray of sand. I've seen my mom show this picture to clients when she explains the ritual. Looking at it now makes me think of the paper on the Morins' dining table, *FREE ME* scrawled in soggy but unmistakable letters. A shiver runs through me.

I keep flipping through and land on a two-page spread covered in cut-out images. Across the top, my mom wrote *to bind or trap a spirit/demon*. Most of the pictures are computer printouts, but one is an actual photograph. It's glossy and slightly blurred, showing a dark red jar sealed with wax. A strip of paper is fastened to its narrow mouth, bearing a row of Chinese characters. The words are barely legible, but I'm pretty sure one is "bind."

Wait, is that our coffee table? A memory swims to the surface:

Wàipó sits on our couch, writing in Chinese on a thin strip of paper with a slow, careful hand. I try to sound the words out as she writes them, but I'm having a hard time. Maybe I can't read them yet. She turns to me, her face serious.

"A spell is much more than words," she says in Mandarin. "Its power is also in the paper, in the ink, and—most of all—in the clarity of your mind and intentions. Be careless with any of these and terrible things can happen."

"Like it won't work?" I ask.

"Worse than that. Dangerous spirits can take advantage of your mistakes."

I think of my haphazard fújī setup: no incense offering, paper ripped out of my history notebook, an old red pen with a chewed-up lid. My gut hardens as I run through my many mistakes. We're lucky nothing worse happened.

I study the rest of the images taped to the page and in each I find a strip of paper like the one I remember Wàipó writing. One picture is a close-up of an ancient-looking scroll covered in distorted writing, mostly strange symbols that don't mean anything to me. But among them are two Chinese characters I recognize: "bind" and "ghost." Another looks like a still from a bad horror movie: Four pale figures in black robes stand shoulder to shoulder in a dark room, a yellow paper covered in red Chinese characters stuck to each of their foreheads. "Bind" is one of the words on those papers too.

My eyes ache as I strain to read the blurry writing, but I notice a pattern: The word "bind" appears in Chinese on every paper I can read. Wait—I've seen something else like this recently. The jars on Maddie's altar. One of them had a piece of paper just like this. A spirit jar, Blythe called it. Was that what Wàipó was making that day? It feels odd to imagine it ending up somewhere like Sylvia's living room. But it doesn't really matter; I don't think this can help us free Maddie.

I turn to the next page, and a plastic sleeve holding a bunch of red paper tumbles out. On the back, there's a diagram showing how to fold the paper into a lotus flower, like the one my mom was making the other day. As I scan down the page, a sentence catches my attention: *Guide lost spirits to the afterlife with paper lotus lanterns and candles, released on water.* There's an arrow to another note scrawled in the margin: *If specific spirit, add object (hair or nails best) to lure/snare it.*

Nails? Like, fingernail clippings?

Disgusting.

How many times did my mom and I make these flowers for the Hungry Ghost Festival and watch them float across the lake? When I was little, I imagined that each of the little lights in the flock we sent winking across the water was a fairy. When I got older and realized how much garbage is in Lake Ontario, I convinced my mom to stop. But I never thought we were actually *guiding ghosts to the afterlife.*

I don't believe in ghosts. I don't believe in the afterlife.

Or . . . I didn't. After today, I'm not sure what I believe.

All I know is something happened in the Morins' kitchen. Something strange and terrifying and probably connected to the other strange and terrifying things I've experienced there. Blythe is convinced it's Maddie, and, if I ignore the voice in my head screaming that this is all absurd . . . it makes sense. If that's the case, if Maddie's ghost is somehow lost or stuck, pleading to be freed—

My mom thought something similar happened to Mrs. Paul's husband. Her plan was to release the lotus flower on the lake, to guide him to the afterlife.

This is it. This is how we help Maddie, too.

I tuck my mom's notebook in my backpack, relieved to have a plan. I poke through what's left in the box, in case I missed anything else that might help. The shiny corner of a photograph pokes out from the pile, revealing the bottom half of a man's face, pale and grinning, a slight snaggle tooth on the right side of his smile.

I freeze. I would know that smile anywhere.

I pick up the photo of my dad.

His arm is flung around my mom's shoulder—a younger, more carefree version of my mom. She's wearing bright red lipstick. I don't remember the last time she wore lipstick. My dad is looking directly at the camera, but my mom is staring at him with raw adoration. The picture is so close-up that their heads fill most of the frame. I've never seen this photo before. I've only seen one photo of my dad, until now.

I stare at the man's face. Frank's face. My father's face. Mom said she was bad at remembering to take pictures before she had me, never mind print them. That's why she only had the one on the altar.

Did she forget about this one? Or did she keep it from me on purpose?

Why would she do that?

My dad's the same in this photo but also different. His nose isn't sunburned, and from this angle he has more freckles than I realized; they dot his neck as well as his cheeks. He's wearing a black T-shirt, and my heart contracts as I realize the shapes cut off by the bottom of the photo are the tips of a crown. Queen Elizabeth II's crown. He's wearing the same Sex Pistols T-shirt as the one I bought at the vintage show last year.

I turn back to the shoebox and start digging out relics of their brief romance: a movie ticket stub, a faded bus transfer, a button with a cartoon raccoon on it. I pull out a thin white envelope with my mom's name in the middle. The name *Frank Yalden* is written in the top left corner, and the return address below reads *University of Brighton, United Kingdom*. Confusion ripples through me. Yalden? Not Jones? Did my mom date another Frank?

I open the envelope and pull out a piece of paper. It's standard blue-lined paper, stiff with age and creased from handling. A love letter, maybe?

As I read, my delight morphs into nausea.

No. Not a love letter.

HOW DARE YOU CONTACT ME AT MY PLACE OF WORK AND THREATEN TO TELL MY WIFE ABOUT US. I COULD RUIN YOU WITH ONE EMAIL.

YOU KNOW WHAT YOUR OPTIONS ARE. BE SMART, JEN. I KNOW YOU'LL DO THE RIGHT THING.

I WILL ALWAYS CHERISH OUR TIME TOGETHER, BUT THAT TIME IS OVER. DO NOT CONTACT ME AGAIN.

—FRANK

The words my mom said countless times play on a loop in my head.

He died before he met you. He would have loved you very much.

That's what she always said.

But if this letter is from him, if my dad's last name isn't Jones but Yalden, it doesn't sound like he loved me. It sounds like he wanted her to . . .

I can't finish the thought.

I read the letter again and again. A sour taste coats my tongue.

The image I built of my father—effortlessly cool but also kind; a quiet, steady presence to balance my mom's bounding energy; the sort of dad who would spend a Saturday afternoon lying on the living room floor listening to whole albums with me—that dream shatters and stabs me in the throat.

My hand holding the letter trembles, but I don't feel it.

I don't feel anything.

The front door opens. Have I been sitting here all night?

I listen to my mom take off her boots and drop her bags on the floor.

I know I should scramble to put the box away, come up with some excuse for being in her room. But I can't make myself move.

The bedroom door swings open and my mom gasps. I imagine the scene as she must see it: me, sitting in front of her closet, the box holding her secrets gaping open in front of me.

"What are you doing?"

"You said there was an accident," I say. I'm numb as the words fall out of my mouth. "A drunk driver—"

"What are you talking about?" Mom snaps.

But her voice wavers. She's looking at the letter in my hands.

"You said he would have loved me." I choke, and a sound that's half growl, half sob rumbles out of me. I jump to my feet and shove the letter in her face.

"Does this sound like he loved me?"

Mom jerks back. "I can explain—"

"You said his name was Frank *Jones*. You lied to me my whole life!" I'm no longer numb. My pulse is pounding in my forehead, my face is scorching hot.

"I was trying to protect you."

"By lying about my dad's name? And telling me he was dead?"

"He *is* dead!" Mom's outburst shocks us both into silence.

Her face is pinched, like she's in pain. Her face is the most familiar thing in the world to me: the broad curve of her nose, the way her right eyebrow is a little thinner than the left. Even with my eyes closed, I can picture her perfectly. But this feels like the first time I've ever really seen her.

"It's just—he wasn't always. You were so little. I didn't know what to say when you asked about him. I was going to tell you the truth when you got older. But he had a heart attack a few years ago, and . . ." Her words trail off, and she takes a shaky breath.

"And what? That made it okay to keep lying?"

"When he died, the way he treated me, treated us . . . there was no chance he could change anymore. I didn't want him to hurt you like he hurt me."

"So he's an asshole and you're a liar. The perfect couple." I spit the words at her, and she shrinks back like they're daggers. "What did he mean he could ruin you with a single email?"

My mom closes her eyes. Her mouth opens, but no sound comes out.

I drop the letter and it flutters to the floor, landing next to the picture of my mom staring up at my dad like he's a shining star. I will my hands to stop shaking and grab my backpack. As I shove past her, my mom inhales sharply. She has her eyes shut tight, like if she wishes hard enough, she'll wake up.

A thought stops me in the doorway.

"How could you keep his picture on the altar? After he wrote you *that*? How could you look at his face every day?"

"It was for you," she says. "I did it for you."

CHAPTER TWENTY-TWO

MY BODY PROPELS ME out of our apartment, away from my mother and her lies. A frigid wind slices through the black sky, commuters bracing against the gale as they scuttle down the sidewalk. I shove my hands in my coat pockets and count my steps up to ten, then start over again, sinking into the rhythm to keep the tornado of emotions swirling inside of me from bursting out.

When my feet come to a stop, an orange glow is painting the bottom of the horizon and I'm standing in front of the Morins' house.

I should probably be surprised to find myself here, but walking up the path feels like the most natural thing in the world. Only when my hand is hovering above the doorbell do I hesitate. It's not even 7:30 a.m. What am I doing?

Before I can back away, the door opens and Sylvia is standing there, looking at me with such radiant joy that I smile back by reflex.

"Maddie?"

The name comes out of her like a breath, so quiet I think I might have imagined it, but the idea alone is enough to yank me back to reality. I shouldn't be here; this isn't my family. My eyes are suddenly stinging and I look down, blinking hard.

"Rachel," Sylvia says. Her voice is clear and steady. Did she say her daughter's name, or was that in my head?

It doesn't matter because this is real, her hand on my back, guiding me across the threshold. The warm air envelops me like a hug and my fingertips tingle. I didn't realize how cold I was. The smell of rotting flowers hits me sharply, but then Sylvia brushes by me to close the door and the bright, clean scent of her perfume takes over.

"I'll make you a tea, okay?" Sylvia speaks softly but firmly.

The cupboard beside the fireplace is open, Maddie smiling her secret smile from within. The red candle flickers, and the trinkets glint in the light of the flame. I hesitate, as the overwhelming feeling that I shouldn't be here snaps back.

Sylvia's gaze flicks over to the open cupboard and she swallows.

"It was Hector's idea," she says. "He thought it might help if I had somewhere to remember her, talk to her."

"Does it?" I ask.

"To be honest, I mostly feel silly, talking to myself." Sylvia scrunches up her nose, embarrassed. "Don't tell Hector I said that." She takes my arm and guides me into the kitchen.

I avoid looking at the dining table, shoving down memories of yesterday and suppressing a shudder. I sit at the island and trace my fingers along the pale lines in the marble until Sylvia sets a steaming mug in front of me.

"Want to tell me what happened?"

Her soft voice, on top of the familiar sweet smell of the tea and my exhaustion, makes something in me crack. Hot tears gather in my eyes, and I rub my face, trying to catch them before they fall.

"Sorry—"

"You have nothing to apologize for."

I focus on the mug. The solid, smooth warmth of the porcelain is reassuring. "I had a fight with my mom," I finally say. "It was . . . bad."

"Did she hurt you?"

"What? No, I just—" I try to take a deep breath, but it sounds like a wheeze. "I can't go back there." As I hear what that sounds like, a tight, panicked feeling overtakes me. "I don't know why I came here. I'm so sorry. Thank you for the tea, I—"

"I'm glad you're here," Sylvia says. "You can stay as long as you like."

The tension in my muscles dissolves, leaving me lightheaded. I didn't want to admit this is what I wanted. How selfish can I be? Barging in on these people who have been so kind to me, given me so much more than they needed to, especially when they're struggling, even if they try to hide it. What right do I have to ask for more? But the truth is that, even after what happened here yesterday, I feel safe with the Morins. And it's not like I have anywhere else to go. The only other person I could call is Yas and . . .

I choke through the lump in my throat and whisper a thank-you.

"Are you up for school today?" Sylvia asks.

I hadn't even thought about school.

Sylvia must see the dread in my face because she says, "Don't worry about it. I'll call them."

When I start to protest, she just shakes her head and tells me to let her handle it. I don't know how Sylvia plans to do that, but I'm too tired to question it. I follow her upstairs, hurrying past Blythe's room when I think I hear Hector's voice through the door.

But when Sylvia walks into Maddie's room, I hesitate. It's just a room, I tell myself. Still, I linger in the threshold as Sylvia puts fresh sheets on the bed.

"Feel free to use anything you need. If you can't find something, just ask." Sylvia tucks the last corner of the duvet in place. "Don't worry about picking Blythe up today. I'll duck out of work early. When I get home, we'll talk. Okay?"

I nod. I want to thank her, to tell her how much this means to me, but the words stick in my throat. Her face softens, and she pulls me into a hug.

"It's good that you're here."

Sylvia gives me another squeeze before she steps away. Then she closes the door behind her, and I'm alone in Maddie's room.

I take a watery breath and wrap my arms around myself. Except for the bed that Sylvia just made, the room is the same as the last time I was in here. But everything else is different.

I take out my phone to find twelve missed calls and eight unread text messages, all from my mom.

I'm sorry

Please come home

I'm so sorry you found out like that

Pick up?

I can explain

Call me please

Just tell me you're ok

I love you

My thumbs hover over the keyboard. She's sorry I found out *like that*? How else was I going to find out? She clearly wasn't planning to tell me. She would have been happy to keep lying forever. I close the app without replying.

I start up my dad's playlist, but instead of comforting me, the first notes of "Pretty Vacant" are jarring. So much of myself came from who I imagined my dad was, but it was all built on a lie.

My mom isn't who I thought she was either.

Who does that make me?

I turn off the music and toss my phone on the bedside table. Heavy quiet descends, pulling me down to the bed. I curl into a ball on top of the covers and let sleep fold me into a cocoon.

CHAPTER TWENTY-THREE

A WEIGHT PRESSES ON the center of my chest, pushing me down, down, down. Panic surges through my body, but I can't move, I can't breathe. The mattress is sucking me in like quicksand. Everything is dark, but I feel eyes trained on me, the gaze as solid and invisible as the boulder on top of me. My ribs are about to splinter, pierce my lungs, crush my heart. In a flash of certainty, I know this is the end.

Then the pressure is gone.

I'm standing on the other side of the room, staring at myself pinned to the bed. I watch my body writhe like a giant bug impaled on a spike. But there's nothing there except a thick, black shadow. My body grunts in rage and pain, limbs flailing, trying to strike the unseen force holding it down. I can't feel anything, but I know it's hurting me.

STOP! I shout.

But I make no sound.

I rush to the bed and I *know* I'm reaching out, but I can't see my arms or my hands. I shove at the shadow hovering over my body, but my touch passes right through—not only through the shadow but also through my thrashing body on the bed, through the mattress and the frame below it.

I'm not just invisible.

I'm nonexistent.

All I can do is stare helplessly as the solid version of me fights to rise from the bed and snaps its teeth like an animal, struggling in vain against the shadow.

• • •

I wake up coughing, bent over the side of Maddie's bed with my forehead almost touching the floor. The stench of rotting flowers is overwhelming. I cover my face and push up to sitting, taking shallow sips of air as my eyes adjust to the piercing white light streaming in through the window.

My right hand twinges with a cramp, and I realize I'm clutching the locket with all my strength. I loosen my grip and trace my thumb over the smooth face, the thin ridges of the hinge, the dents fusing the clasp shut. Calm radiates through me as the metal grows warm under my touch. The air is a little stale, but the awful smell is gone.

It was a dream. Another awful, terrifying dream.

But only a dream.

My shirt is damp and fused to the middle of my chest, the wettest part right where the locket sits when I let it go. Gross. I swing my feet to the floor. They land in a puddle, sending a cold shock coursing up my legs. Where did that come from? My brain, long past the edge of exhaustion, whirs and stutters. I can't make sense of this right now.

I stumble to the bathroom and flip on the light, bending over the sink to splash my face with cool water. I turn the tap off and meet my own eyes in the mirror. Red rims, dark circles. I look terrible. My neck is slick with sweat, the collar of my T-shirt a damp ring. My throat aches like a fresh bruise. My T-shirt is darker in the middle of my chest, the wet spot like a halo around the locket. The shape is weird for a sweat stain. Sort of round but also . . .

I pull the hem tight and a river of goosebumps runs up my arms.

It's a handprint.

My heart is pounding so hard, I almost expect it to rip through my shirt.

I raise my hand, contorting my wrist to try to line up my fingers with the wet stain. The position is awkward, and my hand is smaller than the wet mark. But it must be my hand. It has to be.

Doesn't it?

A different answer pulses in a dark corner of my mind. My rational brain is screaming that it's impossible, that there has to be another explanation, even as acceptance settles in my bones.

I want to deny it. This time yesterday, I would have. I would have stared at the handprint and convinced myself that it was mine. I had a nightmare and I was sweating, clawing at my shirt. It's strange and improbable, but it's the only explanation.

But I was a different person then.

Now, my life is split in two: before and after—the dividing line between the two the moment a pen wrote *FREE ME* under its own power, while the Morins' house shook around me.

Staring at the handprint on my shirt, the final piece slots into place. It isn't only the things that have happened *in* the Morins' house. It's also the nightmares, the insomnia, the hallucinations—the root of everything that's gone wrong lately with my mom, with school, with Yas.

All of it started when I met the Morins, when I stepped into Maddie's home.

The answer is stamped on my chest, so clear, so simple, now that I'm willing to see it.

The handprint is Maddie's.

She doesn't want you here, Blythe said.

Maddie is trying to scare me or hurt me, anything to make me leave. I'm surprised that the thought doesn't frighten me. Instead, I feel a pang of sadness. Maddie became trapped here because she wasn't properly honored after her death, and her spirit is lost, confused. She was trying to ask Blythe for help.

Then I showed up.

I can see why she might feel like I'm taking her place. Even though it's not true, I can't blame her for being angry with me. But she's a spirit. She doesn't belong here. Not anymore.

It's time for her to move on, to be free.

And I know how to help her.

CHAPTER TWENTY-FOUR

"WHAT DO YOU MEAN she's staying with us?"

Hector's voice turns me to stone at the top of the stairs. I creep back onto the landing and tuck myself out of sight.

"What part of that sentence is confusing you?" Sylvia's reply sounds like a dare.

"I'm sorry Rachel's having a rough time at home. But you said so yourself, she's not in any danger. We can't handle this right now. We're still grieving. You have a daughter who—"

"I have *two* daughters." Sylvia is seething. I've never heard her like this before.

"I know, Sylvia. They're my kids too."

"You sure don't act like it."

No response from Hector, but the silence is oppressive. I suspect they've had a version of this argument before. Maybe more than once.

The doorbell rings, the cheery tone cutting off any further discussion. I hear the deadbolt turn.

"Is Rachel here? Rachel!"

My mom's voice ricochets up the stairs, and my whole body goes rigid. What's she doing here? How did she find me?

My stomach twists. My phone—she turned the location tracking on, after the party. I didn't think to turn on airplane mode. So now she's here, making a scene.

"Sorry, who are you?" Sylvia sounds suspicious.

"I'm Rachel's mother."

If Mom wasn't mad before, she is now. She used to snap at people who assumed she was my nanny. Once, she made another mother cry. *I swear, I'm not racist*, the woman sobbed. I wanted to melt into the ground.

"She doesn't want—"

"Please, come in." Hector's calm voice cuts Sylvia off. "This is Sylvia, and I'm Hector. You probably know Rachel's been babysitting our daughter, Blythe."

The door clicks shut, cutting off the whistling wind outside.

"I'll go get Rachel," Hector says.

I dart back into Maddie's room, flopping on the bed. The missed calls and unanswered texts from my mom have been piling up all day, but I never thought she'd just show up.

Moments later, a knock at the door.

"Come in."

Hector steps inside, his thinning hair sticking up like he was running his hands over his head. "Hey, Rachel," he says. "Your mom's here."

I try to look surprised. It feels more like a grimace, but it must be convincing enough because Hector's face softens.

"Sylvia told me you had a fight. Sounds like it was a big one. I think you should talk to her. But you're still welcome to stay here, if you're not ready to go home."

My surprise is real this time. That's the opposite of what he just said to Sylvia. Did he change his mind? Or is he lying, hoping I'll leave with my mom?

"Give her five minutes," he says.

I nod and a smile flits across Hector's face before he backs out of the room, leaving me staring at the half-open door.

I used to think if my dad had lived he would have kept the peace between me and Mom. Maybe he would have broken the tension with stupid jokes and coaxed us into apologizing. Maybe things would have been easier, if it wasn't just the two of us.

What a ridiculous dream.

Now I know the truth: He was alive for most of my life, but he chose not to be with us. He chose not to say a single word to me. Not *happy birthday*, not *you need to listen to this song*, not *what did you learn at school?* I spent my childhood daydreaming about the perfect father who would have loved me, instead of coming to terms with the truth that he was a selfish asshole. How could my mom let me believe that lie? Would she have let me go on believing it forever?

My cheek throbs and I realize I'm gritting my teeth, hard. I force myself to relax, moving my jaw side to side. I guess I better get this over with.

I pause at the top of the stairs. Hector and Sylvia are nowhere to be seen. My mom is standing alone in the entryway, her parka unzipped. She's dressed in her work uniform—safety shoes, baggy jeans, a sweater with the company logo—and her hair is slicked back into a ponytail. She twists her ID badge in her hands and stares down at her boots, which are still planted on the doormat. She looks small and uncertain. Drained.

A painful lump swells in my throat. It's my fault she's stuck here, scraping through this tiny, difficult life. She didn't want to be a mother. I messed up all her plans. And I didn't even have the courtesy to be the daughter she wanted. She wants some kind of super computer whiz, not the introverted, music-obsessed weirdo she actually produced. She must wonder how I came from her at all.

Well, she might not have wanted me, but I didn't ask for this either. My heart pounds as rage coils against my ribs, consuming the brief flare of guilt.

The floor creaks and Mom looks up, her red-rimmed eyes meeting mine.

"You're going to be late," I say.

"I'm sorry, Rachel."

I snort, heat flushing through my veins. She's only sorry she got caught. As I make my way down the stairs, her eyes narrow and her mouth pulls into a thin line. It's like my anger is contagious. When I stop in front of her, tension crackles between us.

"I understand that you're angry." She doesn't sound understanding. She sounds furious. "Maybe I was wrong to keep the truth from you."

"*Maybe* you were wrong?"

"I told you, I can explain—"

"I don't want your excuses."

"You need to come home. You're imposing on these people."

"*These people* invited me to stay." My pulse is a hammer in my throat. "And I can take care of myself."

"No, you can't." She's not listening to a single thing I'm saying. She never has. "Trust me, I know."

"Well, I'm not knocked up with a deadbeat's baby, so I think I'm doing fine."

My eyes burn and I spin away, leaping up the stairs two at a time.

"Rachel—"

The crack in her voice sinks a hook into me, and I pause.

"I didn't come here to fight." Mom's voice is softer now, trembling. "You're right. I should have told you about your father. I know I'm not perfect. I kept telling myself it was better for you, but maybe . . . maybe I did it because it was easier on me."

I turn to face her. Her mascara is running, pooling in the lines under her eyes, and the laminated ID for her dead-end job glints under the pot lights. She couldn't be more out of place in the Morins' pristine entryway. I feel sorry for her, and that pisses me off.

"I know I haven't been a very good listener. But I want to do better." She draws a shaky breath, swipes at her face with the back of her hand. "I can help you—"

"You can help *me*?" The skin around my neck feels too tight, too hot. "*I'm* the one who got you out of bed after Wàipó died. *I* make sure we have clean sheets and vegetables in the fridge. *I* stop the building from burning down when you forget to put the incense out *again*. You think 'listening' is enough to make you a good mother?" I scoff, and my mom winces like the sound cut her. "I know I can take care of myself because *I already am*."

I turn away from my mom's shocked face. I expect her to call my name again, maybe run after me. But only silence follows me up the stairs. It eats my anger and leaves me empty. I slam Maddie's bedroom door, fling myself on the bed, and let the sobs take me. I don't know how long I lie there, but eventually I run out of tears. My throat is raw and my lungs ache.

There's a soft knock at the door and Sylvia walks in, setting a mug down on the bedside table. When I breathe in the familiar, sweet scent, my eyes sting again.

Sylvia brushes the sweaty hair off my face with a gentle hand. I close my eyes, but I can't hold back a new flood of tears. Sylvia gathers me in her arms and lets me cry into her shoulder.

• • •

Three soft knocks pull me out of a dazed half-sleep.

My face is stiff and my nose is stuffed. I'm tucked under the covers, the blanket pulled up under my chin. Blythe's face appears in the doorway.

"Dinner's ready," she says.

"Thanks, Blythe."

I peel myself off the bed, my stiff muscles protesting. I tilt my head to the side and press my fingers into a knot at the base of my neck. The pressure sends a dull ache through my shoulders.

Blythe is still staring at me, chewing her bottom lip. She's squeezing something in her hands; my guess is it's the lighter.

"I'll be down in a minute." I force my wooden face into what I hope is a reassuring smile.

"My mom says you had a fight with your mom, so you're staying with us for a while."

"Is that okay?"

Blythe nods, but her anxious gaze flits over my shoulder. "Do you have to stay in here?" She lowers her voice to a whisper. "What if she gets mad?"

Goosebumps race up my arms.

"I found out how to help her." I sound more confident than I feel. "We can do it tomorrow. I'll be okay for one night."

"Are you sure?"

"I'm sure." I have to be.

• • •

Dinner is a big chicken salad, and I keep my mouth full of oversized, crunchy leaves so I have an excuse not to talk. The energy is different from the evenings I stayed after babysitting. Hector keeps staring into the distance, lost in his own world, and seems startled when anyone speaks to him. Blythe is unnervingly quiet, and Sylvia is trying so hard to pretend things are normal, she's talking almost nonstop. I catch her staring at me more than once. Does she regret inviting me to stay? If she heard any part of the fight with my mom, I wouldn't blame her.

But later, as Sylvia and I are clearing the table, she seems to relax. She hums as I help her load the dishwasher, and when she smiles at me, it feels warm and genuine.

A familiar guitar riff shimmers through the speakers. I look up and find Hector carefully closing the lid over a spinning record. Siouxsie's voice crackles and, when our eyes meet, he gives me a small smile. The tension behind my ribs loosens a notch, and I smile back.

After we say goodnight, I close the door to Maddie's room and spot my crumpled T-shirt on the floor. The one Maddie marked with her handprint during my nightmare earlier today. I took it off and went back to bed in just my sweater, but I'm going to have to find something else to wear tomorrow. Anxiety seeps back in when I look at Maddie's closet. Do I actually smell rotting flowers, or is my mind playing tricks on me?

I root around in my backpack for allergy pills, but I come up empty. I didn't stop to pack an actual bag when I stormed out this morning. I don't even have a toothbrush. Thankfully, Sylvia left an unopened one for me in the bathroom. But I'm less concerned about bad breath than I am about having another nightmare. It's almost nine o'clock; if I go out now Sylvia and Hector will want to know why. I can't exactly tell them I need allergy pills to help me sleep because the ghost of their daughter is haunting me in my dreams. My head is too foggy to think of an excuse that makes sense.

Without the pills, my only option is to stay awake. I'm worried that my welcome is already wearing thin. I can't stay here too long, but I need time to figure out what to do next. And I need to keep this job. It's only one night. Tomorrow, Blythe and I will do the ritual and guide Maddie to the afterlife. Her spirit will find its way to where it belongs, and I'll finally be able to sleep again. Easy.

I can't believe this is actually my plan.

I sit at Maddie's desk and scroll through my phone with the brightness turned all the way up. I type my dad's name into the search—his real name, Frank Yalden—and add *university of brighton*.

How many times did I wish I had enough information to look him up, to learn more about him, to find my grandparents, even? Of course they'd be shocked to learn their son had a long-lost daughter, but after that wore off, they'd be thrilled. They'd want to meet me right away. Maybe they'd offer to fly me out to visit them . . . but now I know that's not how it would have happened. Not even close.

If I do this, it will all be real. The dream will be chased away by the truth. But I'm done with being in denial. I press Enter, and the search results load.

Within seconds, the number of things I know about my father doubles, then quadruples. He was a professor at the University of Brighton. In computer science. What a coincidence. His bio is full of long, complicated words. He has a 3.3 on Rate My Professors and there are only a handful of comments, but I drink in every one.

Good slides, lectures are a waste of time.

Tries hard to make a boring subject interesting.

Smart, funny, interactive.

They only knew him as a teacher, but they still knew him better than I ever will.

He played bass in a cover band called the Worn Pistols. They have a Facebook page with grainy photos of them playing in tiny venues. The last post is a memorial. *In loving memory of Frank Yalden.*

It shows a picture of my dad on stage, looking intently at his fingers curled around the neck of his guitar, the front of his Joy Division shirt stained dark with sweat. I stare at the photo, blinking back tears.

Not everything I thought I knew about him was a lie.

But as I read on, a bitter taste floods my mouth.

It was a tragedy, a heart attack taking someone so young, especially this loving husband of twenty years, this doting father of three children, this dependable pillar of the community. I find a photograph of him with his family, his real family. They're in front of a roaring fire, wearing matching grins and Christmas sweaters. One of his children, the only boy, is almost certainly older than me. Which means he was already married, already had a *kid*, when he was with my mom.

What was my mom thinking? How could she have been so stupid? But then, she wasn't that much older than I am now, and I betrayed my best friend, my only friend, really, because some guy I just met kissed me. I'm not in any position to judge.

I stare at the Yalden family in their Christmas sweaters for a long time, zooming in close and back out again. Studying their expressions, their body language, waiting for a spark of recognition or revulsion or . . . something. But whatever I'm looking for, I don't find it. They just look like strangers.

I stand up, shaking the pins and needles out of my legs. I consider sneaking downstairs for a snack, but I know there's nothing caffeinated in the kitchen and eating more will probably make me sleepy. I eye the bed. It should be fine if I don't lie down. I prop myself up against the headboard, trying not to get too comfortable, and rest my phone against the lamp glowing on the bedside table. There's no way I can sleep with the bulb shining right in my eyes like a miniature sun.

The Worn Pistols have a bunch of videos on their page, recordings of their gigs taken on shaky phones. I pop my earbuds in and start with one that shows my dad in the thumbnail. I run my thumb over the locket while the videos play.

CHAPTER TWENTY-FIVE

THE FOUR OF US are in the kitchen: Sylvia rummages through the fridge, Hector fastens the lid on his travel mug, and Blythe and I sit side by side at the island. She crunches on a piece of toast slathered in peanut butter, and I try to convince myself that the tea Sylvia set in front of me is actually a bitter dark roast. It's not the candy tea this time. This stuff tastes like burnt moss and has me craving coffee with a desperation that's a little frightening.

But I did it. I stayed up all night. No sleepwalking, no nightmares, except the one I'm living in. I'm so ready to tuck myself under the covers and let sleep carry me away, without worrying about waking up screaming, or in an unfamiliar place, or with some unexplained injury. I want to wake up re-energized and content instead of afraid. Maybe then I can figure out how to fix the mess I've made of my life.

The ritual *has* to work.

I glance up from the mug to find Sylvia looking at me expectantly, and my face heats up.

"I'm sorry, what did you say?"

"Are you sure you don't want to stay home today?"

A little thrill sparks in my gut at the way she says *home*. Like it's mine too.

But I shake my head. "I'm okay. I'll pick Blythe up too."

I see Blythe staring at me from the corner of my eye, but I don't look directly at her. I don't want Sylvia to think anything's up, in case she does something that might disrupt our plan.

"Wonderful." Sylvia sets two lunch bags on the counter, a blue one in front of Blythe and a red one in front of me. In one corner of the red fabric, *Maddie* is written in permanent marker. The dot over the *i* is a little heart.

Sylvia nudges the red lunch bag toward me with a wistful smile. This must be so strange for her. I'm wearing one of Maddie's sweatsuits; it's forest green and a size too big, which suits me just fine. Sylvia insisted I borrow something while she washed the clothes I showed up in. So now I'm here in Sylvia's kitchen after spending a night in her daughter's room, wearing her daughter's clothes, her daughter's lunch bag resting in front of me.

I can see why Maddie would be angry.

But I'm here and she's not. Not in the same way. And, as Sylvia's smile brightens and her eyes crinkle at the corners, I feel like I'm where I belong.

• • •

I get out of Sylvia's car with the lunch bag tucked safely in my backpack and a warm glow in my chest. I watch her car until it disappears around the corner.

"So they've adopted you now?" Yas stares at me with her arms crossed.

"It's none of your business," I snap.

Yas starts to say something, but she presses her lips together before any words escape. The blue in her hair is growing out. There's almost an inch of black at the roots, yet somehow it suits her, like everything always does. But it hangs limp around her face, greasy and unbrushed, and she has circles under her eyes, a cluster of pimples on her chin. She looks almost as drained as I feel.

My throat constricts and my annoyance dissolves. "I'm sorry," I say. "I know I haven't been . . . myself lately."

A muscle in Yas's jaw twitches as she studies me, like I'm some kind of puzzle she's trying to solve.

"I've been having these intense dreams." My mouth feels like a desert. "Nightmares really, where it's like . . . I'm not in control of my body. It's worse than sleepwalking. I do things I don't want to. I think that's what happened at the party."

Yas's eyes narrow and a flush spreads across her cheeks.

"At first I thought it was just from stress or insomnia," I rush on. "But now I think—this is going to sound ridiculous—but I think maybe I'm being haunted?"

"Let me get this straight." Yas's laugh is sharp and humorless. "First, it was because you were drunk. But now, it's because you were, what? Possessed?"

"I know how it sounds—"

"I don't think you have any idea how you sound."

"Yas, wait—"

But she's already turned away from me.

Before Yas is swallowed by the crowd, Dell appears and puts their arm around her shoulders. I watch them go, trying to hold on to the anger shimmering beneath my skin, to avoid the needles of shame underneath.

All morning, I keep my head down and one earbud in, obscuring it with my hair and keeping the music to a background hum. It doesn't help. I can't shake this crawling sensation, the feeling of being judged and found wanting. I'm sure that every face I pass turns in my direction and twists into a sneer.

When the lunch bell rings, I leave and don't look back.

I walk toward home, even though I have no intention of going there. The crisp air stings my cheeks and dark clouds obscure the sun like iron doors, turning the sky a sickly gray that matches the piles of dirty snow lining the street.

I reach a narrow store with a sign that reads FRIEND CONVENIENCE in English and Chinese. Tucked between a shawarma restaurant and a phone repair shop, the store's varied contents spill out onto the sidewalk: yellow bags of road salt, a jumble of foldable shopping bags on wheels, a rack stuffed with 2-for-$10 T-shirts. Mom says you can get anything here, at half the price of anywhere else.

Bells tinkle as I enter, but the guy behind the cash doesn't look up. His eyes are glued to a tiny TV, which is playing what looks like an old horror movie. Blurry actors run across the screen, their faces contorted in exaggerated terror.

I weave through the narrow aisles to the back of the store, where the shelves are packed with elaborate joss paper sculptures. There are thick bundles of hell money but also toothbrushes, sticks of deodorant, and collared shirts folded flat in boxes, like they're from a department store. There are life-sized laptops and cell phones, packs of cigarettes, cans of soda, even a full dim sum feast packaged in a bamboo steamer. Every single item is made of paper. I pick up a bundle of hell money and a package of joss sticks, then consider the other sculptures.

What would Maddie want in the afterlife?

How am I considering this as a serious question?

I can't think about it too hard or I start to feel dizzy.

I choose a small box that holds a few delicate, detailed items, including a cell phone, a credit card, a gold necklace, and a watch. If I wasn't looking closely, it would be easy to mistake any of these for the real thing. But they're all made out of paper, meant to be burned as gifts to departed loved ones. I never thought about it before, but it's impressive. These are works of art.

As I place my selections on the counter, I brace myself for a judgmental look from the cashier. But he barely looks at me as he picks up the scanner, glancing back at the TV between each beep. On the screen, men in black robes stand in a line. Each one has a long yellow piece of paper covered in red Chinese writing tacked to his forehead, obscuring his face. I realize I've seen this scene before, in my mom's notebook. Another man in a black robe leaps into the frame. There's no paper on his powdered white face, and his lips are pulled back to reveal long vampire teeth. In a blur of motion, someone else tackles him and slaps a piece of yellow paper on his forehead. The vampire goes rigid, stuck in place.

To bind or trap a spirit/demon.

That's what mom wrote in her notebook, on the page with all the papers that said "bind." Did she get that from this movie?

The man behind the cash clears his throat. Judging from his look, this isn't the first time he's asked me to pay. I look at the joss paper gifts with renewed doubt. Do I really think that when I burn these, they'll pass to Maddie in the afterlife? If my mom's treating horror movies like textbooks, how can I believe anything she says?

But no—there was also the photo of the spirit jar Wàipó made, and I remember her writing the spell. I know what happened with the fújī was real. I know that yesterday, I woke up in an empty house with Maddie's handprint on my chest. I also know that this is the only plan that I have.

It has to work.

CHAPTER TWENTY-SIX

BLYTHE IS QUIET THE whole way back to her house, but as we walk through the park, she slips her hand into mine. I open the front door to a welcome rush of warm air, but neither of us take off our coats. Blythe follows my instructions without question, even when I ask her to find Maddie's brush.

When we have everything we need, we leave through the backyard. Even though I know the gate leads to the park, I'm still stunned when I swing it open and the vast expanse of lake and sky are right there before me. The sun shouldn't set for another hour, but the sky is already dimmed by gray clouds that hang low over the lake. At the bottom of the cliff, the water is restless and white-capped. Glancing back at the house, I picture Maddie shimmying out of Blythe's window and down into the garden below. I can't imagine dropping from that height.

I follow Blythe as she strides across the park. She ducks under the wire barrier, batting branches away and disappearing into the brush. There's a narrow path where patches of frozen dirt poke through the dead grass, but it's still slow going through the tangle of hibernating bushes.

I duck around another skeletal branch and all at once I'm at the cliff edge. In front of me, the earth falls away into air. The sandy cliff drops hundreds of feet down until it meets the thrashing lake below. My stomach does a slow backflip.

But Blythe doesn't pause. She veers to the right and down, disappearing from sight. I creep closer to the edge, and my stomach lurches again. The path continues almost sideways, carving thin switchbacks down the sandy cliff. Blythe moves at a steady pace, the distance between us widening. I suck in a breath and go after her.

The ground is steep and packed hard, though a few pebbles tumble down alongside me. We're lucky there isn't much ice. Blythe moves confidently, like she's made this trip many times before. Did Maddie show her this path? Blythe said they used to go down to the beach together. But this is so dangerous . . . one wrong step—is that what happened to Maddie, the night she died?

The thought rattles me, and I focus on finding stable spots to put my feet.

It feels like hours, though it's probably no more than ten minutes, before we reach the base and the ground levels out. My boots don't sink into the sand like I expect. Instead, it crackles under my weight without giving. It's frozen. Blythe and I are the only people in sight. The rasp of my hood scraping against my hair sounds like it's blasting over giant speakers.

The farther down the beach we go, the closer the base of the cliffs and the edge of the water squeeze together, eventually forcing us into single file. My left sleeve catches on a scraggly tangle of bushes, and the most ambitious waves splash over our boots. I'm starting to wonder if we're going to end up wading in the water, when the beach abruptly widens again and Blythe stops.

Then I see it: a white cross stuck in the sand, framed by a shock of branches so red they seem fake. A waterlogged teddy bear and several wilted bouquets sit on the sand in front of it. My throat feels like it's closing up, but I force myself to continue forward.

I trudge past the cross to the wall of fire-red bushes at the back of the clearing. It's instantly warmer here, the noise of the wind and water muted by the half-circle of dense brush. I lay down a square of red cloth, and Blythe puts a rock on each corner, then gets to work arranging tealights around the edges. I pull out a mason jar filled with rice and set three joss sticks in it, as Blythe places a sleeve of chocolate peanut butter cups, a can of cream soda, and a green apple on the cloth. Maddie's favorite snacks.

In the center of it all goes a big metal bowl, another one of my purchases from earlier today. Mom would be proud.

Or horrified.

I can't believe I'm doing this.

I take out the paper lotus flower I made earlier, the red bloom as big as my palm. Will it float? What if the wind pushes it back to shore?

"Now what?" Blythe asks.

"We need to add something of Maddie's to it. Do you have her brush?"

Blythe hands the brush to me, and I pluck a few strands from the bristles.

"The wind could blow that away," Blythe says. "We should use this instead." She takes a wooden box out of her bag. Maddie's urn.

"Blythe . . ." I shake my head. "Your parents, we shouldn't—"

"They never want to talk about her. They won't even notice."

"I'm not sure—"

She ignores me and opens the lid. There's a plastic bag inside, filled with pale ashes and cinched shut by a thick metal twist tie. Blythe starts to undo it. I feel like I should stop her . . . but what if she's right?

Blythe picks up a spoon, which she must have brought for this exact purpose, and dips it in the bag. The wind seems to hold its breath as a stream of Maddie's ashes flows into the paper flower. When the center is full, Blythe gently replaces the urn's lid.

"Okay," she whispers, more to herself than to me.

I sit back on my knees and close my eyes, bringing my focus to my breath. My mind stills and my muscles relax as my lungs expand and contract in a slow, soothing rhythm. Tiny icicles tickle the inside of my nose. When I open my eyes, I find Blythe watching me.

I bow at the waist and Blythe mirrors me, our bulky coats making our movements stiff. We rest our foreheads briefly on the cool sand, then straighten and repeat the gesture twice more. I cup a hand around a stick of incense and hold the lighter to it until it flares and releases a sweet-smelling tendril of smoke. I use it to light the rest of the incense and then turn to the tealights.

"Can I do it?" Blythe asks. I hand her the lighter and she sets the candles aflame, one by one, her brow creased with concentration.

I think of the message board Yas and Dell showed me, the comments about Sylvia being down here for weeks. If she had candles . . . well, it's no different from what we're doing now. More normal, really, since she was grieving while we're attempting to guide Maddie's ghost to the afterlife.

Blythe's eyes bulge when I take out the stack of hell money and the joss paper cell phone, credit card, and jewelry. "We're going to burn those?"

"It's a Chinese tradition," I say. "Some people believe that spirits need money and other things to live well in the afterlife. They make those things out of special paper. When we burn them, it's like we're sending them to Maddie as gifts. It's a way to honor her."

Blythe picks up the paper cell phone and looks at me, amused. "I think she'll like this."

"I hope so," I say. I'm surprised to find that I mean it.

I pick up a hell money banknote and flick the lighter on. When the paper flares and begins to curl in on itself, I place it gently in the bowl. Blythe and I feed the bank notes to the fire one by one, and soon it's burning steadily, the flames warming our faces.

"What do you believe?" Blythe asks, as she adds the paper cell phone to the fire.

"About what?"

"You said some people believe spirits need money and other stuff. What do you believe?"

I stare at the spread before us: the cross standing vigil over the red cloth crowded with snacks and candles, orange flames flickering in the metal bowl. I thought my mom was foolish, spending her scraps of free time playing make-believe. But I was wrong. I was wrong about a lot of things.

Just a week ago, there was nothing on this earth that would have made me do something like this on my own, never mind with the kid I babysit. But now, here I am. Hoping it will work. Needing it to work, for my safety and my sanity. For Blythe too, and her parents. Even for Maddie.

The thought startles me, but I realize it's the truth. This ghost has made my life hell, but knowing that she's trapped and unhappy . . . I don't want her to suffer. I want her to be at peace, and if I can help with that somehow, it feels like my responsibility. God, I sound like my mom.

Can a person change so much, so fast?

"I'm not sure what I believe anymore."

Blythe and I feed the last pieces of joss paper to the flames, then watch the fire sputter and dance in the wind. The clouds over the lake beyond glow violet and peach as the sun sinks behind them.

"You can talk to her, if you want."

"What do I say?"

"Anything you need to."

Blythe twists her hands together, looking intently into the fire like she can see her sister there.

"Maddie, I miss you so much. I'm sorry I didn't tell anyone when you didn't come home. Maybe if I had—" Her voice cracks and I place a hand on her back. She takes a shuddering breath. "We're going to help you. We know you're trapped, but Rachel knows how to get you out—"

Blythe gasps and my mouth goes dry.

There's a shadow looming beside the fire, next to the cross. It's too large, too smooth, to be cast by the bushes or by anything else I can see.

Like the shadow face in the painting above the Morins' fireplace.

Like the shadow that spread across the table, while the fújī pen moved on its own.

Like the shadow that loomed over my body, as I watched myself struggle to get up from Maddie's bed.

The shadow peels itself up off the sand and becomes a pillar of solid darkness looming before us. Darkness in a human shape. The smell of rotting flowers claws up my nostrils, and a cough sputters out of my throat.

"Maddie?" Blythe is standing now.

The shadow ripples, and suddenly Maddie is there.

She's less solid than the shadow was, her image soft-edged and grainy. I can see right through her to the lake crashing against the shore in the fading daylight. But I can also see *her.*

There's no doubt in my mind that this is Madeline Morin: the girl in the graduation photo I've stared at, whose close-lipped smile I've tried to imitate. Except she's soaking wet. Her long, blond hair is plastered to her forehead and water drips off her chin, runs down her fingers, trickles from the hem of her shorts and down her bare legs. The sand beneath her bare feet soaks the water up, grows darker.

My disbelief splinters, leaving me raw and reeling.

"Maddie?" Blythe gasps.

But Maddie isn't looking at her sister. She's staring at the fire, fingers reaching toward the flames, drawn to it like a moth. Her translucent body stutters like a video call lagging.

Then her gaze flicks up, and she's looking straight at me.

Her eyes narrow.

She strikes a fist into my chest.

I brace myself, but there's no impact. A damp cold seeps from her hand through my coat and my sweater, down to my skin. The locket is a block of ice, and every breath I take scrapes my lungs raw.

Maddie's lips move, but no sound comes out. The fire blazes behind her, through her.

YOU, she mouths, her face distorted by fury. *YOU.*

The locket burns suddenly hot and I jerk back, scratching at the soaking front of my coat, trying to get the metal off my skin. I stumble to avoid our smoldering offerings, and pain shoots up my tailbone as I hit the ground.

"No!" Blythe jumps between me and the ghost of her sister, holding the coin charm I gave her like a shield. Maddie flinches, then her face softens and her mouth makes the shape of her sister's name. She reaches for Blythe, and Blythe reaches back, but their hands pass through each other like air.

"Maddie," Blythe sobs. "We're going to set you free—"

Maddie shakes her head. Her gaze slides over to me and her eyes narrow. The anger in her face slices through any doubts I might have had: She'll kill me if she can. I need to do something, fast.

Blythe stays between us, pleading with her sister to listen. Her desperation must get Maddie's attention because the ghost falls to her knees so that she's eye level with Blythe, speaking rapidly, soundlessly, her rage and desperation clear despite her silence.

I watch them from the corner of my eye as I place one of the tealights in the center of the lotus flower. I pick the whole thing up, careful not to spill the ashes it holds. I creep sideways, keeping Maddie and Blythe in my sights as I move toward the water's edge as fast as I dare.

Blythe and Maddie are still talking when I kneel and set the paper flower in the water. The red petals darken, but it floats and the candle stays lit. I focus on my breath as Wàipó taught me, tamping down my racing thoughts by grounding my mind in the things I can feel right now: my lungs filling and emptying, the smooth paper between my fingers, the frigid water lapping at my wrist. The wind dies down suddenly, and the lake flattens into a mirror-smooth sheet.

"Maddie!" My voice reverberates across the beach like I have a megaphone.

The ghost of Madeline Morin turns to me. When she sees the paper flower bobbing on the water, her face twists with confusion.

"It's time for you to move on," I say. "This will show you the way."

"We're setting you free, Maddie," Blythe says. "You can be happy now."

I let go of the flower, giving it a gentle push out into the water. It trembles and starts to float toward the horizon. I wait for the waves to rise or the wind to push it back to shore. But everything remains still and the red flower sails out as easily as if it were traveling down a canal.

The flower pulls Maddie with it, like an anchor tied around her waist. She resists, her translucent body straining against an invisible rope, both of her arms stretched toward Blythe as she's dragged toward the lake. But when she reaches the water, she doesn't sink. Like the paper flower, she floats on the surface as she's drawn away from shore.

Maddie's eyes lock with mine. I meet her gaze, pushing my shoulders back.

She can't hurt me anymore.

Maddie points a finger at me and starts to speak, soundlessly, urgently. But I'm no lip reader, especially now that the sun has sunk below the horizon, and I can't understand what she's trying to say. Maddie must realize this because her mouth stops moving abruptly. She raises her arm and points straight at me, as her lips move slowly, deliberately, forming the unmistakable shape of two words that feel like a blade straight through my ribs:

KILL YOU

It's the last thing Maddie says. She stops fighting then, her arms dropping to her sides. She looks at Blythe, who sobs and staggers toward the lake. When Blythe's boots splash into the shallow water, I catch the back of her coat and pull her to a stop. I squeeze Blythe's shoulder, and we watch the ghost of Madeline Morin drift away. We stand there until Maddie's outline blurs and blends with the horizon; until I can no longer see the flower or the faint glow of the candle; until all the color seeps out of the sky and is replaced by the navy of early twilight.

Blythe suddenly spins toward me, shrugging my hand off. She unzips the top of my coat and yanks the necklace out from under my sweater, then backs away like it burned her.

"What are you doing?" I feel far away, like I'm floating out of time.

"You need to take off her necklace." Blythe glares at my chest. There's accusation in her eyes but fear underneath.

"What?" I clutch the locket. My sweater is wet from Maddie's hand, but the metal is warm.

"That's Maddie's. She says you shouldn't have it."

"What? It's from your mom's work. She gave it to me."

"No, it's Maddie's." Blythe's voice grows shrill. "She said there are teeth inside."

"What does that mean?"

"Maddie said take it off!" Blythe screeches.

"Fine!" I unclasp the chain with trembling fingers and hold it up. "Better?"

Blythe nods, biting her lip. She's shaking as she holds a hand out, gesturing for me to give her the necklace. When I hesitate, she snatches it from me and stuffs it in her coat pocket.

A pit of longing opens in my stomach, an unexpected emptiness that makes my eyes sting. I imagine shoving Blythe down into the sand and tearing the locket away from her, placing it back around my neck where it belongs . . .

What's wrong with me? It's just a necklace.

Why do I care so much? Because Sylvia gave it to me?

But why would Sylvia give me her daughter's necklace . . . and lie about it?

I turn back to the lake, a storm of questions swirling in my mind. The sky is nearly black and the wind has returned, thrashing the water into frenzied waves. There are a few small lights bobbing in the distance, but I can't tell if any are resting in a red paper flower.

CHAPTER TWENTY-SEVEN

THERE'S NO DRUG BETTER than a good night's sleep.

I wake up exactly where I dozed off, on my side with my hand tucked under the pillow, now numb from being trapped under my head. I flex my fingers, and pins and needles spiral down my arm.

When Blythe and I got back to the house last night, we both agreed something was different. There was a new sort of lightness that we both felt but couldn't quite explain. I didn't see strange shadows or smell rotting flowers. I went to sleep early, without the help of a single allergy pill, and I don't think I dreamed at all. There's no dread heavy in my gut, no menacing presence lurking behind me. I sit on the side of the bed and I examine my body for mysterious bruises or unexplained cuts. I find nothing out of place and my stomach flutters with relief. It really is over. The only thing that feels off is how bare my neck is without the locket.

Even the revelations about my dad feel less overwhelming. There's a new string of messages from my mom, but for the first time, her apologies and pleas for me to come home don't make me want to throw my phone at the wall. I do think she's sorry. I'm still angry with her, but I can kind of see why she didn't tell me. I didn't exactly take it well.

It makes me wonder how much of my mom's life has been shaped by my dad's betrayal. Is that why she's so obsessed with landing a boring nine-to-five job and having me work at some fancy tech company? Is she trying to prove something to him? Or to herself? It isn't an excuse, but looking at the situation from her perspective softens the edges. I know I need to talk to her.

But not today.

Today, I'm going to enjoy waking up well rested and being here, with the Morins, where I have space to think things through.

I slide Maddie's closet open and an image blazes in my mind: *Maddie glares at me with violence in her eyes, her dripping finger pointing at my face, her mouth forming silent words—KILL YOU.*

It runs through me like an electric shock. Every muscle in my body tenses. But I gulp down a shuddering breath and force myself to relax.

She's gone. I'm safe.

I flip through Maddie's sweaters and land on a dark gray hoodie. I press it against my chest and turn to look in the mirror, bracing myself for something strange. A moving shadow, or a face that isn't mine. But it's just me, holding what looks like my favorite sweater but isn't. The color's a little lighter, the cuffs are less worn, and the brand is one that I could never afford. It's like looking at a version of myself from an alternate universe.

• • •

I'm in the kitchen, peeling a lid off a cup of yogurt, when Sylvia walks in. She inhales sharply when she sees me, her smile wide and watery.

"It looks perfect on you," she says. "Just perfect."

My throat tightens and my eyes sting, a mirror of the emotions playing on Sylvia's face.

"Thank you," I say. "For everything."

"Thank *you.*" She reaches out and grips my hand. Then, she sets the locket on the counter. "I think you misplaced this."

"Oh—" A hunger flares in my belly at the sight of the shining golden face. I barely resist the urge to scoop it up immediately.

Then I remember the terror in Blythe's face when she demanded I take it off.

"Blythe—" I have no idea how to say this. "Blythe saw I was wearing this and she was . . . unhappy. She said it was Maddie's?"

Sylvia sighs, her face tight with grief.

"Yes," she says. "It was. I'm sorry I didn't tell you."

"Why didn't you?"

"I didn't want to make you uncomfortable. This was one of Maddie's favorite things. We gave it to her for her thirteenth birthday. I couldn't bear it sitting in some box forever, forgotten."

I wonder why she didn't give it to Blythe, but when I remember the way Blythe looked at it, the question evaporates. It seemed painful for Blythe to touch it, even for the second it took to shove it in her pocket. She would never wear it.

"When you found it that day, it felt like it was meant to be," Sylvia continues. "I could tell that you liked it. So I thought, why not give it to you? But I was afraid you wouldn't take it, if you knew it was hers." She tugs the sleeve of my sweater, Maddie's sweater, and smiles. "We didn't know each other as well back then." When her eyes meet mine again, they're bright with tears. "It would mean a lot to me if you kept it."

"I'd be honored," I say, and I mean it.

Sylvia unfastens the necklace and drapes the open chain around my neck. I brush my hair out of the way and the clasp clicks shut, the locket settling below my collarbone. My skin warms beneath it. I reach up to touch it, almost dizzy from the relief that rushes through me as my fingers brush the metal.

"But maybe—" Sylvia hesitates, a sheepish look crossing her face. "Don't tell Blythe? There's no reason to upset her."

I nod and tuck the locket under my sweater. Sylvia's done so much for me, how can I refuse? Blythe might not like it, but she doesn't need to know. Maybe she'll relax now that she knows Maddie is safely on her way to the afterlife.

It's a new day, for all of us.

• • •

My optimism is extinguished the moment I walk into school and a group of girls by the door breaks into cackles, making crosses with their fingers. I find a fresh pile of garlic scattered in front of my locker, and in second period, I come back from the bathroom to find my backpack stabbed with a crude stake, fake blood soaking the front pocket. I spend my lunch period scrubbing the fabric with soap and water, but it only makes the stain darker.

I'm tempted to skip my afternoon classes again, but no—today is supposed to be a fresh start. If I want to have a hope of passing Mr. Savoca's class, I actually need to go to it. Yas looks up when I walk in, and I cautiously raise my hand to wave.

She looks away.

I slump into a seat at the very back of the room. I take out my phone, pulling up my last exchange with Yas. It's still her harassing me to come to the party. My heart aches, like it's stuck in a vise. I miss her so much. I miss who we were before Eric and Maddie and all my mistakes. I want my best friend back.

I start to type.

I'm sorry about eric, i drank too much and—

I think of my mom standing by the Morins' front door. "I can explain—" she said. But I don't want her excuses. I want her to apologize and mean it. I hold my thumb down on the Delete key and watch the words disappear. I stop when only the first two remain.

I'm sorry

I hit Send.

"What are you doing out in the daylight?" Cameron slides into the desk next to me, sneering. "I thought the sun burned your kind's skin right off."

I refuse to look at him. I shove my phone in my bag and place my textbook and notebook on my desk, aligning them so the edges are perfectly parallel with each other. Cameron flicks a garlic skin at me, and I brush it away without looking at him. I'm not going to give him the reaction he wants. I'm not going to give him anything.

Mr. Savoca calls for the class's attention, and I open my textbook to the page he gives us. I'm copying the equations he's writing on the board when something bounces off my arm and lands next to my foot.

It's a clove of garlic, its white half-smile mocking me from the floor.

I see Cameron's matching smirk out of the corner of my eye.

I turn back to my notebook and the impossible calculation Mr. Savoca is walking us through. A clove of garlic sails onto my desk, skittering across the scratched wood. Another hits my cheek and falls onto my open notebook. I press my pencil into the paper so hard, the tip snaps. As snickers erupt throughout the room, Mr. Savoca turns around. He eyes the class with suspicion, but everyone is watching him silently, innocent and studious. I grab my sharpener and twist my pencil against the blade forcefully.

Mr. Savoca scowls and turns back to the board.

A whole head of garlic plunks down in front of me.

I jump, scattering papery cloves across my notes. The room stays quiet, but everyone's watching the show. Cameron puffs up at the attention and reaches across the aisle between us, smashing a clove of garlic under his meaty palm. He grins as he grinds the stinking mess into my notebook. I focus so hard on not responding that I feel like I'm floating outside myself, like I'm on the other side of the room, watching the scene play out before me like a movie.

I watch my hands clench so hard around my pencil that my knuckles turn white. I watch Mr. Savoca scribble nonsense on the board, while behind him every face swivels toward Cameron and me. A low hum vibrates the air as I watch Cameron flatten another clove of garlic on my desk with his huge, disgusting hand. I see my nostrils flare and my jaw twitch.

It happens so fast.

In one moment, Cameron is smearing his garlic-covered palm over my notebook.

In the next, my pencil is stuck in the back of his hand.

I watch myself—

No.

It's my body, but it's not me.

I'm not the one looking up at Cameron, my eyes vacant and unfocused. I'm not the one whose lips are stretching into a sharp, sinister smile. I'm not the one who is digging the pencil further into his flesh.

STOP! I yell. But there's no sound.

Crimson drops of blood well up around the wound and Cameron's mouth drops open. In the breath before the scream escapes Cameron's throat, I watch myself yank the pencil out of his hand and raise the point to my mouth.

Then chaos erupts.

Cameron is howling and cradling his bloody hand. Everyone else is shrieking and jumping out of their seats, scrambling to get away from us. Mr. Savoca is yelling too, but he's the only one trying to get closer.

I watch my body twirl the bloody pencil against the flat of my tongue. Mr. Savoca pushes out of the crowd and slams his hands on my desk. My body flinches, loses its balance, and slides backward out of the chair—

The world tilts sideways.

When it snaps back into focus, I'm on the floor.

I'm slumped between two desks, and my left ankle is trapped underneath me, throbbing. My tongue stings as I pull the pencil out of my mouth. I drop it on the ground beside me, and it leaves a streak of spit and blood across the mashed garlic cloves. The taste of wood and iron is overwhelming.

My classmates stand in a frenzied circle around me, and Cameron cradles his hand, whimpering and trailing blood on the floor. This has to be a nightmare.

I will myself to wake up.

This isn't real.

It can't be.

Mr. Savoca stoops in front of me, and when I look up, there's something in his face I never expected to see: fear.

It jolts me into action.

I scramble up, prepared to shove my way out, but people are stepping back, tripping over each other to get away from me, and before I know it I'm bursting out of the classroom, into the empty hallway, out the front doors. My ankle twinges when my feet hit the pavement, but I ignore it and start to run.

CHAPTER TWENTY-EIGHT

I RUN UNTIL MY lungs ache and my ankle throbs too much to ignore, and then I walk. I walk and walk, turning left and right at random. The heat and adrenaline start to wear off, and a chill slices through my sweater. I'm lucky it's not too cold out, even though the clouds are low and the air is dense, like it's thinking of snowing. Still, I duck into a library to warm up.

I find a secluded bench in the nonfiction section and examine my ankle, which is tender but not swelling too badly. I put in my earbuds, grateful that I grabbed my backpack by instinct. Who needs a coat when I have Siouxsie's rasping whisper, soaring high then plunging low, vibrating with loneliness and fury. Siouxsie sings like she's here with me, inside my churning body.

My body. How many times have I imagined lashing back at Cameron like that?

But I never did, I never would. And I didn't.

I know that *I* didn't stab him.

It felt like one of those dreams . . . but that was Maddie, and Maddie's gone.

Isn't she?

I speed-walk out of the library, as though I can ditch my unsettling swirl of thoughts if I move fast enough. I pull my hood up, stuff my hands into the sweater's front pocket, and focus on Siouxsie's voice to keep my racing thoughts at bay.

I end up back in the Morins' neighborhood. I walk through the park, all the way to the fence at the edge of the bluffs. I lean on the thin wire and peer down at the beach below, watching the water lap at the shore. A few wet snowflakes drift down from the gray sky.

I take out my phone and find a stream of notifications, all of them from Yas. I dismiss them so I can see the time. Somehow, it's almost three. Nearly time to get Blythe but too early to start walking to her school. Sylvia and Hector should both be at work. I can pop into their house, borrow a coat, then go pick up Blythe.

After that . . . I don't know.

How am I going to go back to school tomorrow? *Can* I even go back? My mom is going to hear about this soon. Will she show up again? I want to ask for her help, but I don't want her to tell me what to do. I'm so messed up. How am I going to explain this to Sylvia and Hector?

I grip the locket and run my thumb back and forth over its smooth face. The motion smooths my turbulent thoughts as well. I don't need to figure everything out yet. One thing at a time.

I let myself in the Morins' front door, and a flicker of light in the living room catches my eye.

Beside the fireplace is a sea of candles, their flames tall and fluttering. So many candles. The cupboard that holds Maddie's picture is open. Seeing her staring out at me from behind the orange glow makes the hairs on the back of my neck stand up. The scene makes me think of that message board post: *She had hundreds of candles lit around her, like some kind of cult ritual.* Sylvia may have left the beach, but she brought her grief home with her.

The Morins wouldn't have all these candles lit unsupervised. Someone must be home. I don't want to intrude on Sylvia and Hector's privacy more than I already have. I turn back toward the door; I can slip out before—

"Rachel?"

I turn around and Sylvia is there, her hand reaching for my arm as she studies my face intently.

"Is everything okay?"

"I-I wasn't feeling well." When did lying become so easy? "The office sent me home."

"Do you have a fever?" Sylvia presses a warm hand to my forehead, her eyes boring into mine.

"Just a headache." I look away, worried she'll catch the lie. "I'm feeling a lot better now."

"You should rest. The school wouldn't send you home for nothing."

"I have to pick up Blythe—"

"I'll pick her up." She guides me toward the stairs. "Go lie down. I'll bring you some tea."

I know I should refuse. I have a job to do; that's the reason I'm here in the first place. But all I want is to sink into bed and let the soft nothing of sleep erase today's disasters, for a few hours at least. I let Sylvia lead me up the stairs, and at the top she makes a playful *shoo* gesture with her hand.

I flop onto Maddie's bed and take out my phone. A dozen more missed calls from Yas, plus a string of frantic texts. Variations on *Where are you? Are you okay?*

Am I okay?

I have no idea.

I try to imagine what happened after I left. Everyone clustering around Cameron, checking to see how badly I hurt him. He probably got sent to the office. Would they call his parents? Would the school call my mom? Maybe they have a standard message, a robo-caller: *Hello, parent. Your child assaulted another student today. You will need to fill out these forms—*

"You're still up!"

Sylvia walks in, a mug in hand, and I push myself up to sitting, sliding my phone into my hoodie's pocket so I can take the tea from her. The candy-scented steam feels good on my face. The hot liquid singes the inside of my lips, turning them numb and cottony. But my muscles start to relax as warmth radiates through my body from the inside out. Sylvia's right: I need to rest. Ironing out the mess I've made of my life can wait.

I take another swig of tea. My limbs are heavy, like someone turned up the gravity. It's a relief to stop fighting the pull, to let myself fall back against the pillows. The bed is so soft, it feels like I'm sinking underwater. It's nice. My eyes slide shut and the blackness is so sweet.

Don't be rude. My mom's voice. I force my eyes to open, but a long yawn comes out of my mouth instead of the words. Sylvia doesn't seem to mind. She's smiling at me. Her face feels very close. It's hard to keep her in focus. She's holding the mug. When did I finish the tea?

"Finally." Sylvia's hand is hot on my cheek. "It's time for you to come home."

She sounds like she's standing on the other side of a waterfall. What does she mean? The current is carrying me away too fast to voice the question. I feel her fingers trace down my neck, following the line of the necklace where it rests against my skin. When her touch stops on the locket, it's like an anvil on my chest.

Then the darkness takes me.

CHAPTER TWENTY-NINE

MY FOREHEAD BOUNCES AGAINST something solid. The earth hums beneath me. My eyelids are weighed down, sticky. I pry them open, and blurry houses whip by outside the window. Music drifts into my awareness, and I focus on the sound like a lifeline, but the song cuts off before I can place it. It's replaced by a baritone voice, murmuring words I can't make out. Is this a dream? The car turns a sharp corner, angling down along a ribbon of asphalt between dense walls of trees. I try to swallow, to speak, but no sound comes out. *A dream then*, I think, as my eyes slide shut—

• • •

A rhythmic crash fills my head, and suddenly I'm facing endless, thrashing water. A layer of mist swirls above the lake, so dense it looks fake. I stumble and the ground shifts. My hands and knees sink into sand before I realize I'm falling, the cold grains shifting and sending me off-balance. I'm yanked to my feet and pain vibrates up my arm. Then Sylvia—Sylvia?—swings my arm over her shoulders and drags me across the beach. I feel my phone slide out of my hoodie's pocket, but I can't make myself move to catch it.

I'm boneless, a sagging flower. The thought makes me giggle, even as I struggle to stay upright. I can't hold the world steady. Everything ripples and spins. I can only lean on Sylvia and go where she goes. *Where are we going, Sylvia?* The question fizzes out somewhere between my brain and my tongue. Sylvia's eyes are fixed straight ahead, on a point where the scraggly bush overtakes the beach. My vision blurs and lists sideways, and I—

• • •

The sand is sharp. It's in my hair, scratching my neck, filling my socks. But all I see is a vast, gray sky. A single gull floats across, oblivious to what's happening below. What *is* happening?

A flash of panic brings my senses into sharper focus. My labored breathing crashes through my skull. I'm lying on my back. My hands are trapped under me. When I try to move them, my wrists strain against something thin and unyielding. Cold seeps through my sweatshirt, stiffens the fabric of my jeans. I try moving my feet, but my ankles are bound together too.

I turn my head and my cheek sinks into the sand. It isn't frozen like it was yesterday. A white cross juts out of the ground a few feet away. Fire-red branches behind, a soggy teddy bear in front. The air is glazed orange, shimmering. Candles—there are candles in the sand, surrounding me.

Is this another dream?

I try to pull the fraying threads in my mind together. In the dreams, I'm outside my body, watching myself. But my shoulders are tingling, my fingers are going numb, and grains of sand scratch my lips.

In the dreams, when I try to speak, no sound comes out.

"Hnnnn—" There's something in my mouth, something pinching the corners of my lips and holding my tongue down.

A hand rakes through my hair, tugging my head back, filling my vision with sky.

Then, Sylvia's face is hovering over me.

She smiles.

It's the same warm smile she's had for me since the first day we met, but something sinister flares behind it. Something rotten.

"Sylvia?" The word is a knife scraping inside my mouth, almost unrecognizable around the gag. But I heard myself say it.

This is not a dream.

Sylvia reaches out, and for a moment I think she's going to untie me. But she only picks up the locket, holding it like it's a holy object.

"I thought it would be enough, you wearing it." Sylvia pulls the chain taut and it digs into the back of my neck as she cups the locket in her palm. "Sometimes I'd look at you, and I could *see* her. Behind your eyes, like she was trying to come through . . . All those warnings about the jar—*don't touch it or you'll be possessed*!" She scowls, and the violence in her face sends a bolt of fear through me. "I should've known it was overblown. What myth isn't?"

Warnings about the jar . . . I think back to the spirit jars on Maddie's altar and Blythe's panic when I reached for them. But what does that have to do with the necklace?

The locket glints like a star in the candlelight. It reflects in Sylvia's eyes, where the black pools of her pupils have consumed all but the thinnest ring of blue. She sets the necklace back on my chest and her eyes snap to my face. Whatever she sees there makes her expression soften into something more familiar, a look of care and concern. It used to make me feel seen, safe.

Now it makes me feel like a rabbit with its leg caught in a trap.

"You want to be part of our family, don't you?" Sylvia strokes my cheek.

I pull away, but I don't get far.

I want to deny it. But I think of how I longed for the afternoons in their quiet, neat home, how I hung around until she invited me to stay for dinner, how easily I slipped into Maddie's place at the table. Was my hunger that transparent?

But as Sylvia says it out loud, while restraints bite into my wrists and a gag strangles my tongue, the spell breaks. The clean white lines, the candy tea, the questions about my day, the family dinners—it was all a veneer, a glossy coat of paint to hide the rot underneath.

"I want you here too. You came to us for a reason. You're going to bring her back." Sylvia's smile takes on a frenzied edge as she touches the locket reverently. "She's still here. And soon, she'll be here to stay."

A flurry of memories whirl through my mind.

Sylvia cradles the locket. "I thought it would be enough, you wearing it—"

Blythe grabs my arm. "If you touch it, the ghost inside can possess you—"

Wàipó's careful pen strokes form the Chinese character "bind" on a strip of paper fixed to a wax-sealed jar—

A shudder sweeps through my body as the pieces click into place. Sylvia thinks she trapped Maddie's spirit in the locket. She gave it to me on purpose because she wanted her daughter to possess my body.

Except Maddie is gone. I watched her ghost float away, tugged across the lake by a paper flower filled with her ashes. I thought that if we freed Maddie, I would be free too. When I didn't have a nightmare last night, I thought it worked. But then today with Cameron—

Blythe yanks the locket out of my sweater. "Maddie said take it off!"

I wasn't wearing the necklace last night.

Sylvia smooths the damp hair back from my face with a tenderness so familiar that tears well in my eyes. It's the same way she looked in the kitchen this morning, when she clasped the locket back around my neck.

The nightmares and the sleepwalking, the sensation of being outside myself, watching my body do unthinkable things—they all happened while I was wearing the locket. *Only* while I was wearing the locket.

I gasp and the gag gets sucked into my throat, setting off a coughing fit. I wheeze and try to spit, but only a thin strand of saliva dribbles down my chin. Sylvia wipes it away with her thumb. She's saying something, but I don't hear her. In my mind, I'm watching Maddie being pulled across the lake. She looks me in the eye and her translucent mouth forms the shape of a silent threat: *KILL YOU.*

But what if it wasn't a threat? What if it was a warning?

A pen moving under its own power, underlining two unmistakable words until the paper rips: FREE ME.

Certainty floods through me, cold and clear. Maddie's spirit isn't in this locket.

But something else is.

Something full of rage, something that's been taking control of my body and making me do terrifying, violent things. Something deadly.

Sylvia reaches around my neck to unclasp the necklace, and I do the only thing I can think of: I open my mouth as wide as I can and sink my teeth into her forearm.

The gag chokes me and carves into the corners of my mouth, forcing me back onto the sand, coughing, but not before Sylvia yelps and loses her balance. When she rights herself, her face is a twisted mask of rage.

She comes at me again, shoving my face into the ground with a clawed hand. Sand digs into my eyelids and worms into my nostrils. I hold my breath, thrashing against the pressure on my skull. The world starts to get soft at the edges. I struggle harder and try to lift my head, make some space to take in air, panic cresting as my lungs burn.

Sylvia finally lets go, and I turn my head to the side, gasping. When I have enough oxygen to focus, I find her standing over me, clutching the locket, radiating spite and triumph. I shrink back, away from the scream or blow I'm sure will follow. But she's interrupted by the sound of sticks breaking behind her.

"Help!" I yell. It comes out as a muffled moan.

Sylvia whips around as the branches bend back and Hector steps into the clearing. He's panting, and his coat is crusted with snow and dirt, like he slid down the bluffs. His shocked eyes meet his wife's and then sweep down to me, bound and gagged on my back, in a circle of candles. He suddenly looks a thousand years old, grief contorting his features. I imagine him rushing over to me, yelling at Sylvia to keep back as he frees my hands from the restraints, pulling me into a tight hug.

Instead, he turns away.

My brief flare of hope shrivels.

"What are you doing here?" Sylvia hisses.

"The door was unlocked and your car was gone. Last time . . ." His gaze drifts back to where I lie in the sand, bound like an animal.

"Where's Blythe?" Sylvia demands. "Did you pick her up?"

"Of course I did. She's at home—"

"You left Blythe alone? Are you stupid?"

"This has got to stop, Sylvia." Hector's voice trembles, undercutting the force of his words. "I tried telling myself that you're grieving, and everyone grieves in their own way, in their own time. But this . . ." He gestures at me with a limp hand.

Look at me, Hector. I plead silently. *Look at me*.

But it's like I don't exist.

"You need help, Sylvia," he says.

"I don't need help, especially not from you," Sylvia spits. "I'm bringing our daughter back."

"What?"

"Don't you want Maddie back?"

"Of course I do." Hector's lips tremble, and he presses a fist to them. "But she's gone, Sylvia. You need to accept reality."

"You give up so easily. It makes me sick." Sylvia points a finger at him, stabbing the air. "*You're* the reason she snuck out that night. Do you tell your *clients* to put their kids under house arrest? You're supposed to be an expert!"

"Sylvia—"

"But I'm used to fixing your mistakes." She holds up the locket, the gold oval swinging from the end of the chain. "I kept her with us. Now all we have to do is set her free."

"You need help, Sylvia," he repeats, taking her hands gently in his. Their eyes lock and there's a glint of gold in their intertwined palms.

Hector's not going to help me. In a choice between me and his family, there's no contest. Just like my dad. The thought brings a lump to my throat. How could I be so stupid? Neither of them chose me. Neither of them were ever going to. The only one looking out for me is me. That's how it's always been.

While Hector continues to plead with Sylvia, I use my elbows to push my torso off the ground, then crunch up to sitting. There's no way I can stand, not with my arms trapped behind me and my ankles bound like this—now that I can see my feet, I realize Sylvia used zip ties. I look around for something, anything that might help me cut them. The beach is barren, except for Maddie's cross. The lake stretches out in front of me, and the cliffs loom beyond the bushes at my back, everything fading into featureless outlines in the rapidly dwindling daylight. I drag my knees in toward my body but lose my balance and rock backward, snuffing out the candles closest to me. *The candles.*

"You think Maddie is in here?" Hector is staring at the locket resting in their joined hands.

"I know she is."

"Sylvia, that doesn't make any sense."

I scoot back so that my feet are next to one of the candles that's still lit. Plastic should melt, I think? I lean on my elbows and hover my feet over the flame, my abs burning with the effort, praying this works, that the tie melts, that my jeans are damp enough not to catch fire too, that I get free before whatever's trapped in that locket does.

"It's true!" Sylvia cries. "I saw her, *right here*. I knew she didn't want to leave us, and I thought maybe the spell, in the spirit jar from Taiwan . . . I didn't know if it would work, but it did. *It did.* I only wanted to keep her close, keep her safe—but then I saw Rachel in her sweater, and I knew. She was sent to us for a reason, Hector! To give Maddie another chance, to give *our family* another chance." Sylvia is pleading, her voice raw and choked. "She's been trying, but her spirit isn't strong enough, trapped in there. She can finish it, if we set her free."

"You think Maddie's spirit is in here." Hector speaks slowly, as though to a small child. He holds the locket up, his thumbs pressing against its sides. "And if we open it, she's going to take over Rachel's body."

There's no mistaking the disbelief in his face, but Sylvia's eyes are fixed on the locket.

I stare at the tiny flame below my ankles, willing it to burn through the plastic. But the zip tie might as well be an iron chain, for all the difference the heat is making. There isn't even any smoke.

"We'll be a family again," Sylvia insists. "Open it and see."

"If I open it, if I prove to you that Maddie's spirit isn't in here—will you get help?"

Dread prickles up my spine. "Don't!" I try to yell, but the gag deadens the sound. Neither of them looks at me.

"Open it." Sylvia's voice is low and impatient.

Hector struggles with the locket, his fingers slipping off the curved edges. He takes out a pocket knife and flips open a slim blade, working it between the two sides of the locket. He fidgets with it for a long minute, as I pull harder against my restraints, my shoulders and ankles stinging from the effort. But the ties don't give at all; they just bite more fiercely into my skin.

Finally, the locket pops open.

A narrow piece of paper flutters out like a tongue and the wind catches it, carrying it toward me as though guided by an invisible hand.

It lands face-up beside me.

The paper is covered in Chinese characters. One immediately leaps out at me: "bind."

But something's off.

The strokes are shaky and the ink is splotched in places, as though smudged by drops of water. Tears? Sylvia was definitely not clear-minded when she wrote this. I don't know if Sylvia reads Chinese, but even if she does . . . If she just copied the spell from the spirit jar, would that even work? And if it didn't—

A shiver rattles my spine, and I hear Wàipó's voice:

Dangerous spirits can take advantage of your mistakes.

CHAPTER THIRTY

SOMETHING MOVES BY THE water. A figure stands facing the lake, shrouded by the dusky sky. My mind tries to tell me it's a person with long hair whipping in the wind, skin so pale it's almost blue in the fading light. But that doesn't match the unnatural length of its limbs, the way its fingers end in sharp, too-long points.

Hector gasps. The locket falls from his hand.

Sylvia falls to her knees, a sob wrenching out of her. "Maddie," she cries, her arms outstretched. "Maddie, Maddie, Maddie . . ." The wretched sound echoes off the cliffs.

The bushes rustle behind me then a pale face looms in the darkness between the branches. A scream rips from my throat, blunted by the gag. The face moves into the candlelight, brown eyes framed by a familiar fur hood.

Blythe presses a finger to her lips, and my muscles go slack with relief. She crouches beside me, fumbling to untie the gag. When the fabric falls away, my chest spasms in a chain of coughs. The corners of my mouth split and burn as I heave deep breaths into my lungs.

I look up at the lake, straining to see in the descending darkness. Sylvia is stumbling toward the figure by the water, her arms thrown wide, ready to embrace the thing she thinks is her daughter. Hector follows behind her in a zombie-like shamble.

"Don't move," Blythe orders.

She pulls the Japanese knife out of its sleeve and cuts the restraints around my ankles. I shuffle sideways so she can reach my hands where they're trapped behind my back. My shoulders pop as my arms swing free, and the shooting pain rocketing up my neck makes me grimace.

"Maddie!" Sylvia's shout pierces the air. Blythe and I turn toward the sound.

So does the thing by the water.

Its features are masked in shadow, but there is no doubt in my mind: That is not Maddie. Every muscle in my body tenses. The instinct to *run* rushes through me, and I'm struck by the sudden, undeniable certainty that this is a predator and I am prey.

I see the same realization hit Sylvia.

She falters and tries to reverse her course, but the sand shifts and her feet slide out from under her. She lands on her back and tries to scramble away, but it's too late. The thing darts forward and pounces, stretching its inhumanly long body over hers.

"Mom!" Blythe shrieks.

Then the monster is gone.

Sylvia lies in the sand, unmoving.

Hector breaks into a run, dropping to his knees at her side.

They're almost at the water's edge, but the wind carries Hector's frantic voice back to us as he calls his wife's name.

This is my chance.

I leap to my feet, step across the circle of sputtering candles, and pick up Sylvia's purse. Relief flows through me when I find the car keys inside. Maddie's locket lies open on the ground where Hector dropped it. Some instinct makes me scoop it up, along with the paper that was inside, and stuff them in the back pocket of my jeans. I'm a breath away from sprinting away, but a yank on my sleeve pulls me to a halt.

"We can't leave them." The panic in Blythe's voice makes me hesitate.

Hector is a dark smear hunched over Sylvia's unmoving body, his back to us as his hands pump up and down on her chest. He bends to breathe into her mouth, then sits up and starts over again. The lake is a pool of black ink, rippling beyond them. There's no monster. But I'm certain it's coming back.

Why should I care if Sylvia is hurt and Hector might be in danger, after what they did to me? The smart thing to do is run. But I can't make myself do it because Blythe is whimpering softly, all the bravado she brought to my rescue gone.

The moon cuts through the clouds, bathing Hector and Sylvia in an eerie glow. As Hector presses on Sylvia's chest, her head lolls to the side, her face turning toward us. Her expression turns all my hesitations to ash.

Under the moon's grisly spotlight, Sylvia's face is twisted in a sharp, vacant smile. The very same smile I've seen in my nightmares, on my own face.

Sylvia grabs Hector's forearm and yanks him down. He collapses on top of her with a yelp. A wet, tearing sound fills the air.

Then someone is screaming.

It's Hector, as the thing inside his wife's body clutches his head in both of her hands.

It's Sylvia, or the monster inside her, a feral silhouette in the rapidly falling night.

It's me, backing away with my hand like a vise around Blythe's wrist.

The pulse in my neck is a fire alarm thrumming through my body—*run*, it says, *run run run*. This time, I obey. Blythe and I crash through the brush, moving as fast as we can while dodging the branches threatening to trip us. When we emerge on the other side, the moon is a full, white eye, illuminating the beach from the narrow end where we stand to what looks like the parking lot ahead. To our left, the lake crashes against the shore in a steady, indifferent rhythm. To our right, the bluffs loom behind clumps of dense forest, dark sentinels hundreds of feet high. There is a single car parked in the lot, glowing under the streetlamps—Sylvia's, it must be. How far is it? Fifty steps? A hundred?

I squeeze Blythe's hand, and she looks down like she forgot it was attached to her.

"We need to run to the car, okay?"

"Are they dead?"

"I don't know." I take the knife from her other hand. "Can you run?"

Blythe looks up at me and blinks, as though stunned. She nods.

I take off, clutching her hand in mine and pulling her with me. The sand keeps sliding underneath our feet. It feels like trying to run up the down escalator, like the ground is working against us. Pain shoots through my ankle, but I push on. The parking lot gets closer. I can see the yellow lines on the asphalt. I can read the car's license plate. I can see the top of the steering wheel through the windshield—

Our boots slap onto the pavement and every one of my muscles strains toward the car. I slam into the driver side door and scramble for the handle, but it's locked. I press the car key buttons frantically and glance over my shoulder at the shadowed beach behind us. Snowflakes drift down from the black sky, staining the sand as they melt. There's no way to know where Sylvia and Hector are, if they're still alive. No way to know how much time we have.

"You're bleeding." Blythe is looking at my hand.

The cut below my left thumb is open again, oozing red. I'm about to tell her I'm fine when she gasps, her gaze fixed behind me. I whirl around, knife first. My heart crawls up into my throat, even though all I see is darkness.

But then a pair of headlights careens down the winding road, turning sharply into the parking lot and barreling straight for us.

We need to run, I think. *Get in the car.*

But the bright lights have me trapped like a deer.

The car stops a few feet away and the door flies open.

"Rachel?" I know that voice. But it can't be—

"Mom?"

"Rachel!"

I reach for her, vaguely aware of the knife and keys clattering to the ground, and then my mom has her arms around me, crushing me to her. She smells like oatmeal body lotion, and as she strokes my hair, the emotions that have been balled like a fist behind my ribs since I first woke up on the beach burst open.

"Mom," I sob. "I'm so sorry—"

"The school called and you weren't picking up"—Mom's speaking too fast, her words running into each other—"I went to their house, but no one was there. Then Yas called—"

I look over her shoulder and, sure enough, there's Yas, lingering by the driver's side of the car. Her car. Of course.

"I was worried about you." Yas's voice is so small, I barely recognize it. "Your mom checked your phone, and it said you were here."

I remember my phone sliding out of the pocket of my hoodie as Sylvia dragged me across the beach. Sylvia—

Fear surges through my veins, reigniting the urge to run.

"We need to go."

Mom pulls back a little and cups my face in her hands. "What happened?"

"We need to go, *now*." There's no time to answer her questions.

"Is that Blythe?" My mom looks past me, to where Blythe is staring at her feet, her arms wrapped around herself. My mom steps over to her and crouches down. "Are you okay?"

Blythe's eyes are grave when they meet my mom's.

"There's a monster," Blythe says. Her voice is small but sure.

My mom straightens. "Okay." There isn't a hint of mockery in her voice as she motions us toward Yas's car and swivels around to scan the shadows at the edges of the parking lot. "Let's go."

One moment I'm moving to follow Blythe, and the next I'm on the ground. My head rings like I'm inside a gong. I squeeze my eyes shut, pressing my hands against the fierce pounding in my skull. I taste blood, and my tongue aches where my teeth sunk into it.

I wrench my eyes open and my mom is there—but so is Sylvia. Mom stands between us, her back to me, blocking me with her body. Sylvia paces in front of her like a wild cat.

Sylvia's mouth, her coat, her hands, her hair . . . all of her is stained red. She licks her lips and her mouth stretches into that menacing, vacant smile.

That's not Sylvia.

My mom knows it too. Her purse is lying at her feet, crumpled tissues and loose change strewn around it. In her hands, she clutches the peach-wood sword.

Mom takes a step forward, thrusting the sword in front of her. Sylvia skitters sideways, swinging an arm in a wide arc, trying to slash at my mom around the sword between them. Mom stabs again, and the monster wearing Sylvia's face squirms back. Sylvia's swipes grow increasingly desperate, while my mom continues to weave and sidestep, luring Sylvia away from us.

"Run!" my mom yells without taking her eyes off Sylvia.

Yas and Blythe are frozen in the headlights, their faces twisted with terror. A gust of snow swirls into my face, and the cold snaps me into action. I scramble to my feet, steadying myself as dizziness threatens to overtake me. I rush to Yas's car and open the passenger door.

"Blythe," I hiss. "Blythe!"

Blythe starts at the sound of her name. She runs to me and slides into the car. But instead of sitting back, she looks me in the eye and grabs my hand. To my surprise, she presses the coin charm into my palm.

"Be careful," she says.

"Thank you." My stomach clenches as I fold my fingers over the coin. "You too."

She sits back and buckles herself in. For the first time in my life, I hope the god of thunder is real.

Yas hasn't moved from her spot in the car's headlights. "Yas!" I keep my voice as low as possible. "You have to go!"

Yas shudders. Her eyes are dazed, but she moves toward the driver's-side door. She gets it half open and pauses, glancing back at where my mom is still dodging Sylvia, leading her away from us. They're almost back at the beach, the peach-wood sword in my mom's hands the only barrier between her and the monster.

"We can't leave her," Yas says.

"No." I shut Blythe's door. "We can't."

Yas's eyes lock on mine and her breaths start coming faster as she gets my meaning.

"Get somewhere safe and call for help," I say. "We're right behind you."

"But—" Yas's mouth opens and closes, searching for words. "I'm not supposed to drive alone—"

"Yas." My voice is steadier than it has any right to be. "You have to go *now.*"

Yas stiffens and nods. She starts to get into the driver's seat, then stops and looks at me. Her eyes glisten with unshed tears.

"I hate you," she whispers. She means *I'm scared, I love you, you better not die.*

"Love you too." I step back from the car. "Now go!"

Yas slams the door and the car peels into a wide arc, racing out of the parking lot.

I'm immediately in motion. I dash back to Sylvia's car, searching for where I dropped the knife. I spot the blade behind one of the front tires. I lunge for it, gripping the handle hard so it doesn't slide out of my sweaty hand.

I turn just as Sylvia feints a swipe to my mom's right, then darts back to her left. My mom staggers and the monster rears up to strike, her fingers bent into claws. Acid horror fills my mouth, but I can't move. The knife is in my hand, but I can't make myself raise it or run toward the danger. It's just like the dreams, when I'm paralyzed, helpless, watching something terrible happen . . .

But this isn't a dream. I still have my voice.

So I scream.

A primal roar wrenches from deep within my gut and rushes out of my mouth, as if my fear and guilt and desperation are solidifying into a terrible noise that slashes through the air.

The monster in Sylvia's body recoils. Its attention snaps toward me, its snarl twisting Sylvia's face into something inhuman. My heartbeat thrashes in my ears, urging me to run. But I plant my feet and keep screaming.

It's just the opportunity my mom needs.

Mom drops to one knee and thrusts the peach-wood sword up, through Sylvia's coat and into the soft flesh of her stomach. I've held that sword a thousand times. I know it's made of wood twice as old as I am. I know the biggest danger it poses is a splinter.

Yet it slices Sylvia open like it's a shard of glass.

Sylvia jerks away, but she doesn't get far. The sword is lodged in her gut, and my mom is clutching it like a lifeline in both hands. Sylvia howls, raking her nails across my mom's face. Blood streaks my mom's torn cheeks, but she doesn't pull back. Instead, she lets out a yell of her own and throws her whole body forward, shoving the sword deeper. Sylvia shrieks, wrenching sideways, and my mom loses her balance. She lets go of the sword to brace herself as she falls, landing on her hands and knees, and scurries back out of Sylvia's reach.

But the monster is focused on the sword hilt sticking out of its stomach. It wraps its hands around the wood, but its skin sizzles and it pulls back with a shriek. It tears at its hair as the wound starts to smoke. A smell like rotten meat mixed with burning rubber makes my eyes water.

The monster moans and looks up. Its eyes meet mine and a shudder runs through me. Because it's no longer the monster.

It's Sylvia.

Sylvia who left me tea every afternoon, who asked me about my day, about my dreams for the future. Sylvia who insisted on driving me home, who made me feel safe talking about my struggles with math, who held me while I cried.

But each of those memories curdles as it surfaces.

That whole time, she was also the Sylvia who lied, who used me, who was prepared to discard me to get what she wanted.

She never really saw me.

She never wanted to.

The look only lasts a second. Then the peach-wood sword clatters to the ground and Sylvia's body follows. She lies motionless, her eyes open but unseeing. Thin curls of smoke waft up from her stomach, but that's the only sign of injury; there's no wound, not even a rip in her coat. The bluffs seem to hold their breath.

My mom stands slowly, staring at Sylvia's body. I call for her and when she turns around, her face is blood-streaked and bewildered. But then she sees me and smiles.

As Mom limps in my direction, the moon ducks behind a cloud and wraps the beach in a black blanket. The streetlamps in the parking lot draw fuzzy circles on the ground, now the only source of light. Thick, wet snowflakes float down around us. Sylvia's body lies unmoving on the asphalt, in the narrow shadow between two pools of orange light.

Then the monster is there, beside her.

It shakes like a dog coming out of the water. Its long hair whips against its translucent skin and its fingernails scratch the pavement. Then it steps forward, into the light, and for the first time I see its face.

Or where a face should be.

Its face is a smooth, featureless stretch of skin, a demonic mirror of the moon re-emerging above us. Instead of eyes, a nose, a mouth—there's nothing.

Still, I can feel it watching me.

The creature rises to its full height in slow, stuttering motion, like a video buffering. Its hair is dark and wet, so long it brushes its ankles. Its limbs are all wrong. Its arms hang long, ending in sharp fingers that brush the ground. Its legs are stretched too thin and bend at unnatural angles.

It turns its awful, blank face toward my mom.

She doesn't see it. Her eyes are locked on mine; she's only steps away. But the monster flickers, that strange buffering movement, and now it's right behind her, reaching with its too-long claws.

I know what it's going to do.

I shove my mom out of the way and leap past her, launching myself at the monster, knife first. I thrust the blade into its chest and it slides in without resistance. I keep pushing until my hands brush its clammy skin and its forehead touches mine. Its skin feels like fog. It smells like the lake.

My vision is filled with the smooth, featureless circle of skin where its face should be. It leans in closer, long ropes of hair falling around us, drawing a curtain that thrusts us into darkness and shields everything beyond from view. I know it has no eyes, no mouth, but trapped in this intimate cave, I can feel its piercing stare, sense its feral grin. Terror runs through me, reigniting the bone-deep urge to run.

But instead, I grit my teeth, push the knife in deeper, and twist.

CHAPTER THIRTY-ONE

THE FLOOR RUMBLES AND déjà vu tickles a corner of my mind. For the second time tonight, I wake up in a car driving too fast along a winding road. It's snowing harder now, or maybe it's hail; I hear heavy drops battering the roof. I'm in the back seat and Mom is hunched over the steering wheel in front of me, her face as close to the windshield as she can get. The wipers sweep frantically, the headlights barely cutting two feet through the darkness ahead. The realization hits me like a hammer: We're in Sylvia's car. We're driving away from the beach.

Quiet notes thump from the speakers, the radio playing on low. I strain to hear the song, and when I finally place it, a feeling bubbles in my stomach that might be a laugh or a sob or both.

It's Destiny's Child singing "Survivor."

We made it.

We're safe.

Mom's fingers clench and release on the steering wheel. Her jaw twitches and her cheek is swollen around four deep gouges, crusted with dried blood. How quickly I went from running as far away from her as I could to being desperate to see her again—but she's right here and so am I. Her chest is rising and falling with each breath, and her hands are guiding us home. Yas and Blythe—they're safe somewhere too. The police are probably on their way. I have no idea what we're going to tell them, but it doesn't matter. The only thing that matters is we're all going to be okay.

"Mom?" I say.

She keeps staring ahead, grim-faced and focused.

I reach for her shoulder, but my hand passes right through.

A sick feeling blooms in my stomach. I try to touch her arm, shake the back of her seat, pound my fist on the center console. But it's like the car is made of mist. My hand slides through all these things that should be solid.

MOM! I yell.

When she doesn't so much as flinch, the sick feeling pulses toward panic.

Am I dreaming?

Mom takes one hand off the wheel and reaches toward the passenger seat. I realize someone is sitting there, slumped against the car door. Mom places her hand on top of theirs, and I lean between the two front seats so I can see the person's face. Static fills my mind, bristling over rising terror, as my brain tries to deny what my eyes are telling me.

The person in the passenger seat is me.

It's my hand Mom is holding, my body swaying limply with each turn, my head bouncing against the window.

It's my body, but it's not *me*.

I'm right here, watching my mom's thumb stroke the back of my hand. The inside of the windshield reflects her pinched face and my body, with my eyes shut and a bruise purpling over my left eyebrow. But as for me, the *real* me, invisible in the back seat with the horrible weight of understanding falling over me like a net . . . there's no reflection of me at all.

My body's eyes open.

It looks up at the windshield and meets my gaze, even though only its face is reflected in the glass. That vacant, hungry grin spreads across its lips. It turns its hand under my mom's and intertwines their fingers. In its other hand, the blade of the Morins' Japanese knife flashes.

NO!

The scream punches out of my lungs but makes no sound.

I lunge forward, trying to place myself between my mom and the monster. But I move right through them, the sensation like cold breath as the monster yanks my mom close and stabs the knife into her thigh. Mom screams and tries to pull away, striking out wildly with her other hand. The steering wheel lurches and the car skids sideways.

Time seems to slow as my mom frantically grabs the wheel and the monster grins maniacally, even as its head cracks against the window—

• • •

Darkness, and a painful pressure against my windpipe. My fingers claw at the seatbelt digging into my neck. I tug it away from my throat with one hand and fumble for the buckle with the other. I mash my thumb into the button, and the belt goes slack and snaps away from me. Gravity pulls me sideways and my head thuds against the car door. I suck in a breath, my hand flying to my temple. My forehead throbs under my fingers.

My fingers. I can feel my fingers.

Relief wells up in a sob, but I force myself to shove down the shock and look around. I'm in Sylvia's car, but it's not moving. It's not even on the road. We're nose-down in a ditch, the vehicle and everything in it tilting to the right. Mom is still strapped in the driver's seat, but her body is limp, her chin lolling on her chest. The stone in my stomach gets a fraction lighter when I see that she's breathing.

"Mom?"

I stare at her, willing her to wake up. Her chest rises and falls, and I sync my breathing to her shallow inhales. But otherwise she doesn't move. Snow is cascading down from the night sky, the thick flakes melting and dripping down the window beside her. A flicker of movement catches my eye, a silhouette moving toward us on the moonlit road. Fear-laced adrenaline floods my muscles.

"Mom!" I shake her arm. "You have to wake up!" She doesn't stir. There's more blood on her cheek than there was before.

The monster's horrible, featureless face appears outside the car window.

My lizard brain wants to take over, to freeze or flee, but I refuse to give into panic. I reach into my pocket for the coin charm Blythe gave me and smack it against the glass.

The monster jerks back and disappears from sight.

It worked.

After everything that's happened, I'm still surprised.

But it won't be long until it's back. We need to go, now.

Mom shifts, a groan escaping with her exhale. But she doesn't open her eyes. She can't run.

But I can. I can draw the monster away, buy my mom more time to wake up, to escape. Or at least get far enough away that I can't hurt her, if the monster takes over my body again.

As I reach for the door handle, my foot kicks something. I look down and see the knife between my feet, its blade crusted in blood. I pick it up, willing myself not to think about who that blood belongs to, and I slide out of the car, grateful for every stinging, shooting pain that rockets through me, because it means I'm *here*.

I slam the door. "Come get me!"

The monster's smooth, pale face appears, glowing in the skewed beam of the car's headlights. I bound down the ditch and sprint into the forest beyond, dodging tree roots and slapping branches away. The moon filters through the canopy and steadily falling snow—disorienting flashes of light that make it hard to tell the difference between what's solid and what's shadow.

I risk a glance behind me, and a long, translucent limb rakes through the air next to my ear. I dodge left, thrusting the coin charm in the monster's direction, but it slips from my fingers. I fumble, trying to catch it, but it disappears into wet snow and decaying leaves. I slow down. Should I look for it? I still have the knife, but—

A glimmer of white through the trees decides for me. Moon or monster, I'm not sure, but it spurs me on, my legs moving faster than my mind, faster than I've ever run before, faster than my muscles can control, and suddenly I'm falling, flying through the air, slamming shoulder-first into a tree. I push away, but its branches grab my sweater, sending me tripping over a root and landing hard on my tailbone. I gulp in a breath, holding the air in my lungs as I glance around.

An army of trees surrounds me, their bare branches slicing the moon's glow into chunks. To my left, the ground slopes down toward faint circles of orange light. The parking lot. A few paces to my right, the forest stops abruptly and a sheer cliff blocks the way, towering against the night sky. Ahead of me is the ragged path I just tore through the woods, and, although I can't see it, I know that beyond lies the road and the wrecked car, where my mom is hopefully waking up and making a run for it. Behind me, trees continue between the bluffs and the beach, dense and unyielding. My hair is dripping with melted snow, and damp flakes continue to float down silently. The only sounds are the whistling wind and my panting.

Did I lose the monster? Should I yell again, in case it's going back for my mom? I push up to my feet, using the tree next to me as leverage. I rest my hand against the rough bark and peer around the other side.

The monster's blank face stares back at me.

I gasp, but determination cuts through my panic, and my muscles cramp as I fight the urge to run. I will not let this thing get my mom. I clench my fist around the knife and drive it into the monster's face with all my strength. Again there's no resistance, like slicing through water. But somehow, the knife sticks in its skull.

I lurch away, slamming into another tree.

The monster doesn't move.

There's no blood, no sign of injury except for the knife's handle jutting out of its smooth, pale face. Like I stabbed a Halloween mask. Still, the monster just stands there, and for a moment I think maybe I killed it. Then its too-long fingers twitch.

I scramble away, slipping on tree roots and scraping my palms on sharp bark, trying to still my whirling mind long enough to see a way out. But that's impossible because there is no way out. I'm pinned in by the lake to my left and the bluffs to my right. There is only the forest behind me and the monster in front, ready to pounce on any path I might take.

It knows this. I can see that as clearly as I see the ferocious grin behind its featureless face. I stabbed the knife right between where its eyes would be, and it made no difference. But as I stare at the knife handle sticking out of the monster's forehead, a spark of recognition sears through my terror. I see a row of vampires standing at attention, frozen, yellowed scrolls covering their faces bearing the Chinese character "bind."

Like the spell Sylvia copied and put into Maddie's locket.

The spell currently in my pocket.

What if—

The monster comes at me then, swiping its claws toward my face. I swerve away, but instead of running, I twist back and grab the knife with both hands. I pull as hard as I can, but it slides out easily, and the extra momentum sends me tumbling backward into the dirt.

My back crashes against something hard, but I ignore it and roll sideways, shoving my hand into my pocket. I pull out the piece of paper that fell from Maddie's locket. It's wet and tattered, but all I can do is hope it's in good enough shape to work. I need to get it on the knife—where's the knife?

Blood pounds in my ears as I twist around, raking my hands through wet snow and dead leaves until I see a glint of silver a few feet away. I lunge for it, but a pale limb arcs through the air, knocking me flat on my back.

The monster stretches over me, its long, sharp fingers circling my throat. My skin burns and the weight on my chest is suddenly immense, like being run over by a cement mixer. I'm sucking in small sips of air, but I know I have only seconds before I can't breathe at all.

The knife. It's so close to my right hand, just finger-lengths away. My vision starts to blur, but I fight to stretch my arm toward the blade and force myself to focus on my breathing, on the fact I'm *still* breathing. The monster is crushing my ribs, pushing them back toward my spine; gravel and sticks bite under my nails as I claw into the ground, desperately searching for the knife; the air is cold when it flows into my nose and warm when it leaves.

My hand brushes a sharp steel edge, splitting the skin on my fingertips. A stilted growl rumbles through me as I stretch farther, blood seeping from my fingers, joints burning, lungs straining.

My hands close around the knife.

With my last ounce of strength, I reach around the monster's arms. I slap the paper onto its smooth face and drive the knife through the middle of it. This time, the blade meets resistance, like trying to cut a lump of wet clay, but I shove harder, fighting to keep my faltering breaths as steady as I can, even as the edges of my vision go dark.

The pressure on my chest disappears.

I fall back, gasping for breath, bright dots swimming behind my eyelids. My throat blazes like I'm breathing in glass. But I'm breathing.

When my vision clears, I'm confronted with a surreal scene.

The monster is pinned to the forest floor. Its long, black hair is spread around it like a demonic halo. Its legs and arms thrash wildly, but some invisible force keeps it pinned firmly to the ground. If it had a mouth, I'm sure it would be screaming. A shard from a dream surfaces, a mirror of this moment:

I'm watching my body writhe on Maddie's bed—my body but not under my control. My limbs are fighting and flailing, but something is stopping me from getting up. Something holds me down against the mattress and won't let go. When I wake up, there is a handprint on my chest. Maddie's handprint.

She held me down, prevented the monster inside me from using my body to satisfy its violent hunger by ripping her family apart. She was protecting us all along.

I take Maddie's locket out of my pocket. It's easy to open now. The inside is marred with scratches, in stark opposition to its smooth face. How could I have let this thing have such a hold on me? Am I really that shallow, that desperate, that I was ready to abandon my life for a few kind words and an old necklace?

I look up, and the rational part of my brain—once the only part I listened to, now a distant afterthought—is surprised that the monster is still there, struggling.

It was once held in this locket. It can be held there again.

"Rachel!"

My mom emerges from the shadows, and her eyes fill with tears when they meet mine. Her hair is flecked with melting snow, and she's limping, a bloody hand pressed against her thigh. I open my mouth to say something, I don't know what—an apology, a question, anything. But nothing comes out.

Mom steps around the monster, careful to stay out of reach of its long, sharp limbs. She sinks down beside me, landing with a thud, her shoulder pressing into mine. We stare at the monster as it struggles in vain, its blank face obscured by the ragged spell pinned to it by the knife. Mom grabs my hand, intertwining our fingers. Her palm is sticky and damp, warm and solid. I can feel her breathing, and I match my inhales and exhales to hers.

When she squeezes my hand, I squeeze back.

EPILOGUE

I PRESS MY FOOT on the gas, flicking on the signal light and checking my blind spot one more time before moving into the right lane. The white BMW that's been riding my bumper zooms past the moment I'm clear, the fierce August sun glinting off its windows. I'm not sure I'll ever be fully comfortable on the highway, but at least I'm no longer hyperventilating every time I need to change lanes.

Yas and Dell haven't noticed how close that was—they're too busy singing along to the LMK track blasting out of the speakers. Beside me, in the passenger seat, Yas shimmies her shoulders and throws her head back, yelling the words at the top of her lungs. It's hard to believe she's the same person who showed up in this very car on that night, six months and a lifetime ago, terrified and confused, or who, a week later, burst into the principal's office and dropped a massive folder on her desk, stuffed with years' worth of evidence of Cameron's bullying. That kicked off an investigation that led to a dozen other students coming forward and ended with Cameron being expelled. "Whenever you were ready, I was going to be ready too," Yas said to me after. "Because we both know you weren't taking notes."

She was right. She's been right about a lot of things.

Including Dell, whose curly mohawk I can see bopping to the music in the rearview mirror. Dell and Yas visited me every day during the two weeks I was suspended for the Cameron incident. The first time Dell came over, they asked me a million questions about the altar in our living room. I thought they were making fun of me until the next day, when they showed up with a gift of homemade sulfur soap, to drive away negative energy. Turns out Dell's mom is a bruja and they've been learning from her for years. I didn't know I wanted a friend who I could talk to about spellcasting or my mom's incense obsession, but now I don't know what I did before them. I'm not sure that I deserve friends like these, but I'm doing my best to earn them now.

The music cuts off abruptly, and my phone rings through the speakers. The caller ID flashes MOM and I reach for *decline*, but Yas moves faster.

"Hi, Ms. Bei," Yas says. "Rachel's driving."

Yas knows I won't look away from the road, but I make a face anyway and see her teasing grin widen out of the corner of my eye.

"Ms. Bei! Hi!" Dell echoes, leaning forward from the back seat.

"Hi, Yas! Hi, Dell!" My mom's voice fills the car. I would be annoyed by how much she loves the two of them, except that's one of the main reasons I'm on my way to Montreal right now. "I'm heading to work soon, so I just wanted to check in."

"Mom, I *said* I'll text when we get there—"

"We're about an hour out," Yas jumps in. "We need to stop for gas, but we should be at Alice's in time for dinner."

"Thank you for the cookies!" Dell says. "They were *so good.*"

I was more surprised when my mom put a container of homemade chocolate chip cookies in my purse this morning than I was when she added Wàipó's peach-wood sword next. I'm still not used to her making me food. It's one of the ways she's working on *showing up while respecting my autonomy*, as our family counselor puts it.

After everything that happened, I expected Mom to ground me until I turned eighteen and start showing up at school to check on me again. But she didn't. She's been a bit overbearing, but it's different from before. She's trying to give me space to live my own life. The fact that I just spent three weeks at U of T—but nerding out about music and film, instead of grinding through the Coding Academy—and that I'm on the way to my dream weekend at Osheaga, is proof of that. Even if she wants hourly updates.

"That's great." Mom sounds relieved, though I'm not sure if it's about the cookies or the drive. We pass a sign announcing there's a rest stop at the next exit.

"We've got to go," I say. "I'll let you know when we get there."

"Okay! Drive safe. Love you!"

"Love you too, Mom."

"Bye, Ms. Bei!" Yas and Dell say in unison.

The music blares back on as I focus on guiding the car off the highway and pulling up to the right side of a gas pump. Yas and Dell clamber out before I even turn off the car, skipping toward the rest stop. Stepping out of the air conditioning into the August heat feels like being slathered in syrup. I stick the nozzle in the tank and press the trigger.

My phone buzzes. *Oh my god, Mom,* I think. *What now?* But when I thumb the message open, my screen fills with a close-up photo of a fat brown worm hanging out of a lizard's yellow mouth. Gross.

Thanks, Blythe.

Reptiles are Blythe's new obsession, since she went to live with her aunt and uncle . . . and their pet bearded dragon, Gandalf. On our first video call after she moved, I told her what I realized in the woods: that Maddie was trying to protect us. That she was never angry at Blythe or at me. She was just scared. Maddie knew something dangerous was trapped in the locket I was wearing, and she was trying to warn her family, to keep them safe. And she did.

Blythe was silent for a moment, then she nodded and told me that bearded dragons have a third eye on the back of their heads. Her way of working through grief is just as unique as she is.

But I know she's working through it because on our weekly calls she talks incessantly about her therapist and always has a new story to share about Maddie. I never thought I'd say this, but I miss the little imp. She's the only other person who really knows what we went through. I'm glad we haven't lost touch. But there could be fewer reptiles involved.

I reply to Blythe with a selfie of my most disgusted face, then finish filling up and park the car. I've only been outside for a few minutes, but I'm already covered in a sticky film of sweat. I need an iced capp, stat.

I head for the rest stop, sending a flock of seagulls scattering. The sun glitters off the roof of the building, and I squint into the glare, raising a hand to shield my eyes. The smell of rotting flowers hits my nostrils, thick and sour, and goosebumps prickle up my arms, despite the heat.

There's an overflowing dumpster at the side of the building. *It's nothing*, I think. *Just garbage.* Still, I round the corner for a closer look. That's when I see it: A thick, dark smear stretching out in front of the dumpster. But the sun is behind me.

A shadow where no shadow should be.

I slide my hand into my purse and find the smooth handle of the peach-wood sword. Its familiar weight is a comfort.

"Rachel?"

I flinch and spin around.

Yas and Dell are behind me with iced capps in hand, their eyes sharp with concern.

"Is everything okay?"

When I finally told Yas and Dell everything that happened—from Wàipó's ghost to Maddie's haunting to the monster on the beach—I waited for them to laugh. Expected them to say they always knew I was a freak and call me *witch bitch* as they walked out the door forever. But instead, they believed me.

I swallow and glance back at the dumpster. The rusted metal glints in the bright sunlight, and a mountain of cardboard spills out of the top. The strange shadow is gone. The humid air smells of gasoline and burger grease, not rotting flowers.

"Yeah," I say, turning back to my friends and plucking the sweating iced capp from Yas's hand. "Everything's perfect." I slurp cold, sweet coffee from the straw, as Yas stomps her foot with an exaggerated scowl and Dell cackles.

Maybe what I saw was nothing, or maybe it was another lost ghost. Now I know they're all around us. But I also know I can handle whatever life throws at me next. Because it's not just me anymore. It's Yas and Dell, linking their sweaty arms with mine. It's Blythe, telling me bearded dragons smell with their tongues. It's my mom, gifting me a vintage Siouxsie T-shirt to celebrate passing physics and pre-calculus and sealing the locket—and the monster imprisoned inside—in a safety deposit box.

It's all of us, together.

ACKNOWLEDGMENTS

First and foremost, thank you to my editors, Kaela Cadieux and Claire Caldwell, who brought this project to life. I'm immensely grateful that you saw something worth pursuing in the jumble of my early drafts and for the enthusiasm, expertise, and patience with which you helped me identify the finest threads in the tangle and weave them into this book.

Thank you to the entire team at Annick Press for the multitude of tasks, big and small, it took to transform my words into a real, beautiful book and for all you've done to get that book into readers' hands. Thank you also for the excellent Annick Press Mentorship Program that gave me the opportunity to work with you.

I'm indebted to the folks who offered their subject matter expertise to help inform key elements of this story. Thank you, Jae, for your wisdom and guidance on Chinese folklore and the spiritual and magical elements of the story; Florence, for answering my many questions about the realities of modern high schools; and Ryan, for your advice on current teenage "cool girl" trends. Any mistakes are mine alone.

Thank you, Linda Pruessen, for your skilled copy edits that greatly improved the clarity and consistency of the story.

Thank you, Mary Ann Blair, for your eagle-eyed proofreading and awe-inspiring attention to detail.

Thank you, Marcela Bolivar, for creating a more gorgeous, haunting cover than I could have imagined.

Thank you, Marilyn Biderman and Brenna English-Loeb, for your invaluable and incisive industry advice.

Thank you to the Toronto Arts Council and the Festival of Literary Diversity for offering grant and mentorship opportunities that are critical supports for early-career authors like me. Thank you, Loretto Maryholme and Gibraltar Point Centre for the Arts, two wonderful retreats where I wrote much of this story.

I've dreamed of being part of a community of writers almost as often as I've dreamed of publishing a book, and I'm grateful to The Writer's Studio at Simon Fraser University for helping me build that community. In particular, thank you to my mentor Leanne Dunic: Your encouragement, guidance, and support helped me believe this was possible and gave me the tools to make it happen. Thank you to the best workshop group, The Writer's Coven, for showing me how amazing a caring creative community can be. Thank you, Cadence and Shawne, for your friendship and your insightful feedback on this story. Our chats/rants helped get me unstuck so many times! I'm grateful to be able to share the highs and lows of this journey we're on together.

I'm fortunate to have so much support and (sometimes unintentional) inspiration from my friends and family. Thank you, Steve and Lois, for owning a knife that scares me so much I had to put it in a horror story. Thank you, Mitch, for sharing wild sleepwalking tales that sent me down a research rabbit hole, which in turn inspired many of Rachel's nightmares. Thank you, Jess and Ben, for the care with which you read this book and offered questions to help me improve it. Thank you, Vic, for our conversations about writing, Chinese culture, and belonging.

Thank you, Pops, for your unwavering support and for passing down your love of art and your excellent taste in books and film. Thank you, Michie, for ensuring I had an endless supply of books while I was young and letting me stay up as late as I wanted if I was reading.

Thank you, Mike, my beloved partner in life and in art. Thank you for the road trip brainstorms and late night read-throughs; for keeping me fed and reminding me to stretch; and for building a life together that makes pursuing our dreams possible.

Thank you, dear reader, for choosing to spend your time with this story.

FUNDED BY
THE CITY OF TORONTO
TORONTO
ARTS _ COUNCIL

A Good Daughter's Ghost was produced with the support of the City of Toronto through Toronto Arts Council.

PHOTO CREDIT: DANICA OLIVA

SAM WILKET writes strange, surreal, and sometimes scary stories. Her work appears in publications including the *Tahoma Literary Review* and *Coven of the East: Reclaiming Asian Women's Magical Histories*. *A Good Daughter's Ghost* is her debut novel.

Sam is a graduate of Simon Fraser University's The Writers Studio, and her writing is influenced by her experiences as a second-generation Canadian of white British and Chinese descent, a member of a blended family, and a voracious reader with wide-ranging taste. She lives in Toronto.

Visit her online at samwilket.com.